Other Books by the Author:

A Bottle of Rain
Nowhere near the Sea of Cortez

As God Looked On

Jim Harris

Livingston Press
at
The University of West Alabama

Typesetting and page layout: Joe Taylor
Proofreading: Maggie Slimp, Jessica Gonzalez, Tricia Taylor, Amy Call
Cover design and layout: Amanda Nolin
Cover art: Bruce New

For Amy

I would also like to give a special mention to my Mother, Inez Downs, who always called me a too quiet child, and would on many occasions when my silence was unbearable, give me a hug, and say, "Aw, honey, you might as well say it as to think it."

At some point in my childhood on this request was honored and has generated smiles sometimes and untold damage too many times, but undoubtedly helped me in my path to being a writer. Thank you, Mom.

This is a work of fiction.
Surely you know the rest: any resemblance
to persons living or dead is coincidental.

Livingston Press is part of The University of West Alabama,
and thereby has non-profit status.
Donations are tax-deductible:
brothers and sisters, we need 'em.

first edition
6 5 4 3 3 2 1

As God Looked On

"It is guilt we must escape from, not God."
—Luis Bunuel

Seymour

There on the east side of a wraparound wooden porch Seymour sat looking at the bark of a catalpa tree and then on through the leaves of the tree to the rolling wheat field that had a lone anvil-shaped little oil well pumping away in the middle of it. The anvil-shaped oil well was bright blue except for the heavy rust around its edges.

That little oil well pumped out five gallons a month. Roger said he kept the equivalent of two of the barrels a month and the rest went back into Seymour's account at the Ridgway Bank. It wasn't much and back in the 70's when his Uncle Bud put that oil well in it produced upwards of fifteen barrels a month.

"It might never stop though," Roger had said. Roger had left moments ago. He had work to do.

Seymour decided to spend some time with Renoir. He had a book on Renoir that was at the top of a box full of art and history books and the one thing about Renoir was that his impressionism was accidental and he really wanted to be a realist but when he tried to be a realist it didn't work out. Renoir's painting, *Bal du moulin de la Galette*, was Seymour's favorite painting. He had a replica of it boxed up somewhere.

"When I tried to be a teacher it didn't work out either," Seymour said. He looked around. There was nothing but a breeze to hear him.

Renoir, for a brief time, from about 1865-1886, tried to paint in a more structured classical style that had less color, more definition, and was ultimately not a very good period for him. Then, in 1890, the same year Groucho Marx and Ho Chi Minh were born, and the same year Vincent Van Gogh shot and killed himself, Renoir returned to lighter colors and vague outlines around the edges of his figures, and focused on nudes (young women exclusively) and domestic scenes.

Seymour nodded. Him too. At the height of his teaching, when he was leading long legged young women to high school volleyball sectionals, he would very carefully pull off Stephanie's panties in a hotel room on Michigan Avenue, and, starting at that area just above her belly button, he would slowly work his way down until her thighs trembled as they clung sweatlocked to his neck . . .

Seymour had this theory that impressionism was more than just an art form that used small strokes of unmixed colors to simulate actual reflected light. It was a philosophy. Why limit attempts to capture visual reality in terms of transient effects of light and color to a square canvas?

Seymour, at the height of his near schizophrenic mental state that would be brought to an end by four cheerleaders and an iPod, Seymour believed that each of his moments in time were nothing more than still captures of his own personal impressionist collection.

The French, who started the impressionist movement, have never fully recovered from it. While the other art movements magnified the word *capture* to establish what they were trying to do, impressionism wasn't at all about capturing anything. It was about expanding, not capturing visual reality. It made perfect sense to Seymour that impressionism could easily become a philosophy in addition to an art form. That's what the French were doing. They were living in impressionistic states of mind all through the 20th Century and on into now. Sartre described the Nazi's march into Paris with such an impressionistic approach, Seymour believed. And Luis Buñuel, though Spanish born, made his most significant movies in France, and Lord were his movies impressionistic.

All the scenes in a Buñuel movie were succinct and encapsulated and even though there were multiple plot lines, all the scenes, in the editing room, could be mixed and matched and presented in virtually any order and if viewed with the appropriate amount of attention, would present the swath of reality Buñuel was after. Like walking through an art gallery with only Renoir paintings.

A strange chill went through Seymour and his body moved enough to rattle the chains of the swinging bench he sat in. It was how he had dealt with his affair with a teenage girl, and with his crumbling marriage, and with his crumbling ability to hold a coherent thought in his history classes. Seymour had convinced himself that he was living impressionistically.

He was living in impressionistic moments in time.

How silly.

Stephanie

After Stephanie killed her husband she didn't know what to do with herself so she went to Florida on a Greyhound bus. She sat like a rag doll with her temple pressed against the glass almost the whole trip. It rained all the way through Georgia and the raindrops stuck to the window like tears.

Stephanie's husband worked construction and after getting tired of her and their year old son, he started doing meth and fucking teenage girls.

"Mind if I sit here?" A young black man said. He sat down hard. He noticed Stephanie's tanned knee peeking out of her ripped jeans. She had on good perfume too. He cleared his throat and got comfortable in the seat. She wore a baseball cap backwards and pulled down over her forehead, and her ears poked through brown stringy blond-streaked hair. She was running from something, he decided. He unzipped his book bag and took out a biology book. He was on his way back from a two-day revival and a visit with his family in Atlanta to classes at Daytona Beach Community College. He had a test coming up.

"I hate biology," he said. Her head finally moved some. Her sad eyes went to his book. She had pretty eyes, too. Green. And a small thin mouth. She was probably younger than him and he was twenty-two.

He tensed when she put one hand on his thigh to steady herself and then used her other hand to close his book enough to see the cover. She was taking biology too. Same book.

"Where?"

"Heartland Community College," Stephanie said, with a bit of a smile. Her voice was weak. She hadn't talked for a while. She started to say "Was," but didn't.

He asked her where she was going. She looked at him briefly. Her son, Jeremiah, was probably still asleep. Her own mother was probably sitting on the couch smoking a cigarette.

"I'll go home with you if you like," Stephanie said. Jeremiah stopped breathing. Her voice was as broken and meek and unconvincing as any voice he had ever heard. Her temple went back to the tear-stained glass. Jeremiah took a breath finally and opened his book more and tried to get comfortable in the seat so he could study. He tried to focus on studying. He really needed to study.

The sun was just coming up way out over the Atlantic Ocean as the

Greyhound bus crossed over the Halifax River and came to a stop just this side of Highway A1A. The bus went on and there on the side of the road were left a tallish, skinny, Cuban-Chinese girl and a short, chunky black young man holding two suitcases.

Stephanie carried a purse, a make-up bag, and an Old Navy cloth sack of clothes. He started walking and then she started walking and then they both stopped. They didn't even know each other's name.

Stephanie and Jeremiah, they told each other.

"That's my son's name," Stephanie said.

Sure it was, he thought, as he started walking. He was a sucker for a pretty face. And a pretty body. And a lighter skin. She had olive skin and large strange slanty green eyes and thin killer legs that went on God only knew how high. He was tired.

"Charley Younger should be okay," he said as he walked. Stephanie trailed behind him.

The road they walked on was part gravel, part pavement.

Stephanie stopped and let out a noise. Jeremiah stopped and half-looked back at this skinny weird beautiful girl. He was looking at his death probably.

It was the blue shiny sliver of the Halifax River starting to illuminate the horizon that caught her attention. She asked if that was the ocean. He started walking again. "Nope," he said. The river. He half-pointed. The ocean was the other way. He half-pointed in the other direction. There was a river on one side and an ocean on the other. Oh. Now she saw the banks on the other side.

"It's beautiful," she said. Her voice was gravelly. A touch husky. He liked her voice. It was a lived-in voice.

"I want to see the ocean. Are we close to the ocean?"

"You'll see the ocean," Jeremiah said. "You'll see a lot of it. And it'll see you and you'll both get along."

This made Stephanie laugh. Her laugh was a deep, deliberate laugh. He liked her laugh and he liked her for some reason.

From nowhere three pelicans swooped over them. Stephanie let out a loud God! as she ducked. She'd never seen such birds. They were so big! They flew over them as straight and in formation like Blue Angels. Had he ever seen an air show? Nope. She lived for a while near Scott Air Force Base. Fighter jets flew by all the time.

"Charley Younger better be okay," Jeremiah said. "He ain't, I'm gonna kill him."

She started to ask who Charley Younger was but everything was too distracting. There by the bridge was a dock and lots of boats. It was all so beautiful. The most water she had ever seen was Crab Orchard Lake. This was too much. She asked if they had to walk far.

"Nope."

The road led to the most beautiful little trailer park Stephanie had ever seen. It was right along this beautiful, beautiful river. The trailers were all the same. Small and white and nothing out of place. No aluminum foil in the windows to hide the meth labs. No run-down, poorly constructed sheds. Just flowers and patches of what looked like crabgrass in the front. A slight fishy scent hung in the clean wonderful air. Jeremiah kept walking.

Stephanie stopped. She couldn't do this. He somehow sensed she stopped. He stopped. A boat horn rang out in the distance. He turned around, his head shaking. He looked tired and distracted but he just didn't look threatening to her.

"If Charley Younger didn't get his butt to work this morning I swear I'll kill him." She asked him who Charley Younger was. He didn't say anything. He just stared right through her. He was chubby but he had a cute round face. His eyes were small. In the emerging daylight he didn't look as black. He sighed so deeply she could almost feel the earth shake. When he turned to continue walking she followed.

Stephanie froze as they turned down the first street in the first row of these perfectly identical white trailers. Jeremiah stopped to switch the heavier bag to his other hand.

He heard Stephanie say something like, "You take care now!" She stepped back nodding at this black man. He scratched his temple.

"You got anywhere to go?"

She gave him a dry look. Of course she had somewhere to go. There was always somewhere to go.

He took another deep breath. And hopefully Charley Younger still had a job and his power's still on and the dogs didn't get his stupid cat.

Stephanie smiled. "You take care, Jeremiah." Jeremiah was looking at the sky. It was a dark but beautiful sky. He started walking. Stephanie was still backing up. There was always some place to go.

And when she turned finally to go to that someplace that's when Stephanie collided head to shorter head with someone.

That someone was Charley Younger.

He screamed when they collided. He had been running. Awkwardly, but running. Stephanie got the worst of it. She fell straight down, a shot to her chin.

Charley Younger started crying, wailing, and right over her. Jeremiah dropped his bags and ran. This scared Charley Younger even more. He wailed even louder.

Charley Younger was a short, thin, dark-haired forty-six year-old man who looked twenty-six. His left eye was crossed some and both eyes squinted close together so badly you couldn't figure out how he could see. He had somewhat of a hunch to his stance and both hands turned inward slightly like he was perpetually riding a bike. Charley Younger had no thumbs. He held a smooth piece of wood in his left hand much of the time, especially when he slept, to keep two of his fingernails from digging into his palm hard enough to draw blood. He carried the piece of wood in his pocket around people. He had a bloody palm. He forgot to hold the wood every night Jeremiah was in Atlanta.

In between wails Charley Younger hunched and bent over this girl and said he was sorry.

Between shut ups to Charley Younger Jeremiah bent over Stephanie, who had sat up, stunned.

An old lady came out on a small concrete patio to check things out. She called out for Charley Younger to calm down. It wasn't helping anything to panic. Charley Younger stopped but he continued to fidget badly.

"I saw you, JJ, that's all," Charley Younger started crying again. "I ran. I ran into her." He pointed with his bent hand, his body moving comically, like he had to go to the bathroom. "She walked the wrong way. No, I did." He let out another wail. He stopped just as abruptly. He turned to the old lady and his whole demeanor changed. "Hi, Mrs. Dottie."

Mrs. Dottie wiped her hands dry with the dishcloth. "Hi, Charley." She wore a pink housecoat and pink slippers that had white fur on the front strap. She turned to straighten a flowerpot she had nudged on her way out. She said it was all right, Charley Younger. That young lady just needed some ice. Mrs. Dottie asked JJ if she needed to get some ice.

"We'll take care of it. She'll need aspirins."

"Ibuprofen's all we have. 500 milligrams. Wal-Mart generic. Bad for your kidneys, Jeremiah," Charley Younger said. Mrs. Dottie smiled.

"Shut up, Charley Younger," Jeremiah said as he helped Stephanie to her feet. She was a bit wobbly. He steadied her with soft, but firm hands.

Thumbs

Charley Younger sat beside Stephanie on the sofa. Her head was back and her eyes were closed and a white washcloth rested on her forehead where she hit when she fell.

"I trust you," Charley Younger said. He didn't trust many people but when he trusted someone it was probably forever. Or close to forever. Jeremiah really believes in forever. Charley Younger said all this while he was staring at the dark, well-worn carpeting. Jeremiah stopped doing the dishes and told Charley Younger to give her a break.

"She's one though. One I trust. Even though I have trouble with forever."

One of Stephanie's eyes opened. The shiner, the attention, both gave her a chance to not think about anything.

"Did you clean the bathroom?" Jeremiah said.

"Twice," Charley Younger said. "I clean it twice a day. It's a small place. Look around. It's spotless."

Jeremiah's voice boomed out a "Damn." He thought he spilled some soft-soap when he got home. Charley Younger was off as if shot.

And the place was indeed immaculate. It was small with a small kitchen that had a small black square table and four matching chairs squeezed around it. A faux wet bar separated the kitchen from the living room. On one wall was the sofa and on the opposite wall was a 19-inch GE TV. It wasn't on. An old black phone hung on the wall over the wet bar. Jeremiah washed dishes behind the wet bar.

Stephanie felt weird. She wasn't scared really. She was sad. A lot sad if she thought about it. Her stomach made her a little sick. She sat up and the washrag fell off but she caught it. Her son wouldn't see her at the end of the day. After she got home from the diner and took her shoes off he wouldn't see her. She adjusted the rag on her head. But her son wouldn't see her today. Jeremiah stopped doing the dishes and asked her if she was okay. No, she wasn't okay at all.

"I'm okay," she said.

Charley Younger rushed back in and sat down and his eyes went back to the carpet.

"Since I trust you," Charley Younger began. Jeremiah froze, and dropped a fork he was washing. "Three trailers down, my mother, God bless her soul go to Heaven, is in a deep freezer we paid fifty dollars for eighteen years ago at the flea market."

Jeremiah, from the kitchen, groaned.

Stephanie looked at Charley Younger. His bent, curled fingers were moving. His squinty unnatural eyes looked barely open as he stared at the floor. Or did they? He wasn't right.

"We," he took a breath. "We had a hard time, a hard time getting the freezer home. I'm no help."

"You want something to drink?" Jeremiah called out. "Diet Coke, ice water, we got ice, Charley Younger? Nothing else until I can get to Winn Dixie." Charley Younger was nodding. Plenty of ice.

"Diet Coke," Stephanie said. Charley Younger went away again. She patted her forehead with the now cooling dishcloth. That boy had no chin and his ears were weird and his eyes were barely open. Retarded! She eased her head back and put her hands in her lap. And there was something wrong with his hands. She had enough money for a hotel on the beach. She'd never seen the ocean. Everything might be over and she might never see her son again but she wanted to see the ocean. It was the fall and the off-season for tourists. She bit down on her bottom lip and glanced at her watch. Her son was asking for her now. Right now he was asking for her. It would be best if her mother said nothing. Just act normal. For now.

Stephanie jumped when the soda got in her face.

Jeremiah didn't know what to do, didn't know what to say. He stood there in the small trailer living room a bit clownish and awkward. He had to pee. He turned the TV on. "No remote," he said. "Just," he shrugged, "just press the button here." He went down the hall.

Stephanie could leave now. Yes. She could bolt and head down to some hotel on the beach and she would be fine. Instead she took a drink of soda. It tasted funny. There were so many strange, unfamiliar smells in this place. Stephanie looked around. The Lord's Prayer in a gold frame was there on an end table. An 8-inch plastic Mother Mary was on top of the very old TV. Fuck me, she thought. Not psychos. Religious freaks. Worse than psychos.

Charley Younger startled her on his abrupt return so much she let out a yell and this made him jump. "Stop that!" he half-yelled. His voice was the only normal thing about him. Stephanie smiled.

He hurried across the room. He stopped against the wet bar. "If, if I stop, people stare. You stare."

"No, I don't."

Charley Younger opened the refrigerator. "Okay, then." He fumbled around for his own soda.

"How'd you meet JJ? I met JJ when I was his age. We grew up kinda together. He beat up a boy who made fun of me." He sat down on the sofa and almost dropped the soda. He had to anchor it with his other hand. His voice sounded almost normal if a little breathless. Stephanie tried not to look at him. He said he was right.

"Right about what?"

"About my thumbs. You saw them. Only stubs. You have beautiful thumbs."

She asked if she could smoke in here. Charley Younger nodded. He'd clean it up. He cleaned up everything. JJ smoked once in a great while when he was nervous about something. JJ was a neat freak too but Charley Younger did all the cleaning. "Even without real thumbs." He smiled and he looked stranger when he smiled. He had no chin. His teeth were smaller than they should be. "I do most everything pretty well except hitchhiking."

Stephanie stopped tapping out the cigarette and gave Charley Younger a What did you say? Look. She followed the look with a blurted out laugh.

Jeremiah's voice boomed from down the hall. "Shouldn't you be at work, Charley Younger?"

Charley Younger cowered some. He should be at work. He should be washing dishes or mopping the floor or cleaning the windows down at the Ken Wan Inn Chinese place just down the road by the pier. But the bus threw him off. He missed JJ. If he didn't show up on time they would make him work the rest of the day for nothing and then JJ would take his pay stub and yell at the little oriental woman who ate rice in her hand. She did. She would carefully put a ball of sticky rice in her palm and with that tiny perfectly formed thumb she would push the ball of rice into her mouth. That's how real Chinese people ate rice. That's why it had to be sticky. Only sticky rice. Flaky rice fell everywhere like if he would try to eat it.

"Shut up, Charley Younger!"

Charley Younger jumped again. Jeremiah was tucking a shirt in. A clean shirt. He had cologne on. "Get down there now! Tell them I had you cleaning something. I don't care. Tell them to call me."

Charley Younger left. The floor of the trailer shook as Jeremiah lumbered hard into the kitchen and Charley Younger went out the door.

"He gotta work." Jeremiah found a soda. "We all gotta work." His hand was big with short, black fingers that engulfed the soda can. He stood there short and chubby and pointed a finger at Stephanie.

"I know a place you can work maybe." He turned to look out a window. He asked her if she could wait tables. An orange flame flared under her nose. Of course she could wait tables. That's what she was doing before. Before killing her husband, she almost said. Smoke spiraled gray and billowy above her.

He had to go to church. He would return in two hours. Did she want to go to church?

"Fuck no," she said, her voice cracked, broken, and weak suddenly. Oddly, her eyes watered up. She puffed harder on her cigarette.

He almost said something but didn't. He pulled out his keys and left.

Like It Should

This made Doc's day, out here on the patio as he watched a harshly beautiful white woman go inside with a black man and a broken man. She would mend them both, he imagined, taking turns, one at a time, and again, for at least four hours at fifty dollars an hour. Two-hundred dollars worth of sexual heaven. Doc crossed his legs, flapped the newspaper hard to read the local section. He slowly, like the sun, peaked his eyes up above the newspaper, looked all around. He had to do something more in his retirement. He had to do something since his wife died. Since his two kids turned their back on him and carved out their lives in Minnesota. Shit. He hated cold weather. Florida was his weather. It always had been.

It was already almost too late this morning to take his five-hundred dollar metal detector out to the beach and search for dropped rings, earrings, change. He smiled. He had this metal detector for a year now. In six more years, at the rate he was finding shit, he would turn a profit. What a life!

The girl didn't really look like a hooker. She looked more like a social worker. Someone might have found out those two put the broken man's old mother in a deep freeze to keep her retirement checks coming. That was the only way to keep Charley out of an institution and save up and buy him a new chin. That would probably never happen. He was living proof nothing ever happened like it should. Sixty years old, living in a trailer with a handful of porn magazines and a metal detector. Jesus Christ. Where was everybody? Where was his life? She would probably do both of them at once. Goddamn, what an ugly image.

He looked at his Daytona Beach coffee mug on the little white plastic table. He was out of coffee.

"Oh," he said, pointing. "Before the blow job could you fetch me a nice hot cup of that cheap-ass Folger's coffee I just made in my brand new 10 dollar Wal-Mart coffee maker?" He gritted his teeth and turned the page of the newspaper. He gave it another angry flap to straighten out the comics. He had to get it read before the sun was all the way up and it was too damn hot to sit where he was.

Pablo

Pablo didn't want to go anywhere. He was six years old and his belly was usually always full and his mother and his uncle had just put in the greatest thing you could put in a tin-sided, cement floored two-room house on the side of a hill in southern Mexico—*a cuarto de baño interiors*—an indoor toilet.

When Pablo first pooped in that toilet he stood over it and watched the water swirl and shortly it was gone just like that. He stood there smiling.

His aunt yelled at him to wipe his butt with a corncob like so (she gestured), then told Pablo to pull his pants up. It was a better life now.

They got a 12 inch television when Pablo was five and now they had a toilet and they finally found enough cardboard to cover the walls of both rooms so when they all slept the spiders and scorpions couldn't get in so easy.

If only Pablo hadn't stolen those Converse in the park. God was watching when he did this, his aunt told him as they, later on, headed towards America in the back of a big, dark truck.

No, Pablo should have just walked on by as those rich kids from the rich part of town took off their new tennis shoes and lined them neatly on the concrete before wading and splashing happy in the Fountain of Redemption in Prestro Park.

But there those blue hi-top Converse were. He scanned them all and that pair he knew would fit was right there and glowing. Pablo slipped them on and sure enough they fit like an oversized pair of gloves. At first he was just going to try them on. But he grimaced and pushed his heart back into his chest as his whole body shivered at the thought of running through the streets and hills and alleys of Xaxace in these blue hi-top Converse.

These tennis shoes would carry Pablo to greatness. He would marry a girl even prettier than his aunt and they would have a tin house with *four* rooms and *two* indoor toilets. Pablo could poop in one and his beautiful wife in the other.

Off he ran in those beautiful blue hi-top Converse tennis shoes.

Pablo got pretty far away too before he went tumbling head over heels. He had forgotten to tie his shoestrings. He didn't know yet how to tie shoestrings. He bunched the pearly white flat soft strings up, stuffed them under the tongue, and off he ran again.

Pablo glanced once behind him as he ran and sure enough. Beautiful golden stars the size of pesos flew fast and thick behind him as he ran.

They were magic shoes and this was a great thing.

But Pablo shouldn't have stolen them.

That's why he and his aunt would end up in the back of a smelly hot truck.

God had watched the whole thing.

Stephanie

This was just too easy. Too magical. This couldn't really be happening. But there it was. There they both were, more exactly. Two shoe boxes full of twenty-dollar bills. Stephanie didn't even have to count it. It was plenty. She had taken them both out from under the bed and taken the lids off. There was a third one under there too just waiting for more twenty-dollar bills. She could take a bus on down to the Keys. She could go anywhere she fucking wanted to. She touched one of the twenties with her finger. She could sit in a bar and find a nice horny old man with some money who would hide her. She blinked. Nothing was all that bad if it was dark enough.

She looked at the picture on the table next to the bed. Jeremiah's family, no doubt. Ten, no twelve kids all sitting around a very large, smiling mother. No father, of course. They were black. A god-fearing family and Jeremiah looked like maybe the oldest and he trusted everyone. She laughed out loud. It was just too crazy. Nuts! She killed her husband yesterday and now look at all that money. Stephanie found herself shivering. She smelled under her arm. God, she needed a shower. Stephanie jumped as her eyes found Jesus again. Right there on the wall next to the window. Aglow in a faded yellow light and staring upward with a strange, foreboding look on his face, like when she would give her drunken husband a blow job.

She went out of the bedroom to get her purse. She stopped halfway. Jeremiah might have forgotten something. Might have gotten sick or something. That retard might show up. Stephanie was shaking so badly with dread and excitement she felt weak and light headed. She spun around in a circle. She hurried over to the aluminum door and turned the little tarnished gold-colored lock set in the handle. She got fucking scared all of a sudden.

Jeremiah

And there Stephanie was a couple years ago, her and Tony were both drunk and she had on a low-cut tight blouse and short jean skirt hiked up as she bent over the trunk of a Saturn. She should have never trusted a man who had just clipped off her thong with a pocket knife. She stared at a trash bin as he sniffed loud and ugly and then let out a groan. He did light her cigarette before ramming inside of her. He could have worked her a bit. He didn't. Her being a little dry, he said, always made him feel big. He wasn't.

Of course she got pregnant in the parking lot of a titty bar, after French-kissing a stripper who was a dumber looking blond than she was. At least that stripper got a couple bucks stuffed in her thong. All Stephanie got was a worthless husband who slapped her so hard right before he came it brought tears to her eyes. (He saw that in a porno movie, he said.)

They were married three months later as his ex-girlfriend and her man witnessed it. (How weird was that?) They went down to Giant City State Park for their honeymoon and Stephanie slipped and fell on a trail and bled that night and she swore she heard Tony praying for her to miscarry. She didn't.

Stephanie had Jeremiah breech and that very same night her husband bent someone new over that ugly green Saturn at that same titty bar but at least that woman had sense enough to make him wear a condom. That woman was Stephanie's younger sister, Alicia.

Alicia would leave, shortly after the birth, to attend Truman State University somewhere in Missouri. She would major in Elementary Education. She was smarter than Stephanie. Stephanie thought most everyone was smarter than she was. Especially about men. Especially about life. About everything.

Then Jeremiah was born and she thought he was the greatest thing that ever happened to her and then her husband got into heroin and Stephanie came home early from her waitress job and caught him shooting up with a teenager, while Jeremiah slept in the next room. Her husband tried to crawl away from Stephanie. He got no farther than an end table. The teenager's nose was leaking green and white gunk and she sat on the couch as if posing. The teenager was naked from the waist down.

"What are you doing?" Stephanie said. The teenager's eyes looked wide and almost bloody, her tanned belly was exposed and she wore a Barbie belly button ring and her perfectly-trimmed brown pubic hair was shaved into the shape of a tiny arrow pointing down. Stephanie came very close to throwing up. The girl was so fucked up she tried to move her head and couldn't.

Stephanie went in to check on Jeremiah, who was sleeping. She eased the door shut and came back into the living room and broke her husband's jaw with the heel of her fake-leather boot. She heard it crack. He should know about the strength in her thighs. She was in tears. Tears of hatred. He started throwing up and appeared to be gagging on his own vomit. He rolled around until he was against a wall. Blood was coming up. He tried to say something. He was turning from beet red to blue. Stephanie ignored him. But you can't kill assholes like him. Impossible.

The teenager at least had managed to close her legs now. She was whimpering. Stephanie was shaking. Shaking with anger. Disgust. She took the flesh colored rubber hose and put it around the girl's neck.

"Don't ki—, don't ki—" The girl couldn't get the words out. Stephanie spotted the girl's cell phone on the table. She flipped it open. Three missed messages. All three were from somebody called *My Lover*. Stephanie called *My Lover*.

"Yeah?" People were calling out pizzas in the background. Laughter, curses. "A large 17 inch supreme without bacon! Get the phone!"

Stephanie told him what street his girlfriend would be laying out on. With a hose around her neck. Stephanie stared at the girl.

She flipped the phone shut, right after hearing an adolescent voice say, "Um, okay."

Thirty

Jeremiah pulled on the emergency brake and stepped out into the hot white sand and there across the ocean horizon was the God Almighty Lord Jesus Christ Reverend Johnson talked about so well today. Reverend Johnson always pumped Jeremiah up about the Lord and there He was in the clouds and the blue sky and the white caps and there in the sails of a boat and at the end of a fishin' pole there on the deck of that charter boat and thank you Lord you are everywhere today, tomorrow and always. Jeremiah was pumped and it was God not that pretty girl, Stephanie. No, his erection came from the blood of the lamb not his thoughts. He tugged. He hid it. God forgave him. Yes, the Lord Jesus Christ is our Savior and forgave all who sinned as he was sinning now. As he was thinking about her curiosity. Her curiosity for his manhood, his mother told him about such women. About the evil ways of the world and God, yes God would save him from eternal damnation and there in the Heavens his cloud would be and there she was, naked and smiling on that cloud, NO! Jeremiah had to think about our Savior not how alcohol brought out the curiosity in such women when alone, his mama told him as she soaped him up there on the verge of puberty, her medals dangling between her ample, slightly wrinkled bosom.

His mother was ill now. That's why he went to Atlanta. His mother, not quite on her deathbed, but she wasn't well. He would try to see her every month but it was too expensive. His younger brother paid for the bus this time. His younger brother, Jacob, who was a lawyer now. A secretive lawyer who didn't have much to do with the family except out of guilt. Guilt drove everything. Drove you everywhere like an evil chauffeur. Dropped you off anywhere you wanted and left you there. Evil, evil guilt, and Jeremiah bet her skin was soft. Soft and pulled warm and tight over tiny bones. Two young girls walked by. In bikinis. In heat. In Heaven was the Savior and what would Jeremiah fix her for supper? What about lunch? She would want to eat and Charley Younger missed his cooking, he bet. He missed his own cooking. The family had bad pizza that last night in Atlanta and one of his younger sisters spent the whole time on a cell phone pacing on the back porch just jabbering away about nothing. To nobody. His mother was going downhill. Every one of his brothers and sisters would fight over everything in the house like coal black hyenas, goddamn it. Forgive me, Lord! Guilt always lost its footrace with Greed every day of the week. But in the Kingdom of heaven everyone was thirty and his mother would be thirty and he would be thirty and Delores, his girlfriend, who had no curiosity about him whatsoever (she didn't drink and there would be nothing until the ring), would be thirty and this sky would always be there as all God's Children would be thirty for eternity. Amen.

If Jeremiah passed all the tests. If Jeremiah kept to the plan. If Jeremiah followed the Lord and not the upward path of those thin, brown thighs into the tight thicket of evil and regret. Besides he was getting fat, fat as life, and the fatter he got the less he could see of such a woman's curiosity and this made him chuckle a deep chuckle. He had to go to the Winn Dixie. He had to get something for lunch and something good for supper.

Thank you, Lord.

Caught in an Agave Field

It was getting late in the day and the sun had gone down behind the mountains. Pablo, mouth open, stared at the pink sky that bled into the pale blue sky. It was so beautiful it didn't look real it looked like lights. His aunt kept talking to herself. They were so late getting home it was not good, she said. They should have left the market earlier but the shrimp market was filled with so many distractions. His aunt tried on every necklace and every bracelet and the one with the blue stone cross made her cry she wanted it so bad. It almost made Pablo cry. He would buy his beautiful aunt this blue stone cross when he grew up.

They left finally and oh Lord if they didn't cut through the big agave field they wouldn't make it home for *carne asada*. They only had *carne asada* on special occasions but tonight their outside brick pit would have *carne asada* on it thank the Lord they could not be late little Pablo. Hurry, hurry, hurry, keep up little Pablo no dawdling they had to get home she wanted to make the tortillas thank you Lord.

Ghosts got them. They were alone and no one was in the big agave field as the sun went down behind the mountains and then they got grabbed from behind by evil voiced men. Ghosts. Damn the luck.

They blindfolded his aunt but not Pablo. They let him see it all because the foul smelling older ghost put his big ugly warted nose to Pablo's tiny button nose and told him he would cut his tongue out if he said a single word.

They were roughly dragged and knocked down as they were pulled and told not to say a single word and one of them punched his aunt in the stomach just so she would stumble and get in a position so she could get pulled along easier. They stopped only once for one of them to stick the barrel of his gun inside the opening of her low-cut blouse so they could see her breasts better and their laughter was wicked like evil birds.

Pablo would kill them all when he grew *cojónes*. He would kill them slow. Pablo spit at them and this surprised them and he got slapped off his feet so hard his bottom lip split open.

Then the bus came. They were pushed into the bus and they sat in the middle. The *patrón* with the rifle standing next to the bus driver yelled out, exalted, that everyone was on their way to America!

Pablo looked around. Some of the people on the bus were crying. Some were beat up badly and everyone else was just sad. His aunt used the blindfold to hold to Pablo's chin to stop his bleeding lip. She held him close and rubbed the back of his neck with her other hand.

They shouldn't have stayed at the market so long. They shouldn't have cut through the agave field.

"We didn't listen to God," she half-whispered, half-spit into Pablo's ear.

Homecoming

Evidently Jeremiah at the beach wasn't the only one who got all sexed up with that new girl in his trailer. So did Charley Younger. She was so pretty and she smelled like springtime back when Charley Younger was a child in Kentucky when there were flowers. Lots of flowers in their backyard and his father used to beat him just for being retarded over by those big white flowers that looked like the popcorn balls his mother used to make. He couldn't hold those popcorn balls very well and he wasn't good at chewing them at all. But they were so good. Even though they stuck to his small teeth and his jaw muscles weren't very good and he would dribble saliva and cough and spit bits of sugar sticky popcorn everywhere. Then his dad would just haul off and slap him just because he worked in a coal mine and thought Charley Younger wasn't worth a shit and a retard. Charley Younger tried not to cry and would just cower and breathe hard and want to kill his fat ugly old coal miner father, as his head bled sometimes and sometimes it hurt so bad Charley Younger would wet himself and this would piss his father off so bad he would then beat Charley Younger with a belt until Charley Younger would pass out.

Charley Younger took a break from the Chinese place and hurried across the street and went through a space between two old Daytona Beach motels and hurried down old gray wooden steps and ran awkwardly through the thick white sand. He passed a pretty girl stretched out dead in an itsy-bitsy bathing suit and there on her leg was a tattoo of a phoenix, a beautiful colorful phoenix rising up towards death, he figured.

Charley Younger stopped and steadied himself. He was out of breath. He didn't run very well. His lungs were bad. He breathed badly his whole life. But he had arrived. He was where he should be. It was all here. All noisy and rolling in. Charley Younger raised his ever-slumping eyes, and still trying to catch his breath, he stared at this magnificent, endless ocean. He took in a huge deep breath of comforting salty air and this was his ocean. He owned it right at this moment in time. It was his and he was just granting these beautiful dead people permission here because he was a nice retarded guy. A nice deformed retarded guy who wanted a chin and better teeth and a chance to put his penis inside that girl in his trailer with the long legs and little butt and did he remember to set the clean plates out for witchy oriental woman who would like to kill him? The buffet didn't open for another hour so maybe if he didn't he still had some time. She could just kiss his retarded ass. His perfect ass, by the way. He was deformed and all, but his ass you could bounce a quarter off of. Whatever that meant. A whore told him this. A whore he paid for almost six years ago and all she did was stroke his hair as he cried and couldn't breathe but she said if he had nothing else, he had a nice ass.

Back in Kentucky his father came home once and yelled so loud and long at Charley Younger his father started coughing up blood and black from his lungs and with his eyes pointing down Charley Younger wanted to be right where he was now, here at this ocean with all this water and life and promised land and a biplane there in the sky floating by, a banner trailing BARBECUE RIBS 9.99. That's part of the reason him and his mother moved to Florida. Because Charley Younger wanted to see the ocean and his mother didn't care and when they found the only island trailer park in the world they fell in love with Florida and have been there ever since.

This was life. This was his. He knew he forgot the plates. Charley Younger turned and ran ever-awkward back the same way he came.

No, Jeremiah didn't look at her legs there on the couch. Nope. When he came home from church and a come to Jesus visit to the ocean and unlocked the door and walked in and saw Stephanie there on the couch he, instead, put his eyes on the Virgin Mary. Yes, he did. No, he didn't catch a glimpse of her blue panties creased in between her folded up olive brown, bare thighs. She was really sleeping hard there on the couch. Her jeans were in a little heap on the carpet in front of the couch. So was her faded, tattered red flannel shirt. Her tank top Jeremiah didn't notice clung to her body so tight her nipples on those small breasts looked about to explode. It was hot in here. Very hot. She could have turned on the window air-conditioner. It was right there in the window beside the couch. Then she wouldn't have had to undress like she did. God, she must have been tired. Her mouth was open and her chest heaved. She slept like she hadn't slept since the beginning of the world. By the look of her, she hadn't slept in years. Jeremiah swallowed hard. There was about four inches of brown flesh above and below a perfect circle of a belly button. He didn't notice there was no fat on this woman. He made certain not to notice anything about this girl. He had God to worry about.

He turned on the window air-conditioner and then held his breath.

It was noisy but she didn't even move. She was so tired.

Jeremiah walked as quietly as he could out of the living room and brought back the softest, thinnest blanket he had. He eased it over her. She stirred but she didn't wake up. She needed this sleep.

Jeremiah didn't know what to do with himself so he grabbed a soda and went outside and sat on the concrete patio. He wanted a cigarette bad. Worse than he could remember in a long time. Not this bad since he put Nettie, Charley Younger's mother, in the deep freeze. God he hated doing that. Nothing was right about that. But Charley Younger needed that pension check. Jeremiah took a drink of soda. He had to calm down.

Then Jeremiah jumped as if shot in the white plastic chair. He had three more twenty dollar bills to put in the box. It was time, as a point of fact, to start filling up the third box. He had to put them away as he always did. Every Sunday. He got up.

Jeremiah went inside and Stephanie was sitting up now in a beautiful position, as one of her knees was up and touching her breast, as her other leg stretched out so far in front of her Jeremiah was certain it magically went several feet into the floor. She was half-smiling.

Jeremiah walked on by Stephanie, walked on by her eternal legs, on by an ass that blended so well with her thighs as to not exist, walked on by the troubles his mother taught him forever and a day to avoid, and on into the bedroom where his boxes were.

Charley Younger's Beach

Charley Younger cleaned the front window so good you would hardly know it was there if it wasn't for the yellowed newspaper clipping stuck to the glass. He had to clean around that dirty piece of paper. It was an article from the Daytona Beach Chamber of Commerce about how this Chinese restaurant made the best sesame chicken in all of Daytona Beach Shores. The article was over ten years old and very faded and yellowed. The Chinese people were smiling uncomfortably over a table with a plate of sesame chicken in the photograph on the newspaper clipping. Charley Younger thought they looked more like they were standing in an overly chilly rice paddy than in their little hole in the wall restaurant. Charley Younger didn't even like the sesame chicken. The sesame seeds stuck to his teeth and for the past two years they went cheap and decided to mix thigh meat with the white meat and everybody said it wasn't as good. The only one who never complained about it and said he loved it each and every time he ate it was Jeremiah. He said that about any food he ate. Jeremiah, Charley Younger believed, would eat shit if they cooked it right. He ate anything they put in front of him.

"You clean dishes now," the Chinese woman whispered hard to Charley Younger. She didn't want the tanned young tourist couple to hear her talking. They were the only ones in the place. She had a plate of pot stickers in her hand.

Charley Younger didn't want to go do the dishes. There was a tanned pretty girl out here. He liked tanned pretty girls. He stopped to straighten some fake flowers on an empty table.

"Go do dishes. No pay."

Charley Younger's droopy eyes blinked. "You pay," he said through his nose. He straightened fake flowers on another table. He glanced at the tanned girl and jumped. She was looking at him. This made Charley Younger mad and embarrassed. He made an odd noise and headed back towards the kitchen. Another couple was coming in. Another pretty girl, and he had to go in the back and do dishes where this seven year old Chinese boy would laugh at Charley Younger and make fun of him as he did his homework. Charley Younger stopped and spun awkwardly around and that girl who just walked in was goddamn looking at him too. He turned and crashed into a table so hard a glass of water fell over and as he tried to catch it that just made matters worse and a plate hit the floor.

The Chinese woman was bent over beside herself. She wanted to kill Charley Younger. She got real close to him and spit out venomous whispers through tight tense smiles. He turned just so that he could feel her breath as he looked up, pieces of the broken plate in his hand. Her breath was garlicky. The chinks all ate too much garlic.

"Be nice to American cripple boy," he said, and then blew out a strange kind of laugh. She slapped him so hard with the back of her hand he dropped all that he held. She immediately got between him and her customers.

"You go home now. No more work today. Go home."

Charley Younger finished picking up the broken pieces. He cut his finger scraping up the tiny bits. Then he kept his head way down as he left. Four people saw it all. Four hundred people staring at him. Four thousand people staring at the clumsy freak show.

Charley Younger squinted as he stood out on the curb. Then he ran as fast as he could across highway A1A. A car laid on the horn. A bent middle finger waved behind him as he ran. He ran to the beach. He ran crazy and as fast as he could and yelling all the way.

"Get off my beach! It's mine! Get off of it! Go home! Get off my beach!"

Two young boys maybe ten stopped and smiled and then laughed at the retard.

The retard stopped suddenly, his awkward limbs trying to stop too. Charley Younger turned to face the boys and double-pumped both middle fingers and then started running again.

It was a beautiful day at Charley Younger's beach today.

Death Angels

Stephanie sat on the patio and stared at her cell phone beside her pack of cigarettes on this little metal mesh table out on the patio. She stared at the cell phone and nothing else through two cigarettes. It wasn't on. It couldn't be turned on. It was an old Motorola V400 flip phone pay as you go and if it was on the display would glow blue. But she wouldn't turn it on. She would see no blue glow. She wouldn't hear her mother ask her why she killed Tony. Her mother might even ask if it was her who killed Tony. Of course she killed Tony. Her mother would tell her to say it was self-defense. Yes. Walking into the living room while he was watching a porn movie and shoot him twice in the face. He had a beer in one hand and his dick in the other. Self-defense.

She snuffed out the second cigarette and put the phone finally in her purse just as Charley Younger opened the door. A huge whiff of frying fish came out of that trailer door. It made Stephanie's belly rumble suddenly. She hadn't had anything or even thought about eating in well over two days. But suddenly now, the smell, she was hungry.

Charley Younger asked her if she wanted a beer. Her eyes lit up. They had beer? Charley Younger fidgeted and pointed off somewhere. Of course they had beer. Bud Light. Light beer. Light as air beer. He gestured weirdly, pointing off into space it seemed.

"JJ drinks two or three a night. Every night when he's home. He works late. I'm sleeping and these beer cans show up on the counter." He laughed. "Except when Dolores is over."

Delores?

"His girlfriend. Very sweet." Charley Younger bent up funny. He had odd body movements in general, Stephanie thought. "Kinda cute," he said. "Kinda not cute."

Stephanie laughed as she got to her feet. And then it struck her. She was in Florida and she had never been to Florida before. Never seen the ocean. She had wanted to see the ocean. She had planned it all out. She grabbed Charley Younger's sleeve. He froze. Was the ocean far away? The real ocean. Not that beautiful, beautiful river. The Ocean. With a beach. She'd never seen a real beach in her life. She had never seen an ocean of any kind.

Charley Younger lost his breath. He could smell her. It was the sweat of angels he was smelling. Death angels carrying him up. They would smell like she smelled right now. He lurched some. He had to find a breath somewhere. He told her to follow him. He spit out a strange word with his request. It was angel but it didn't get past his missing chin and broken teeth. He started to run and then stopped. He skipped a couple times. She was an ocean virgin. Come ocean virgin! She came. She followed.

Jeremiah was in the doorway. "Get back here. The food'll be done in an hour!"

They kept running.

"I'll eat without y'all!"

They kept running.

Him

It was the roar that got to Stephanie first. The ocean was big and endless but the noise! She was stunned. Charley Younger pulled a piece of wood from his pocket to hold in his palm as he talked and pointed out where a dolphin fin protruded out of the blue water. Stephanie gasped when the dark gray body surfaced and then vanished. This brought tears to her eyes. This was the ocean she had dreamed of. And it roared so loudly she couldn't hear what Charley Younger was saying. She didn't care about the people ambling about. Or the cars parked on the beach. Or the father and son heaving a football back and forth just down aways. She was listening but she could hear nothing but the wonderful loud drone of this wonderful huge noisy ocean.

It was all as it should be. She looked down and the sand was hot and thick but that noise. That wonderful fucking noise.

She had wanted him to live up to his promise. She had made love to him in that house and she had bought a white nightie just for him and it fit her badly and was embarrassingly cheap really but it was off her in two seconds anyway and they made love so many times she was sore the next day and there in the dark he told her about the ocean he wanted to take her to. Ocean's roar, he said. He couldn't believe she'd never seen the ocean. But he told her about the ocean and he described it so well. He always described everything so well. And it was just like he described and this was making Stephanie cry. He told her he would take her to see the ocean. He promised. She made him promise her several times that night. But there is nothing in a promise. She loved him and there she stood in a baseball cap, her hair pulled into a cute pony tail through a St. Louis Cardinals cap and her arms crossed just above her tanned seventeen year old belly he went so crazy over and he told her they couldn't see each other anymore. It was over and his wife might be pregnant (even though she wasn't) and there was nothing between them anymore. Even though his wife was lying for some reason she would never know about.

Through the noise Stephanie caught sight of a toddler staggering through the cooling, thick sand, his wobbly chubby legs and tiny fat feet and that was it. That was what put her back on track.

Stephanie headed down towards the water.

Charley Younger followed. Charley Younger skipped as he followed. He learned to skip as a little boy and, deformed or not, he was a great skipper.

He stopped and yelled out, "My Ocean!" Stephanie heard this. Through the hurt and pain and dulled anticipation she heard him yell out "My Ocean!"

His ocean. The thought struck her hard and painful. Stephanie had nothing anymore and even this retard had something. She cried even harder and kept marching towards the water.

Stephanie crossed the path the cars made through the white sand. She passed an empty wooden lifeguard station until she came to wet, hard dark sand and there at her feet through the thick tears she saw broken shells. She missed her son and she would never see him again and that's why it was easy now to do what she had planned to do.

She looked around. She looked at the endless now ugly ocean.

Stephanie, her tears blurring out the white caps, broke into a run towards the water. She could run fast. She had always been a fast runner. She was an okay swimmer as long as she didn't stay under too long.

But she planned to go under now.

Frozen in the sand behind her, Charley Younger said very softly, "Stephanie?"

Catfish

As three whole catfish fried in a hundred-year-old cast iron skillet and Charley Younger was trying to save Stephanie from drowning, Jeremiah happily cut up carrots and onions and potatoes while singing a gospel song in a rich, rather feminine voice. He shook his shoulders, shuffled his feet even. He loved to cook. Jeremiah, in his mind, was as good a cook as there was. That's why Charley Younger always brought home the fish they had planned to throw away at the restaurant. If the Chinaman bought too much on a Friday night and didn't get it all sold over the weekend Charley Younger would bring home as many as ten whole blue cats they had bought at the Flea Market Fish shop. Why they gave them to Charley Younger no one knew. Guilt, Jeremiah believed. They treated Charley Younger bad and Charley Younger was the best worker they had. In any case, there were three frying and four more waiting to be fried. They were dipped in egg, then rolled in flour with a touch of baking powder, a handful of spices, and plopped easy into a skillet full of sizzling, good old fashioned lard. Not Crisco or Canola. Just plain old lard that came in a square metal container that they could only get at the Winn Dixie in Ormand Beach. That's the only grocery store Jeremiah shopped at. There were mostly people of color who worked there and they enjoyed a good laugh and they treated you right there. Not like the scary white trash that worked at the super Wal-Mart down the road. No, everyone knew that was a shithole place run by white shirts and white skins from Arkansas.

He turned the first batch of catfish over. The puffy white flesh was poking beautiful through the brown, crunchy surface where his tongs hit. Jeremiah sighed. He was very hungry. He would eat three of these and they probably would pick over one a piece. They were over a pound each anyway. She might not even like catfish. He didn't have much else. He had to get to work in a few hours. He sipped from a glass of ice tea and leaned heavy against the counter.

Jeremiah worked at the Crab Inn down at the end of Ponce Inlet. It would probably be a slow night. Sunday nights without anything going on in Daytona meant a slow night. They might even let him cook. He made better crab cakes than anyone. They all knew that. He stared at the frying fish. Stephanie would get a job there and run home with one of the handsome young server boys like all those other pretty girls did. He laughed. And then she would join all the others out back who, on their breaks, would smoke and smoke and bitch and bitch. He figured she would fit right in.

Jeremiah carefully took out the batch of crispy whole catfish and stacked them on a plate and then put the rest of them in the skillet. He opened up the oven and peeked at the corn bread. It was almost done also. He eased the oven door shut and just stood there and shivered. He loved catfish.

Loveless

So the ocean didn't want her today, but as Stephanie drifted deeper and thicker into that darkening water her thoughts went deeper and thicker and down into her past where in that musty dim apartment he played the droning loud music he called shoegazer and she smoked a joint with him and listened to him rage on about music and oh did he know music and life and was he so smart, he especially believed he was smart, the way he was talking and all, and it was her who had to seduce him. He was just stupid about those things. Or maybe he wasn't so stupid. Maybe he knew all along he could ease her panties off her and slide his finger into her as if she were a delicate pastry. And he did something the young boys never did. He tasted her. He eased his finger inside for a while and easy back out and put his finger in his mouth as he talked about the seminal band, My Bloody Valentine, and how significant their album, *Loveless*, was to everything. Everything. Loveless. He was Loveless, he said. After his wife left him. If she left him. If he was telling the truth. In his finger went again, and it was joined by another finger this time. He sure knew where to put those fingers. Gentle and firm. She lightly rubbed the hair on his arm. Even though she tried not to, Stephanie came. A tense, quiet shiver and then she got a bit ugly all of a sudden. Loveless. His wife was just out of town, she bet. Was he through with his little gynecological exam? He put another CD in. He tried not to touch the hole in the plastic with his wettest fingers. This made her laugh. The music was just this droning loud stuff with scary waves of vocals washing over her like the ocean was doing to her now, five years later. Shoegazer. Loveless. My Bloody Valentine. Stephanie remembered all this for some reason. Being with an older married man was this ugly magical experience but he made her feel like she was real. And that's why she was remembering it here and now and right on the brink of her death. It's all anyone wanted really. To feel real. Something collided with her head. She had done it, she believed.

Stephanie had brought her own self to death.

Pablo Meets a Friend

Pablo was so tired and his Aunt's lap felt so good when he laid his head in it he fell asleep immediately. The truck hit many bumps and slid everyone inside all around but, oh was he tired.

He made friends with a *niño mongolico,* a mongoloid child, who was nice and chubby and about his age and her slant eyes were kind. She had metal stars and a ball but it was too bumpy to play jacks. She let him play with the ball though as she held the metal stars up in her chubby hand and laughed.

Still Pablo was so tired. He gave her back the ball and wanted to sleep but the truck stopped suddenly and they ate tortillas and tamales from a big cardboard box they threw in the back but they needed something to drink. They didn't give them anything to drink. They were all thirsty.

It got very dark in the back of the covered truck as they came upon night but the ride was still fast and bumpy and noisy. People tried to sleep.

There were only women and children in the truck and the women were all about his aunt's age and the children all about Pablo's age. A young woman was matched up to her child or like Pablo, her nephew or brother or sister.

Except the *niño mongolico.* The *patrón* had something else planned for her that they didn't know about.

Pablo asked her who she was with. She looked around and looked sad for a moment and then smiled. No one.

Pablo fell asleep in his aunt's lap and his friend fell asleep against his aunt too.

His aunt couldn't sleep. She hadn't slept at all.

She could pray though.

She kept praying.

Saved

Stephanie opened her eyes and found herself breathing so heavy it was like her lungs were touching her tail bone on each breath. There were bright streaks of white and blue and black but her eyes wouldn't focus. One eye was particularly black. She wiped at that eye and it was filled with blood. It smelled of blood and was thick and dark but it didn't hurt. The hurt came higher on her head. She realized suddenly that she wasn't dead. She tried to get her elbows underneath her and sit up but each limb was dull and weighed five hundred pounds. She finally got her eyes clear and discovered that the blood and the stinging were coming from right at the top of her forehead.

Beside her was Charley Younger, and he was stretched out and panting as hard as she had been panting. He had a big bump on his forehead also. Stephanie seemed to have gotten the worst of it. Again. His was just swollen and purple. He seemed out cold until she said his name. He bolted up.

"Ouch!" He grabbed his head. "You're the strongest person I know."

"Did you save me?"

"I was going to. I kept you from going way out. Some kid helped after that." Charley Younger looked around. He didn't know where the kid went. "He felt you up, I think."

"He did?"

"Yep." Charley Younger grabbed his head again and winced. "You shouldn't go in the water if you can't swim."

"We hit heads?"

Charley Younger rolled his almost shut eyes. She could really put two and two together. He would have gotten her to shore. The kid just helped. There were precious few things in life Charley Younger could do better than others but swimming was at the very top of the list. No one taught him. In fact, his dad threw him into a rock pit when he was seven years old and down he went and it was peaceful and cool and dark down there and when he felt like it he came back up and this scared the shit out of his dad but right there that day when he was seven years old Charley Younger realized he could swim better than anyone. He remembered his dad saying one thing over and over again for a long time.

"What?" Stephanie asked him.

"Like a damn dog!"

Stephanie smiled. Then she brushed more blood out of her eye and eased back into the sand to tilt her head back and help stop the bleeding. She didn't die. She had wanted to die. She closed her eyes.

Stephanie didn't die and now there was only one thing left to do. It was what she should have planned to do all along. Now it was time to plot and plan and fight and scratch and kill again if she had to and she would do this regardless of what anyone thought because she only had one thing left that made her real and that was her son. Jeremiah. Thick, determined tears pushed the blood out of her eye. She would get her son back. Stephanie would feel his little toes again and feel his chubby little arms around her neck again and fucking glory hallelujah the end would justify the means and the only thing even God would be able to do was just look on.

Stephanie would get her son back.

Postcards

The upright metal stand held postcards. It creaked when Stephanie eased it around. It made a tinny sound as it spun. There were postcards of big-breasted tanned women in skimpy bikinis and muscle bound tanned men in bulging tiny swimming trunks and airplane shots of the beach and one of the Halifax River on one side and the white strip of beautiful beach on the other. The words Daytona Beach stretched in all colors and fonts across virtually all of the postcards. Pink Flamingos were on many of the cards. Seymour was here somewhere, too. It was that precise time of year when he would bring his perfect little ass to Daytona Beach and stretch out beside his perfect little wife with her perfect little tan and expensively blond hair cut in that disgusting ugly yuppie bob, like she'd stolen the ass of a duck and set it on her head.

Stephanie didn't plan it this way. Didn't plan to kill her husband and run away to Daytona during the same week *Seymour* always brought his family here. Of course she didn't. She hadn't seen *him* in over five years. What had he called fate one evening after fucking her twice late one hot night on the grass of the reservoir? Bad timing? She liked his lips though. They weren't thin like her husband's. They were thick. Perhaps he didn't come here this year. Things always change.

Earlier as Stephanie stood in front of the postcards Charley Younger kept pointing his finger where his chin should be. Finally Stephanie got the message. She brushed at her own chin and a big crumb of fried batter from one of the three whole catfish she ate fell from her face.

She didn't fight Charley Younger when he grabbed her around the waist there in the darkening ocean. The water that felt so warm and cold and thick all at once. She truly did want to die. A long sleep struck her heavy and appealing there in the ocean. As she sank. As her ears filled up and her mouth filled up. It was the absence of pain that she found most attractive.

If Charley Younger hadn't tried to say something to her in the water his head may not have fallen so hard against hers. He got the worst of it, but he saved her life. Good or bad she was alive.

And when Jeremiah put that first whole catfish in front of Stephanie she devoured it. Scarfed it down like it was a cocktail shrimp. The tiny translucent bones Jeremiah warned her about she picked clean and stacked in a little pile beside her plate. She knew how to eat catfish. She didn't like cornbread or raw onion but she liked catfish. Jeremiah watched a bit shocked and totally amazed as Stephanie picked that whole catfish as naked of flesh as he had ever seen. And he hadn't taken six bites. He got up and put another one in front of her and she lit into it just like the first one.

Charley Younger sat in the living room picking very carefully at his catfish. He put his face close to the plate when he ate the cornbread and made sure no one was watching. He never ate at the table with company. He would if it was only Jeremiah and him but never with company. Stephanie stopped eating only once to tell Charley Younger to come to the table. He didn't answer and Jeremiah shook his head and she just shrugged and went back to grazing.

Jeremiah wasn't quite finished with his first piece as he ate onion and two pieces of cornbread with butter when he stopped and got up and put the third whole catfish in front of her. He fully expected her to say she was full. She just shrugged and smiled and wiped her mouth. She said she was hungry.

"And I love catfish." She smiled and her teeth were so white. He didn't know many people with teeth that white. "It's the best I've ever ate."

Jeremiah looked down at the only piece he would get of this batch. "Thank you," he said.

So they drove down to the Winn-Dixie where the parking lot was mostly empty on a Sunday afternoon and in the parking lot Stephanie rummaged through her purse as they walked and slipped a twenty-dollar bill into Jeremiah's hand. He didn't refuse it. He was pretty much broke until payday. Charley Younger dawdled in front of the store like he always did. He gently poked at a stack of lawn chairs. Then he wiggled a stand-alone umbrella. Then he pulled his arm back and let out a yell. His arm was sore from an accidental elbow he got saving this pretty girl's life. He yelled out that he was a hero. They were already inside. He finally went in, too.

They didn't have any whole catfish so Jeremiah got a pound and a half of fillets. The old tiny black lady carefully took the fillets and wrapped them in white paper. Her shiny black hair was pulled back tight and covered with black netting. She was older than even Jeremiah's mother. Maybe older than his grandmother. He knew her name. Mrs. Jackson.

Mrs. Jackson weighed out the fillets then put two more on and winked before taping the white paper shut. She said what she always said to Jeremiah when she did this. When she gave him extras.

"You a friend of Mr. Dixie?"

Jeremiah smiled. "I'm a friend of Mr. Dixie."

The old lady cackled.

Jeremiah said he didn't see her in church today. Mrs. Jackson said she had to come to work. Had to come in at seven. "Make Mr. Dixie happy."

"And pay your bills."

"That's right."

They both laughed.

Back at the twirling postcards Stephanie jabbed at the swirling metal stand so hard a couple fell as it stopped spinning so abruptly. She very carefully bent down and removed the one postcard that caused her to stop the spinning.

It was of a fat little baby boy in a sailor uniform sitting in the sand with brightly colored plastic toys surrounding him. The words Daytona Beach stretched all across the sky behind him. Charley Younger had been looking over her shoulder. Charley Younger saw her eyes. Charley Younger saw her expression.

"You have a child," he said.

After a long pause, Stephanie said, "Yes, I do."

Her Last Night on Earth

There was a phone ringing in a house eleven hundred, forty-seven miles and nineteen feet, three inches away. No one would answer. But in his head Doc watched his wife ball up the dish cloth and plop it on the island kitchen and walk in that hurried beautiful way and then pick up the phone, press the right button, and in that voice he had heard for over thirty-five years, she would deadpan, "Hello?"

"Hi, Honey."

The phone kept ringing. Out the window he watched an old car ease by. The air outside was hot and dry and dead. He absently scratched himself as the phone kept ringing. The skin of his inner thigh was sticking to his balls. And vice-versa. He smiled as the phone kept ringing. He finally moved his leg to separate his two aged body parts. His underwear was old and baggy. Who cared? No one saw it anymore.

The phone kept ringing. No one would answer because his wife was dead and he still hadn't sold the house and he didn't plan on disconnecting the phone any time soon.

This time, as the phone kept ringing, he decided that sooner or later he would have to put his house up for sale. And, even more importantly, he would have to get over his wife dying.

She died quietly in her sleep. She had been dreaming. She had been dreaming about a time when her husband *didn't* call her at the worst possible time. That's the only time he called. At the worst possible time. Always.

"It is?" He would say, referring to the worst possible time she spoke of.

"I love you though."

"You were busy?"

"I'm always busy, Honey," she would say. "It's a big house."

And it was a big house. There were five bedrooms and three bathrooms and she was anal-retentive and he dropped everything he had no use for any longer wherever he happened to be. And half of his kids did exactly the same thing. The other half of his kids were always busy and they didn't like to answer the phone either. He blinked. Out the window now was that very pretty girl. She was walking into Jeremiah's house with Jeremiah and Charley Younger. He imagined she looked very nice naked.

His wife looked nice naked. Even in her death she had a very nice body and for her entire fifty-eight years she never carried any extra pounds anywhere. He loved to lay in bed with her and look for any extra pounds and though he never found any he always found lots of other wonderful things.

He let the phone ring a little while longer.

He thought briefly about pulling his pants down and thinking about that girl out there. But he wasn't up for it. That girl, at this very moment, was making him think about his dead wife. His beautiful dead wife who died in her sleep of a very efficient stroke, after she had finished cleaning up the house and picking up all the things he left laying around. And after cooking the most brilliant meal he had ever tasted. And he had forgotten to help her clean up. He could have at least helped her clean up the kitchen on her last night on earth.

He hung up the phone.

Lonely

As the sun set on the other side of the world two active feet dangled from the wooden lifeguard chair there just down from the pier. The beach was pleasantly empty and the tide was inching itself up over the white sand and it was the perfect time of day according to Charley Younger.

When the sky eased into burnt orange and mixed with the streaks of black and browns everywhere this was when the ocean became his and his alone. Charley Younger stopped peeling his orange. Every evening, when he had an orange, he would bring it here and climb up into the empty lifeguard chair and dream of rescuing a beautiful woman. A beautiful deaf and dumb woman. Who could not hear him or see him but who knew he saved her. Instead he rescued a beautiful woman who could see him and hear him.

In fact, Stephanie had insisted on Charley Younger eating with them. Not where he always ate embarrassed, when there was company at the table. She had insisted he come out of the living room and sit at the table with Jeremiah and her. Insisted! This agitated Jeremiah, but she kept insisting so Charley Younger inched his way up to the table. Jeremiah should have said something. Jeremiah should have told her the truth, that Charley Younger had a fear of people watching him eat. He had a fear they would laugh at him or be grossed out. One person became a hundred people to Charley Younger and then a million people grossed out or laughing at him. Jeremiah should have told her this. He said nothing. But Stephanie said something when he finally made it to the table.

"Chill," she'd said, tearing into another fillet. She was so hungry she even cut the big slices of onion Jeremiah had made into pieces and ate them and they were the sweetest onions she had ever tasted.

"Vidalias," Jeremiah had said. Then he had asked her what her story was. Charley Younger had stopped picking at his food and trying to hide his mouth. Stephanie stopped eating too. Then she took a large drink of her third beer. Jeremiah wasn't halfway through his first beer. He had to go to work tonight. Then she smiled a sheepish, beautiful smile.

Now, Charley Younger tossed the orange peels, one at a time, into the rising evening tide. They vanished black and silent into the darkening gray foamy water. There was very little orange in the sky now. More brown and black than orange. It was beautiful. The colors he felt right before dark were always beautiful. Lights far out on the water from a distant boat twinkled. The pier glowed incandescent to his left. There were a few fishermen on the far end of the pier but it was too dark to see their faces and the softening roar of ocean made it impossible to hear them talking.

"It was the last time he would touch me," Stephanie had said, after saying she shot her husband twice in the face with a .45 caliber hand gun her husband bought to kill stray cats with.

Charley Younger coughed out his unfinished bite. Jeremiah froze a piece of bread in one hand and a beer glass in the other, his mouth full of onion and catfish. He did finally swallow.

She stared into her beer as she spoke.

"He officially raped me that night," she'd said. She didn't want to have sex and more than that even she would not ever have sex with him ever again, she told him. Him and his porn movies. She had just put medicine in Jeremiah's ears since he had a double ear-infection and had finally got to sleep.

"He hit me so hard in my stomach I doubled over. I couldn't breathe."

Then he leveled her with another punch to the face. Stephanie pointed to a brown spot on her cheek. She didn't get that running into Charley Younger.

Charley Younger and Jeremiah were looking at each other as she dead-panned what her husband did to her next.

Now, Charley Younger froze in his lifeguard chair. There was no chill in the air but he felt cold and for the first time in a long time he felt lonely. There was usually nothing lonely about his ocean and his beach or maybe it was just that lonely was so everywhere he had made it a good thing. It wasn't a good thing right now.

Stephanie took her son to her mother's and she took off on a bus and she was here now and she wasn't hungry anymore and needed a cigarette. She got up from the table. Charley Younger couldn't eat anymore either and Jeremiah didn't eat much more either. He had to take a shower and get to work. He was closing tonight so he'd leave his key under the stone frog.

Stephanie went out and had a cigarette and Charley Younger cleaned everything up. He cleaned the table twice and even cleaned the stupid old chairs twice. There was not a crumb left on the floor. He started to clean it twice too.

Instead he peeked out the slit in the crank window of the aluminum front door and watched Stephanie smoke a cigarette. She had set a dead cell phone on the rusty metal table beside her. It wasn't turned on.

Everything was all black and a little gray now. It was the only time of the day when the ocean's roar was only a whimper.

And Charley Younger was as lonely as he could ever remember being. Her eyes were wet and red finally when she said she took her son to her mother's.

So lonely Charley Younger felt like going to the freezer and thawing out his mother. When she thawed out she would be just like before. She wasn't dead. Ice was healing her. He read that somewhere on the Internet and believed it.

Charley Younger coughed and wrung his hands and his feet did not move for a long time.

Then he climbed down off the lifeguard station and headed home.

Larry

Larry was more than tanned, more than weather beaten by the hot Florida sun. Larry looked more like he'd been dipped into the bowels of hell and seared for a few minutes and then returned to earth, crisp and aged. He wore a *Gone Fishin'* cap that looked older than he was and he looked old. He had a wrinkle on his face for every hundred packs of Marlboro Lights. He was fifty-seven going on six years past legal retirement age. And Larry was skinny. Every steak and cheeseburger and lobster tail most people packed into their body Larry replaced with a cigarette and six pack. He liked to eat actually but almost always managed to replace the entree with his next Budweiser.

Yes sir indeed he was an alcoholic. He was an alcoholic for the same reason many people were alcoholics: he drank too much. A waitress one time, a hard-looking woman who proudly told every man she could that she never wore underwear unless she was in a dress, asked Larry one time what his liver probably looked like. Larry thought about this through two cigarettes and a free shot of whiskey.

"A charred piece of damp coal," he said. He smiled and she laughed. But Larry earned his skinny, wrinkled dried up body. Earned every ounce of it. Vietnam, three wives, a couple kids, a short stint in a Georgia prison for robbery. By God, he would tell you, you come out of all that any better.

And now, here he was, gainfully employed at Bate's Bait Shop right on the Halifax River and happy as he had ever been in his life. He blew smoke into a rack of dusty lures.

Not really. Larry was lonely. He lived in a trailer in a bad trailer park up in Ormond Beach all by himself and he probably hadn't talked to his last remaining kid in four years. Maybe more like six years. Time flew by in a blink of an eye.

That's the one thing he'd a done better in his life. Get along with his kids more. His oldest, god bless his soul, died last year in a car wreck in Jersey City, and his youngest, a thirty year old daughter, wanted nothing to do with him. Larry made sure the freezer was shut. There wasn't one tub of frozen shrimp left. He'd have to figure out that goddamned computer and how to order more with the fucking Internet, his boss told him. Larry didn't care one iota about the Internet and as he stared at the drop-dead pretty girl standing all nervous at the counter as she pointed at the cigarettes, he thought, "What the goddamn hell is the Internet?"

As Stephanie carefully opened her purse and removed one of the twenties in such a way that this man could not see the rest of the twenties stacked neatly inside, she paused and said, "Island?"

Yes sir indeed. If she lived in the Pelican Island Mobile Home Park, and Larry seriously doubted she did, as it was a supposed senior community, then she lived on the only island trailer park in the entire world.

"It's documented somewhere," Larry said, as he, with precision, undid the plastic from her pack of unfiltered Camels with one hand, tapped it lightly but firmly on the counter, just once to get just one to pop straight out the end, then flipped open his Zippo with his other hand and flicked it opened and it flamed simultaneously. Stephanie smiled. Very impressive. She took the cigarette and eased her thin warm hand upon his wrist and leaned toward him to let Larry light the cigarette.

Larry got a hard on. He hadn't done that for a woman in, fuck, he couldn't remember how long. Memories from when he could flitted and floated everywhere in that bait shop.

Stephanie, as she stood there and stared with a look of measured indifference out the window, stared into the dark night where the most beautiful river she had ever seen was, stated,

"I live there."

Crab Cakes

The restaurant down at the tip of Ponce Inlet, where the Atlantic converged with the Halifax, was busier than it should have been on a Sunday night and everybody wanted a window seat as two dolphins eased through the water alongside the dock on the Atlantic side of the restaurant and on the left side two men coming in from fishing were cleaning and dressing big tuna and groupers under bright white lights. It was a good show tonight and a steady stream of tourists lined the windows as the locals sat at the bar. The place was hopping.

Jeremiah cleaned tables most of the night because they were a waitress short of course but then, Annie, a steel-haired twenty-six year veteran waitress, grabbed him finally by the back of his belt and told him to get his brown ass into the kitchen and make those one of a kind crab cakes. They were out of shrimp and she just talked a party of eight into his crab cakes. She wanted a big tip to end the night and she might even share it. She slapped his ass.

That's all Jeremiah needed. He wadded up his white rag, tossed it into a pile of dirty dishes and headed back into the kitchen.

Seymour

Outside on the second floor of the Ocean Palm Inn, Seymour Belmo leaned over the white-painted metal round railing and mused about the dime-sized mole on the inside thigh of the Cuban-Chinese girl who had smiled so pretty and talked so coarse and cried when he made love to her. Down below dull bright lights lit the empty pool. White plastic deck chairs encircled the pool like techno tombstones. A thin gray line of ocean rippled vaginal out in the near-dark. It was a beautiful ocean. God she smiled so pretty and didn't talk much really. He talked all the time around her and she just listened mostly. And smiled. He promised Stephanie, those many years ago, that he would take her right here and make love to her right out there in the deep white sand but that never happened.

Seymour never left his wife and the girl tried to kill herself in a warm tub with a razor and a half a bottle of Vicoden. She didn't die, however. Their relationship died. He vowed to stay on track and never stare for very long at the panties of students in jean mini-skirts.

It was history he would stick to teaching, not bad behavior. But that mole. It hovered there alive on her thigh, just inches from trouble. Wet, tight trouble.

Seymour was drunk. He sat at the Top of Daytona Restaurant and drank six Jack and Cokes. Six! He laughed when an old bi-plane eased by at eye-level trailing a banner for BBQ BEEF Sandwiches. The bartender looked at him. That wasn't particularly funny. Seymour staggered to the elevator and down the twenty-nine floors and here he was musing over a mole.

A young musician had saved Stephanie's life that day. He played drums in an emo band and lived in the apartment down from her and he had a key to her apartment and he got high and naked and hiding in the louvered linen closet he prepared to jack off watching Stephanie take a bath. It was just a fluke thing, him doing that, he said. He stopped pulling when she eased the razor blade gently across her left wrist. Was that a razor blade? He said he yelled this next:

"Jesus Fucking Christ!"

This startled her. The bath water rattled. Then Stephanie switched the razor blade to her other hand and sliced her other wrist.

Stephanie passed out and didn't remember anything after that. Didn't remember her naked neighbor wrapping up her wrists with first small towels and then big towels and cords and calling 911. He stopped briefly to get dressed.

Later, several weeks later, over a cup of coffee, Stephanie asked the emo musician if he fucked her.

He looked genuinely disappointed. He flicked at the silver ring through the left side of his nose. He hadn't thought of that. He shrugged. "They got there pretty quickly actually." Then he asked her if she loved that asshole.

Stephanie, there in a Starbucks in Granite City a few years back, rubbed her still tingling wrists and said, "I must have."

The musician laughed a dark, very dry laugh. "What about now?"

Stephanie didn't answer right away. She watched a young mother with her daughter cross the street. Then finally she spoke. "I don't think so. No."

Oh, if that mole could talk. Seymour sighed and tipped the plastic cup of warm jack and water up to his mouth. But it couldn't and neither could he when he was where that mole was. He sniffed and smiled. Funny. She seemed like she was out there right now. There in the darkness. He could smell her. Smell her soap. He swore he saw her shadow. He smiled a painful smile.

Chicago

And Stephanie was out there on the beach in front of the Ocean Palm Inn, actually, if Mr. See Nothing, her ex-history teacher and object of her obsession at one time, would have looked hard enough. If he hadn't have been so drunk. Stephanie was standing there staring into the void as the quiet rumble of the Atlantic clarified a few things for her. Purified a few other things. The hot air was finally cooling. And though she didn't look behind her, didn't turn to see the solitary drunken man hanging on the railing there in the distance as he contemplated her mole, Stephanie knew Seymour was here in Daytona somewhere.

Because it was the second week in May and his pretty little wife was on a cruise with her four pretty little sisters and they would be stopping in that same bar in Jamaica and they would all get drunk and there would be only one condom they would draw Margarita straws for. Then the winner would place it solidly over the ebony maple tree of a coal-black stripper and, with hoots and whoops, insane laughter and red faces, give him a blow job.

"Well," Seymour's wife had said, recalling how they had all swore not to tell this yearly tradition to their spouses, and then recalling how she had caught her husband in a parked car with that Stephanie girl one time, told Seymour everything. Told him every graphic detail. How she worried for weeks that a little might have gotten on her lip in her zeal. "Tradition is tradition."

Not that Stephanie planned this all. To come where asshole Seymour was. Daytona was just this place that popped into her head at the bus station. And it happened to be the same week she killed her husband. Stephanie blew out a perfect smoke ring that hung over the ocean much longer than she thought it would. Stephanie knew nothing about irony. A light from a boat twinkled in the distant darkening horizon. She lit another cigarette.

But Seymour, the asshole teacher, kept Stephanie here in this moment, her purse glutted with twenty-dollar bills. She sat down in the sand, brushed perfectly white sand off her thin, tanned knee, tucked both those knees up to her chin and stared. He always spoke of moments. Chunks of moments. It all made sense to her now. She thought she had him and he knew there were just these moments together. The little fucker.

It had sure been an exasperating moment late one evening in the dull yellow musty choking light of an Amtrak train ride back from a harrowing happy trip to Chicago where they fucked each other in a corner 19th floor hotel room on Michigan Avenue for the very first time. Seymour had promised not to do anything. She kept staying on the verge of a smile and saying okay and then he got the tickets. Stephanie had never ridden a train before. She lived her sheltered life in the shadow of a smelly tire factory in Granite City all of her seventeen years and had never ridden a train or flew in a plane or ever seen the ocean. She was seventeen years old! It would be harmless, he told her. He had to give a talk at a seminar at a conference of high school history teachers on the topography of modern music and how history is influenced as much by the song as by the lyric. Whatever, she had thought, her bare foot resting on the bulge in his jeans as they sat there in Forest Park that day. She knew he would fuck her. And he did. But not right away.

The whole city of Chicago scared Stephanie. The buildings were too tall and the streets too dark and that lake Seymour said looked like a huge beautiful ocean was just scary and didn't look like an ocean at all. No, she had never seen an ocean but she knew it didn't look like that, no matter what he nervously said. They shouldn't have come to Chicago at night.

Union Station was dark and dreary and noisy and smelly and that green river looked like green alien mud and as they both sat in that stupid diner-like place on State Street, Seymour looked like he felt the same way. This wasn't how he wanted it to turn out at all. There was no lusty magic here. This supposed romantic illicit excursion had left this thirty-six year old married man as sick as she was feeling all of a sudden. All anticipation, all titillation was gone. There was abject anxiety and regret and a frightened young girl who kept filling her lungs with cigarette after cigarette and really couldn't wait to get home. She didn't really want any of this. He was the one who started it all. What? Well, it was. He started it. Always calling her back when she left a message on his phone. What? She wasn't hungry. Maybe just some fries. Where was their room? They had been walking forever, she said, her eyes sagging and damp. Was it a double-bed like he said it would be? Was it?

Then the subcutaneous gears shifted. The hotel was awesome. A huge glass façade and this long white limousine out front with some hidden celebrity inside and look at that fucking waterfall! Right inside with open oval glass elevators on either side! She giggled and lost her breath on the way up, the Chicago skyline through the wide-open huge glass left her thin, pretty young mouth wide open. It was all fucking good now. Seymour marveled at how the fuck word rolled so casually off the sweet little tongue of Stephanie.

But he was still sick to his stomach. As the elevator came to a stop and as those golden mirrored doors opened he fully expected her to go into full cardiac arrest for no good reason. He would be able to explain none of it. He froze stiff more than once wondering if seventeen was indeed "of age." Hell, he didn't know. Hadn't cared before. His wife just got a new job. Fuck a duck. What had he gotten himself into?

"Oooh . . ." Stephanie said in the hallway. "The carpet's so thick!"

Seymour could barely bring himself to smile. He felt diarrhea coming on. He couldn't poop in the same hotel room with this girl he didn't know. Jesus Christ.

Seymour, as he stared at a chubby young woman snap at her thick macramé like bikini before diving into the empty well-lit pool there in Daytona, still dizzy from all those drinks, jumped as if shot when his cell phone vibrated in his pocket. It was his wife. They were in Jamaica. It sounded like a lively Caribbean party going on. She was drunk. She got the wrong straw this time and had to watch her younger sister. And the black man wasn't as well-built as last year.

"Seymour?"

Silence.

"Am I getting fat?"

Seymour looked at his cell phone as if something strangely new had suddenly appeared in his palm. He put it back to his ear. Of course she wasn't getting fat. She barely weighed one-ten. She looked better than she ever had. The mid-thirties was the most wonderful time of beauty for any woman.

"Is there anyone there with you?" she asked.

"No."

"We should have a kid, Seymour. All my sisters have kids."

Again he looked at the phone.

Then out of the Jamaican blue, "Can I sleep with someone while I'm here, Seymour?"

"What?"

"Honest. Would you care or not?"

Would he care was what she was asking. Seymour said again of course he would care. He took a deep, nervous breath. He didn't like the silence on the other end.

It was the end, he surmised. The shelf life of his marriage was expiring. There were no children and there was no love between Betsy and him any longer. He closed his eyes. He would not care one single bit. The phone went dead. He could hear no party.

Seymour put the phone back into his pocket and leaned over the railing to watch the full-bodied young woman navigate slowly through the clear-lit pool and gracefully make her way to the deep end.

It was too beautiful of a night, Seymour decided, to be so goddamn miserable.

1986

The bar and grill in the middle of Sun Glow Pier had a lot of people in it tonight. Stephanie stared out the screenless cranked-out wooden windows and could see all the lights of the high rises and hotels that lined the north side of the ocean. She sipped a draft beer in a plastic cup. She closed her eyes and then those large green Cuban-Chinese eyes bolted open. Her son was crying. Of this she was certain. He missed her and he needed her. She stared down at the dead cell phone there beside her cigarettes. Then finally she let her tense body go. She took another drink of beer. It hit Stephanie suddenly that her mother, though only in her forties, would not be able to take care of her son. She might not be able to take care of anyone. Her father lived in St. Charles with a horrible bitch maybe three years older than Stephanie.

Drunk one night several years ago, her father revealed something to Stephanie. Something he should have kept from Stephanie but for some odd fucking reason, told her anyway.

He talked about Holiday Dance 1986 in a small town called Red Bud and this papier-mâché high school gym was poorly lit and flashing sparks from a spinning mirror ball had turned everyone funny colors. He sat in a corner table with a plastic glass of cheap wine and a partially hidden joint and all night long her mother was agitated and weird and her face had been all puffy for days, maybe longer, weeks, and she kept talking and talking about this commune in the Northwest where her friend Dorothy went, for she didn't know what reason really, she was a free spirit, Dorothy was, and it was time for her to go somewhere, anywhere but Red Bud, Dead Bud, she kept calling it and let's dance, no, let's not dance, I'm so fucking bloated, and if Dorothy would have been here she could have gotten her hair right. Don't say a word I know my hair is a mess. Don't say a damn word and then she doubled over and almost hit her head on the table and if he hadn't been so fucked up himself he might have helped but she was alright. She just needed some air, for Christ's sake, so they went outside that gymnasium and it was a beautiful black and snowy, crisp night. The snow fell light and he couldn't remember such a night because you looked up and you couldn't tell if you were looking at stars or snowflakes. Honest to God. Oh, I can tell, your mother said, still standing there swiveling all around, so nervous and agitated and she looked, yeah, puffy, but tall and beautiful like never before. Oh, she might have been a little heavier than she had been in those early years, but I always liked every inch. He still likes heavier women. You need some weight on you, daughter.

He couldn't remember how long they stood out there but they were starting to shiver and she was talking trash about everybody, her mom and dad, and how Dorothy just up and left for no goddamn reason but she had every reason! Your mother threw her palms at the stars and snow. This was Dead Bud! Dead Bud, Illinois! Then she dropped like she'd been shot right into the snow. Something was pissing her off. Something she ate or just some mental something.

Stephanie's father paused here in his story. He sat there in that beat up recliner, it was Christmas and her mother was with her folks and every Christmas after her parents split Stephanie had to spend with her father. Not a single Christmas was Stephanie allowed by her mother to spend Christmas with her. Only her father. Every other holiday she spent with her mother, and most weekends when she should have been with her lousy father, her mother made up some excuse to keep Stephanie with her. But Christmas was a different story. Every Christmas, like here now, with her father. For the longest time, her father kept repeating this through his yellow teeth until it made him laugh way down deep. So deep it made him cough. He dropped his cigarette on the carpet. Stephanie picked it up.

She was her father's gift and there doubled over and cursing so loud out front of that gymnasium even he was embarrassed. The world, her life, him, everyone her mother.

Finally, her mother, back there in 1986, got to her feet and stormed back into that gym and he kind of followed. He was drunk and high but not so much that he wasn't embarrassed.

Her mother stormed right into the bathroom. He knew it was time to go. He knew she didn't want to be around people when she was like she was. He put his blue bow-tie into the jacket of his stupid tuxedo and just leaned against a yellow painted brick wall. He was out of cigarettes and definitely out of dope and everything else really. The band was playing "Stairway to Heaven." Swear to God. He didn't know how long she was in there. A long time maybe. Time was slow that evening.

Her mother came out finally. She looked better. Even though she was white as a ghost she looked better. Now it was time to go. They'd go to his house and his parents would be asleep and he'd get some tail on the living room floor.

Stephanie was already curled up into a ball and turned away from her father on the couch with her head buried so deep into the cushion you could hardly see it.

She didn't have to hear what her father said next. Stephanie wasn't stupid. She wasn't particularly smart but she wasn't stupid either.

Her mother stopped in the doorway of the Red Bud High School Gymnasium and since her father was right on her heels, he actually collided with her and bounced right off. It was snowing really heavy now and the stars were blowing through that open door.

"Oh, Merry Christmas." Nancy Ann Smith spit and snarled at her stupid-ass no account ignorant boyfriend, Steve.

"Your gift's in the trash in there."

His gift. After he had bounced off his date he looked at his hand. Something wet was all over the bottom of her peach-colored dress. That something was thick and looked black in the ugly light of that night, 1986. It was blood.

The year, the day, the hour when Stephanie was born.

Happy birthday, Daughter.

Temptation

It wasn't the fresh crab or the filler or anything like that. The secret to Jeremiah's crab cakes was the cayenne pepper he got from an organic grocery store back home in Atlanta. It was just down the street from where he grew up and right next to the worst Chinese restaurant in America. Way worse than Charley Younger's Chinese restaurant. It had mice that would stare at you and just blink. And the Chinese people behind the counter would just stare at you and blink too. But the crab rangoons were the best in America so sometimes he would weather the mice.

But the West Indies Organic Grocery Store owned by Jackson Whittaker had this homemade cayenne pepper Jackson made himself from the Charleston Hot variety that he got from a Louisiana farmer back in 1946. The Charleston Hot variety of the cayenne pepper was the biggest and the hottest. "Like I used to be," Jackson would tell Jeremiah. Then laugh. Jackson even sold that cayenne pepper in a gallon jug for people who wanted to keep cats out of their yards. In fact, this is all it said in black on a plain white label on each bottle:

Jackson Whittaker's Cayenne Pepper
Will Make a Cat Go Blind

It wasn't just hot. It was alive. It didn't just heat your mouth and lips right away. It was timed-released, Jackson said. Organically timed-released and when you swallowed it and then ate a little more, there would be a time when it would finally rise up so slow you'll be half way through something and then your chest would go numb and then eventually your throat would go numb. Happy numb. It made Jeremiah's balls tingle. He didn't like to be coarse and talk about this but he made some jambalaya one time and he put a little too much of Jackson's cayenne pepper in on purpose and it was the best jambalaya him and Charley Younger ever had and Jeremiah drank the rest of his fourth beer and God was it good with beer and then he asked Charley Younger, who had just ate about half the bowl. Charley Younger didn't even touch his cornbread. He just scarfed that jambalaya down with three glasses of big ice water. Charley Younger thought about it.

"Yeah," Charley Younger said. "My balls are tingling."

They ate the whole pot that night.

Tonight, as Jeremiah absently looked over the kitchen counter at the dolphins rising up out of the water there out the window he moved aside some bottles and there was his bottle of Jackson's Cayenne Pepper. None of the other cooks ever touched it. Jeremiah rolled it right into the fresh crab meat and then rolled everything else into it and made the nice perfectly round patties. He baked them in a 450 degree oven for fifteen minutes.

Jeremiah made at least thirty-six patties that night. Two a plate. It was about all they had left outside of some dried up and overcooked and oversalted prime rib and the three waitresses were talking his crab cakes up, and sliding dollar bills into his pants. Jeremiah, as the night wore on, got sweaty and tired and it was finally close to closing time. Then that tall, big-breasted German girl, Tilly, pressed against him and put her hand almost down his crack. He liked Tilly. She wore costume jewelry and he remembered her first day of work last year when on the very next day they told her she couldn't wear that cheap perfume to work anymore. Tilly told him that couple out there wanted to talk to the chef. Wanted to talk to the maker of the greatest crab cakes they had ever had.

Jeremiah said this to Tilly very seriously, even though he was kidding: "Do they know I'm black?" She slapped his ass and almost fell off her platform sandals.

And they were a white couple. Of course they were. They were more than a little drunk and talking loud and laughing. Jeremiah eased himself out towards the table. He'd had to do this maybe three times before. And he didn't like it at all. And it was always white folk who wanted to see him. Not once did any black folk want to see the chef. They just wanted to eat. He looked sheepishly at their drinks. He was certain they were drinking Manhattans.

The man told him he hadn't tasted crab cakes so good in his life. Not even the Maryland crab cakes he had in Washington, DC were as good as these. Were these Louisiana crab cakes? No, sir. Atlanta crab cakes, Jeremiah told him. The man had gray hair even though he didn't look that old and she had tanned pencil-thin calves and thick curly blond hair she wore over the wrinkles in the corner of her eyes. Her teeth were big. She looked older than him.

She asked him what the secret was to those crab cakes. Was there a secret? Yes, Ma'am. Jeremiah guessed you could call it a secret. He started to tell her about Jackson's cayenne pepper but she shushed him up and laughed some more. She didn't want to know. More laughter. You tell secrets, and they become, well, they aren't secrets anymore. They laughed some more and sipped their drinks. Jeremiah smiled. That made sense. Was he a full time chef? The man asked him. No. He wanted to be someday. He was working on it. Jeremiah said he had to get back into the kitchen now. The man stood up and shook his hand. The lady, one of her pencil thin calves rising and falling real fast as she sat there with her crossed legs, extended her hand and flashed those big teeth and wide mouth. He shook her hand and she felt cold to touch. He almost jumped. She had been good in her youth, Jeremiah concluded. He eased himself away and back into the kitchen.

And there Tilly was, standing right where he left her. Right over the last four crab cakes. There were only two left now. She was chewing. She looked up at Jeremiah, brushed a crumb from her lip and said, "Oops." She stopped chewing long enough to say one thing.

"Temptation is more powerful than life itself, Jeremiah. Man, those are good crab cakes."

This statement made Jeremiah freeze. His legs went weak. He had to leave right now. He had to go home.

The System

To the Mexicans that river was the Rio Bravo, to the Americans it was the Rio Grande, but to Colonel Bob, it was neither grand nor brave when someone tried to cross over to the American side. It was more often than not, death. Just like the Battle of Palo Alto, his men would stop the Mexies dead in their tracks. Any Mexican caught in their sights was plugged. It was how it was and just where did all of them come from? I'll tell you, Brandon. Time for your education. Stand there tall, man, every day and listen to the squawk box spew out the litany of Mexican voices and wait here on this bluff and look through those mounted binoculars and get educated. It was a great wide blue river but those mother fucking Mexies did not own this part of Texas where Bush had a vacation house just up the road and the Battle of Palo Alto showed just how Texans understood the power of gunpowder and the Mexicans didn't. Nothing has changed. Nothing ever changes, boy. We have Texas and the Mexies want it back.

Three quarters of a million illegal Mexicans every year try to cross that river just in this part of Texas alone and by God they just keep coming and in their shanties way down in Mexico they just keep fucking and conceiving Jesus Christ their birth rate is three times the American birth rate. Why? Why they're goddamn Catholics is why. Yeah, I know you're a Protestant. I can tell you're a Protestant. It's okay. Goddamn relax. You're here and the checks'll keep coming but when your goddamn country is 97% Catholic fuck man, you know what happens when the Catholics roll into your third world shantytown? The condoms sneak out the back door. Birth control pills shipped in by the government get dumped into the contaminated by Amoco and Exxon and Monsanto rivers.

But there are systems, Brandon. Look at those five buses there across the great river. That's how you do it correctly. That's how you siphon off the great American dream systematically.

Colonel Bob stopped to catch his breath.

Brandon, barely thirty, stood on their mountain lookout and peered through the lens at the five bus loads of Mexicans on a flat area on the other side of the river. They were getting out of the buses. He could barely hear the Mariachi band playing in front of one of the buses because the wind was too loud but it still came out weakly from the mounted speaker next to him.

Colonel Bob pointed. That was the same Mariachi band every time. They played in a Palo Alto Tex-Mex restaurant every night. The leader of the band was a Mexie named Guervo. He had been playing in his band for thirty-eight years and not a single time did his wife ever come with him when his band played. And why was that?

"You never know when you might get lucky," Guervo said. The Colonel laughed and showed teeth that looked too large for his mouth and one of his big front ones was turning black.

Watch closely, Brandon. This was a system. Those Mexicans and their five buses came there every month. Those Mexicans had papers. They were legal Mexicans.

Those Mexicans traveled up North and picked asparagus in Indiana and Illinois. No, they weren't legal in Mexico. They were kidnapped down in south Mexico systematically. It was a system, Brandon, and you're right. It don't make sense. Mexico don't make sense.

Mexico cries itself to sleep every night because it don't make sense. Everything dangerous to the world comes in threes. Ask the Catholics. Hell, ask the Protestants, for that matter. Mexico comes in threes. The north, the south, and the middle.

Colonel Bob lit a Cuban cigar. He lit it with a silver Aztec lighter.

The North is a Nafta-Inspired haven of factories and pristine Universities and Mexies with stucco houses and two-car garages and gas grills in their backyard barbecue pits. Nafta created this wonderful symbiotic Shangri-la with their kind and gentle American friends and who cares who runs towards the river in their backyards? These northern Mexies were the Mexies who slept good at night.

But you move down toward the middle part of Mexico, the liberal part, the free-thinking part, the shit-disturbing part filled with those liberal pussies who clog up the middle class universities and government offices with their righteous cries of freedom and justice and shit, I mean fuck, that's where they have all those cry baby indigenous Indian populations who want their country back, the goddamn Aztecs came from there, Brandon. Brave Aztec warriors in battle bling bling like you've never seen, who fought off the Europeans, first the Spanish and then the French and even the goddamn English tried to horn in on the Aztec nation and eventually those Aztecs didn't have a prayer. I mean come on, an Aztec warrior dies in battle he turns into a hummingbird and flies into the sun.

Fuck, man, is there anything more pussy than that? Not like those killer Al-Qaeda's huh? Seventeen virgins over and over again for all eternity? Give me that goddamn suicide jacket. And you wonder it took us so long to find Bin Laden?

Colonel Bob laughed and coughed at the same time. Brandon kept peering through the lens. The Mexicans from the bus were getting in a big circle. There were Mexicans with guns scattered all around the outside of the circle. The Mexicans in a circle were all women and children.

And the southern part of Mexico? Brandon. That's where the action is. That's where the Catholics taught the illiterates to breed like Spanish flies. Along the hillsides and sprawling out of the third world shantytowns they procreated, and that's where all the immigrants were coming from, from the south, and that's where all the gangs came from. The drug lords and horror show killers who burned police and their enemies in vats of acid and decapitated whole families if you fucked with them and they knew where the money was.

America!

It's revenge time, Brandon. Remember the Alamo? Santa Anna kicked our ass at the Alamo and then him and his army got their ass kicked right up the road a few weeks later and forced Santa Anna to sell Texas for about 15 million dollars. That comes to about 11 dollars an acre. What a deal!

Shortly after that Santa Anna sold the rest of the southwest for 10 million. Tax free. What another deal!

The Mexies are still pissed at that. And now they are getting it all back. And then some.

With the rich Mexies up north here and the literati shitheads in the middle, and the bad soil and babies popping out like zits in the south, it's a perfect storm. Tornadic Mexican conditions and those goddamn southern Mexies are just plain wrong. They're mean. No, they don't have condoms or conscious but they sure as hell can find an American made assault rifle.

And they're coming. And it's more than just your typical revolution. No, Jesus Christ, this ain't like a bunch of powder wigged Englishmen reading John Locke and writing up laws and boundaries based on their god-given right to bear dominion over inferior creatures like women, Indians, and niggers. Fuck no, this ain't 1776. This is the new millennium. This is the Mexie millennium.

They don't need to climb into trees with a musket and pick us off one by one. They just need to blow leaves off concrete and put shingles on our roofs.

It's all history, Brandon. Life is your binoculars, Brandon. Look in the middle of that circle of women and children. It's about to happen. We've all seen it happen. You're new. You're a virgin to this kind of thing. You got family, right? You want to keep your family, right? You don't want your family decapitated one night because you get self-righteous and mouthy, do you? Focus right on the gringo in the middle of the circle with the pistol in his hand.

Focus, Brandon.

The Fountain of Youth

Flat on his back, the great white beacon of light from the tallest lighthouse in Florida shining its big French light bulb twenty miles out to sea, Seymour concluded his head was just a bit too close to the road, as a late model mid-sized Chevy, driven by a large black man sailed fast by his forehead. Gravel struck his drunken cheek.

The chubby young woman, her body as solid and smooth and round as an erotic armadillo, giggled ironically and sniffed her pinkie finger. She had just a touch of stuff left from a party last night. She sat smartly on a park bench beside the road, a beach towel stretched tightly around her torso. She sipped a large plastic cup of gin and Red Bull. She wanted to see the lighthouse at night. She kissed Seymour once and let him feel her up. "I like older men," she said. "But not much."

But here they were. Seymour had kept drinking for some reason. He didn't like to get so drunk but he did this night and he was here on his back alongside a road down at the very end of Ponce Inlet Harbor.

Ponce is short for Ponce De Leon, the Spaniard who discovered Florida, he told this Canadian girl. If you don't count the Timucuan Indians, who were hunting Mastodons and fishing in the creeks and streams and ponds of the Great Atlantic some 15,000 years before the these smelly old Spaniards came to town.

The girl rattled the remaining ice in her cup, cocked her head. "Didn't he discover the Fountain of Youth?"

No, no, no, no, no. He just went looking for the Fountain of Youth. He found Florida and hostile Indians who wanted to kill him instead.

She laughed. "I bet you're looking for the Fountain of Youth."

Seymour sat up. His erotic armadillo was smiling. She had a beautiful face above that massive cleavage. Massive everything really. And all so firm and hard and young. And not embarrassed one bit by any of it (Ah, today's youth).

No, the Fountain of Youth Ponce De Leon thought he discovered is now just a piddly tourist attraction in St. Augustine. For $6.50 you can drink from Ponce De Leon's Fountain of Youth. As long as you sign the disclaimer.

The girl laughed again. "Everything in Florida is a piddly tourist attraction," she said.

And to top it all off, shortly after discovering what he believed was the Fountain of Youth, Ponce man was killed by a poison arrow from the very same Indian tribe he would help exterminate.

"Talk about winning the lottery and dying in a car accident," she said. This made Seymour smile. He liked this girl.

The Spanish killed off all the Indians while they were in Florida and then sold it to America for the price of a time-share.

She asked Seymour if he was some kind of historian. Yes, he was, he said. The worst kind. A high school history teacher. But he was good at it. He made sure he taught only the most important aspect of history to his uninterested young students.

She asked what that was.

"The lies," Seymour said.

The girl stood up. "I want another drink. I'm not drunk yet." She said it was next to impossible to get her drunk. She weighed a hundred and fifty eight pounds dry as a bone and alcohol, she told him with a laugh, had lots of places to hide before it got to her bloodstream. He smiled. He had never heard it put that way.

"Well," she said. "If I get drunk enough, you may be able to put it anyway you like and if you're real lucky, you might even discover the Fountain of Youth tonight."

She started walking towards the oldest bar in Florida, her sandals flopping on the pavement.

Seymour staggered to his feet. What a nice ass on this girl. A nice big ass.

The Juggler

Earlier that evening, after a few more beers, after watching two young lovers feel each other up in the sand just down from the pier, after downing a platter of delicious grouper fingers dipped in tartar sauce, Stephanie overcame her mental lethargy, overcame her desire to steal Jeremiah's money in order to make it quickly back to her very own Jeremiah, and instead asked to speak to the owner. She had moved to the bar. She said she needed another pack of cigarettes and the grungy bartender, a cute, yet homely-looking skinny boy with a silver earring and hundreds of dollars of tattoos all over his body ran and got them for her. She watched him bitch slap the cigarette machine twice before her Camels fell out. When he came back she thanked him with her smile and asked him if he wanted one. He shrugged and took one. He had to turn sideways and cup his hand all around the end of that cigarette before it would light. The ocean breeze was strong through those open windows tonight. He blew smoke every which direction and then leaned his palms hard upon the bar in front of Stephanie.

"What did you say?"

Stephanie was staring in the mirror behind the bar at the crowd behind her. She looked finally at the bartender.

"Is the owner around?"

This young bartender studied this nice-looking girl very carefully for a moment. He was looking for what was very important for a bartender to always look for. He had only been out of jail for about six months and only been a bartender for close to six weeks but he knew what was important to look for. Motive.

Bartenders had to keep a constant eye out for motive. Drunks hitting on each other. Women angry at their men. Men looking to dump their women. And vice-versa (with an emphasis on the Vice). He blinked finally. He had no idea really what the fuck this long-legged, mischievous, devious chick wanted with the owner. She couldn't get a job. Everybody tried to get a job here. She had no boobs! Daryl only hired waitresses with big boobs to work the pier. And even though she'd had at least five beers, for some reason she didn't look like the type to sleep her way into a waitress job. He didn't say any of this to her though. He just shrugged and walked away.

In the mirror Stephanie could see a young couple about her age. They had two small children with them and they were animated and the little girl was eating those grouper fingers like Stephanie had eaten them. They were good. Even though it was late the family was tanned and on vacation and having a good time. Stephanie looked at the bar where her cell phone would normally be. But it was in her purse.

Stephanie was a touch startled by the contact the owner made when he came up to her. "You wanted to see the owner." Then he gestured to the bartender, who promptly made him a drink, and her a drink. "Daryl." Daryl was tanned and was once muscular but now a little past forty and chubbing up and had a bleached blond short cut hairdo that made him look gay, Stephanie decided. He wasn't though. He liked the women. He liked women a lot. This she could tell. Some liked him probably, too. He didn't wear a wedding ring. He was married though. To someone. She stared at her drink and then sipped on it. She asked him if he needed a bartender.

This surprised him. His head went back. Bartender? She looked more like a server. In a fancier place. More like a rookie waitress who would drop things. Could she make a blue tail fly? One more sip. She said she could make a lot of things fly and this made him laugh and then he talked about how this place crawled with old people, retirees, through the week, who ordered dumb drinks from the fifties and shit. If she worked here she would have to know about twenty old drinks.

Of course she knew how to make a blue tail fly. A shot and a half of Blue Caracao Liqueur, one shot white crème de cacao, and a half a shot of half and half. Fill the shaker with cracked ice, strain into a cocktail glass, bend over just slightly to show her thong and the tattoo of a Monarch butterfly in the small of her back (Daryl leaned back and observed this one for himself) and ease her pinky over the lip for good measure and smile like this. She smiled like that. She saw his eyebrow raise.

This even made the bartender smile. He was listening to it all. What's that half and half shit?

"Well any cream really. Don't forget it though." Stephanie said. "And still no tip from the old people."

This made the owner smile broadly. She was good. He sipped his drink. She had no boobs. He saw this in the mirror. "No real openings at the moment. Maybe try back later in the summer when everybody starts back to school." He moved his eyes to the crease between those round little breasts. They weren't too bad though. Her nipples poked through that tight thin blue tank top like thorns.

Stephanie eased herself off the barstool and stumbled against Daryl in the process. Sorry. She steadied herself and went behind the bar.

"May I, Brian?" She said. This impressed the bartender. He didn't tell her his name. She must have heard someone else say his name. He liked her even more. Still, he looked at his boss, who just was still a little amused. Sometimes when something like this happened he was amused and then other times he would personally escort this white trash drunk bitch right out of the place. Brian stepped aside. He could see the Boss's amused indifference fading. He tapped ashes.

Stephanie looked around until she found what she was looking for. Three bottles of different liqueurs that she set on the counter. B & B, Drambuie, and Kahlua. Nothing new coming out of that drink, both men were thinking.

Until Stephanie threw one in the air. Fairly high in the air. They both gasped and reflexively reached out. She caught it. Fuck. The next one went even higher in the air.

"Goddamn!" Daryl yelled out, right before she caught that one too.

"Oh, fuck," she heard Brian say as he was reaching behind her like she was some comic imaginary marionette. He didn't know what to do. Fuck!

Then everyone in the place froze. In a matter of seconds, Stephanie was juggling, silently, perfectly, and seemingly without much effort, all three liqueur bottles. She did this for quite some time. The bottles flew so high at times it made people gasp.

Then, one by one, the errant liqueur bottles made their way back to the bar. The entire place erupted in applause. Daryl scrunched his cigarette out.

Stephanie had a job.

Father Harold

Jeremiah drove faster than he usually did. Faster than usual past the empty patrol car that always set on the Oceanside of the road there on the edge of the town, Wilbur By the Sea, an oddly named little town between Ponce Inlet Harbor and Daytona Beach Shores. He wouldn't even have cared if for the first time ever an officer was sitting in that empty patrol car. He wouldn't have stopped. His money was gone. Every dime he had saved. Twenties actually. Only twenties. Every one of those twenty dollar bills he had saved in the last four years was now in the hands of a pretty white girl he never should have trusted. He didn't trust her really. Never trusted her from the minute he sat down beside her there on the bus. He was just busy. And he was dumbstruck looking at her. He never should have been dumbstruck looking at her. His mother warned him about such women. Especially white women. Especially white trash women who kill their husband and leave their kid and he bet she made up the rape. Made up her stories.

And Charley Younger probably sat cross-legged on the bed talking to her the whole time as she filled up that Old Navy bag of hers. Charley Younger probably told her what he told Jeremiah one time. That he didn't want his eyes and his chin fixed. He'd never get laid anyway. Look at these thumbs! That old doctor said he could fix his eyes and chin but not those thumbs. You can't reconstruct thumbs. Who would sleep with a guy with no thumbs? That dirty white girl would pause, probably, take a puff off her cigarette. Shrug. It wouldn't be that bad, she would say, and then back to stuffing in his twenties. You fix your face and treat me nice and I'll fuck you like I mean it.

Jeremiah drove up on a curb thinking this. A car coming the other way swerved and laid on the horn, but Jeremiah got his car right. Then he tried to get his God right.

He asked God for forgiveness. Bitterly at first and then with as much sincerity as he could muster. He should know better than to steal. He should know better than break a Ten Commandment. It was pure selfishness he did it in the first place. Then he couldn't stop doing it. Then he justified it through Charley Younger. It was just wrong. He had to put all the money back. But now it was gone! He was only two thousand short of the twelve thousand that old semi-retired doctor who had an office in the same strip mall as Woody's Barbecue said he would do it for. In between the boobs and eyes he did for rich old ladies. And that was four years ago. And the old doctor was looking old. You got that money yet, Jeremiah? Not yet! I'm working on it!

Lord, Jeremiah thought he was crazy. He told his God once again he thought he was crazy. He should give it all back to the church. Give it all back to Father Harold who stuck his hand into Jeremiah's pants one day and said it was an accident.

An accident. And then Jeremiah started lifting the twenty dollar bills and promising Charley Younger he would have a new chin and new eyes one day.

Jeremiah floored it through the curve and the yellow light of the intersection.

The Oldest Bar in Florida

Her name was Martha. Seymour's mouth fell open. No, it wasn't. That was an old name. You're too young to be named Martha, he said, as he motioned for a drink. They sat at one end of a big horseshoe bar. A very old horseshoe bar. The wood was soft with smoke and age and spilled alcohol and the breeze coming in the opening of the bar that led out to a dock felt good and the ocean behind them was black. There was a big iron pot in the middle of the bar that was used to burn wood in. It was too hot to burn wood this time of year.

Martha laughed and this stirred up her perfume and Seymour liked this. But she liked her name. And anyway, the name Seymour was nothing to write home about. Seymour liked her cute little Canadian accent. She was from Quebec. This was her last trip to Florida with her father before she went off to the University of Washington to study Business Administration. Seymour sipped his whiskey. God that sounded boring. Martha pushed Seymour off his barstool and if someone hadn't caught him, he would have fallen on his ass. Martha and the bartender thought this was funny.

"I write poetry," Martha said.

"So do I," Seymour said. He picked up his drink. "No, I don't."

"Are you married?"

"No." Seymour shrugged. "Not really. Not too much really." He shook his head. The bartender let out a big laugh on that one. She was smoking a cigarette at the end of the bar. She was taking a respite from running drinks. Her hair was dyed-blond and she had one of those burnt local tans and these huge wrinkles in the corners of her eyes that looked well-earned. She tapped Martha's arm. "Honey, he's so married he probably don't get laid twice a month."

Martha laughed.

"Hey," Seymour said. Then he jumped as his phone vibrated once again in his jeans. "Just a second." He staggered outside. It was his wife of course. He said hello and walked towards a big statue of a pirate in front of a rotting old miniature pirate ship.

"I did it," his wife said.

"Did what?"

"Slept with another man."

Seymour stared at the plastic face of the pirate. A white light shined on this plastic face.

"I don't want to hear this."

Silence.

"Then hang up."

More silence. He almost frowned. She sounded like she had been crying. She was crying. She blew her nose into the phone.

"Are you okay?"

Silence.

"Our marriage is over, isn't it, See Mee?"

See Mee. She hadn't called him See Mee in, hell, years. See Mee was from way back when they first met. She slipped and called him See Mee instead of Seymour and they had laughed way back when and this became a term of endearment and for the longest time back in those early days she called him See Mee and then she stopped and never called him that again until now.

"Seymour," she corrected, without laughter.

"Did you come?" Seymour asked.

She exhaled. Silence. Then, "Well of course I came. You know I would work at that regardless."

"What?"

Sniffs. "Seymour, did you love that girl?"

He shoulders slumped. He leaned against the pirate ship. He noticed it was more like half of an old fishing boat really. Here it was again. His wife never had gotten over Stephanie. He was over Stephanie, for the most part, but his wife couldn't get over her. Never could. She was obsessed with Stephanie for a while. How did she feel inside? Did they kiss a lot? They never kissed anymore. Why do people stop kissing when they've been together so long? Did she come? His wife almost always came. Didn't he feel guilty? Etc. etc.

"A little, I suppose."

A noise, then, "You fucker. You asshole fucker." He heard another noise. No, he would have to say that. Not an appropriate *no*. "Not from Seymour Belmo. You have to tell the truth. You lie about many, many things but never about something that would not hurt me!" Real crying now.

"Sounds like you're having a good time."

Click.

Seymour stared at the bright French light of the lighthouse easing in his direction. He wasn't being truthful. It was more than a little. He loved Stephanie with a frightening, exhausting intensity for a time. That would really hurt his wife. Why he enjoyed hurting his wife even a little he couldn't explain. He didn't want to go inside. He didn't want to sleep with a firmly fat girl named Martha. He put his phone back in his pocket. He wanted to be See Mee again. Oh, well. He staggered back into the oldest bar in Florida.

The Right

The Halifax looked so good at night. Chuck grew up just down from here across from the Catholic Church on Route 1 and goddamn he deserved better than the Cubans. He could outwork them any fucking day those silver fish shimmering across the big old Halifax and the big white caps lit up, Chuck wanted all of it and then those goddamn Mexies came with their homegrown meth and fuck they can work nonstop sixteen hour days just non fucking stop. Man, on that meth you go on forever. Until you die. Chuck smiled. Best meth Chuck ever had and he was out now and the fish weren't biting and he could just bust someone up for just one hit and he ain't ate for three days. Not that he wanted to. Food just left him with nothing. You know?

Larry, standing behind the counter of the bait shop, just stared. "You're a fucking loser taking that shit." He had his hand on a billy-club under the counter. He had enough of Chuck. Chuck wasn't right and was getting less right all the time. His long dirty blond hair and tattoos and meth-rattled teeth, what was left, and his shaking fucking hands.

Chuck stiffened, rocked his head back like a very ugly rag doll.

"Larry ain't in no good mood." Chuck twisted his hand in the air, adjusting some strange invisible dial. He just wanted a goddamn pack of cigarettes. Spot him a pack of cigarettes until the next blue moon. He laughed and Larry squeezed the handle of the billy-club harder. He squeezed it hard enough to burst most things. Larry wanted to rattle this man's skull with it. He had a magazine to read before he closed up and went home and turned on his new used window air conditioner in his only bedroom and this man wasn't right. He represented what wasn't right about the Right. Those rich people all over the state of Florida. They produced this man. And billions like him. Larry just wanted his job and he wanted to go home and not just splatter fishing lures and sealed packets of stink bait with the blood of the Right.

"Go home, Chuck. Get out of my place."

"This holy place?" Chuck said.

Chuck said this so quickly it startled Larry. Chuck's eyes weren't right. He needed to die tonight. He needed to die right out back. Old Lady Mollack was sound asleep and wouldn't say anything anyway. Larry could just wipe the blood and brain and gristle of Chuck off into the beautiful Halifax and take the club home tonight and read about Chuck in the little corner of the paper that no one would investigate because the Right never bothered with people excited about the comfort of a new used window air conditioner in a forty year old fifteen-hundred dollar trailer. Larry sighed so deeply it rattled the windows of the bait shop. Larry wanted to close and go home. He told Chuck to leave.

Chuck took a deep breath. The side of his greasy sun burnt face glistened opaque, a charred piece of ceramic broken and tossed into the garbage of the Right.

"A smoke, a joke, another toke."

But Chuck did the right thing. He angled his way out. He smelled his death and he didn't like Larry even when he had money for a pack of smokes. He had nowhere to go tonight. He beat up somebody two days ago where he once lived and she would kill him if he went home tonight. Or tomorrow night. Maybe sometime when she wasn't so sore and he had scored some more meth off the Mexies she would take him and let him hold the holy crinkly tin foil that burned the blistering rocks of life.

"Goodbye, Mr. Larry. Goodbye, goodbye, goodbye." Chuck planned now to lie with the moon to his back on a hard soft aluminum bench and fall asleep with the tiny metal lights of pleasure from those tiny square high-rises slowly blinking off across that huge and happy Halifax River. The Halifax of his youth. The Halifax of his decline.

The Halifax of his death.

Remember the Alamo

While Charley Younger's chin was drooping towards the slumbering beautiful head of Stephanie in his lap his eyes were as wide open as he could get them as he peered at the faded muted 19 inch television. His tear ducts didn't work as well as other people's but still his cheeks were so soaked with tears they dripped off his chin and plucked Stephanie's smoky hair. She did not stir. He started to absently rub them away with his thumb stub but he didn't.

Stephanie had come home so drunk and spent she didn't even bother to put the shoe boxes back in their place under the bed. Instead she sat two of them down and missed setting the third one down and twenty dollar bills scattered all over the thin carpeting. She didn't care. She wanted to sleep. The ocean didn't want her today but the pier did and she was finally drunk and spent and curling fetal on the couch in Charley Younger's lap and this was okay. He was clean and lost in a movie. His crotch smelled of Aqua Velva. She knew Aqua Velva. Her Grandfather used Aqua Velva and God what a wad her tired cheek rested on through his thin plaid ugly pajamas. God's ironic gift to a retarded man. A dick the size of a bull. It didn't stir. It was as languid and soft as a rag full of sand. Stephanie was asleep instantaneously.

Charley Younger ignored her completely. Wasn't even aware she was there really. He was frozen and crying like a retarded baby. It was the end. He had watched this movie over three hundred times. The movie killed him a little bit each time he watched it. When he died, Jeremiah told him, his death dream would be a new ending to this movie. A new ending to the Alamo.

But until that happened the ending was always the same and Charley Younger would cry like a baby each and every time as that sea of well-dressed uniformed Mexies parted and that woman and child marched their way through the desolate barren Texas landscape.

He made a low, droning noise of Charley Younger sadness as the credits eased themselves over that poor quality VHS-formatted landscape.

One Jeremiah Now

Well, there was only one Jeremiah now. He was a little boy way up north, twelve hundred miles away and sleeping, his left eye blackened and bleeding a bit through a crusty edge of dried blood brought on by the fist of his mean and volatile grandmother. But that story would have to wait.

Down along the Halifax River, just inside the entrance to the only island trailer park in the entire world, the yellowed and salt-dirty light of Jeremiah's car lights shot clear across the river and faded somewhere into the darkness of the other side.

Jeremiah was dead. So was Chuck, the drug addict. Larry, having just come out of the bait shop, was rattled more than irritated actually. He tossed his cigarette into the crab grass and waited for the police he had called.

It seemed Jeremiah in his haste to get to his twenty dollar bills took a wider turn than normal and clipped Chuck pretty good. There was even a thump. More from an angry palm than anything else but Jeremiah didn't know that. But he knew Chuck. He gave him leftovers more than once over the years.

Jeremiah slammed on his brakes and got out shaking his head and talking things no one heard and as he first bent over Chuck who lay flat on his back in the half-gravel, half-paved road, Chuck rose up like a devil Phoenix, fillet knife jabbing and slicing random into Jeremiah's body. It stung but just irritated Jeremiah more than anything.

He went to pin this dumb drug addict's arms down and then finally went for his throat when he wouldn't stop the jabbing.

Until the knife blade pierced a main artery in Jeremiah's neck.

Then there was this frozen moment in time as the breath of life oozed out of Jeremiah, almost real. His large round body eased itself down upon a startled and suddenly repentant drug addict named Chuck.

So repentant was Chuck that he had meekly flipped the knife around and offered up the handle to Jeremiah, who was really a nice black. One of the nice blacks. Not like a goddamn Mexie. A nice black, Chuck thought. His last thought. The blade, forced by the dying weight of Jeremiah, into the stomach of Chuck, the empty stomach of Chuck, slowly twisted the life out of him also. They both died.

Their cheeks ended up side by side upon the road.

"Goddamn," Larry said. He didn't even want to go home now. His new used air-conditioner would have to wait. It would have to wait until he drank himself sober somewhere.

"Goddamn," Larry said again.

The Pool

And there that vaginal ocean was again opening and closing, the quiet dark roar soothing droning towards something. Something final, she decided, as her body separated and drifted through the white-lit blue concrete pool of the Ocean Palm Inn again.

This was how her evening started. She shouldn't have gone drinking with a man named Seymour. Another married man and why did they never care how heavy you've gotten? Especially the older ones. Especially if it was one night and out. Especially. And then the humiliation there beside those two dead men, stacked on top of each other. And was that top one the big one! And of course this man she just met had to see it. Had to follow the flashing police lights. The ambulance. She would have driven on by. She wasn't one of those people who stopped to look at death. She never stopped for such things. Car wrecks were for pervs to ogle over.

And that girl. That beautiful ugly girl. Her and this man she met stood on either side of the death pile like zombie mannequins. It was chilling. It was weird.

And that odd handicapped man whimpering and brushing the white sheet there on his knees. His hands were crippled, and curled fetal like into his palms.

A chill went through Martha there in the tepid thick pool water. Perhaps her enlarged heart stopped for a moment. And then her mother came to mind. Her powdery dead mother and all those flowers. Her mother loved flowers. And everyone kept reminding her of how much her mother loved flowers and how beautiful all the flowers were and she, not old enough to take it all in, kept thinking over and over again that all people loved flowers. It wasn't just her mother, for Christ's sake.

Arms moving gently slowly through the water, Martha suddenly thought how weird death was. How weird life was and even more weirdly, oddly, if she were to ever love anyone as powerfully as she had loved her mother. She rolled over on her back in the water. She doubted it.

Martha let herself float with just that minimal movement of her large and powerful legs, a light wavering of her graceful puffy fingers, as a huge unavoidable smile eased itself wide across her pretty face. The sky wasn't quite dark. Just a mushy, muted gray. She kept smiling and all she could hear was the slight gurgling of the stream of cleansing filtered pool water and the purring roar of the ocean. Had she heard that beautiful ugly girl correctly?

At first nothing was said. But after a moment that girl breezed almost awkwardly around the dead bodies and buried her head into Seymour's shoulder. Martha stepped back and for the longest time it seemed like, still nothing was said. But there was something between these two people. His arm went round her so oddly comfortably.

And then they went to the car and Martha more or less trailed behind them and before she got into the backseat, before the other girl slid herself into the front seat, before Seymour got behind the wheel, before the thin young woman with the tear-burnt cheeks said the oddest of statements, Martha gave the whole scene one final look.

The physically challenged man now lay atop the mound of death, his cheek firmly upon the sheet, and was droning out the oddest of wails. It caught Martha somewhere. Her throat perhaps. More people had oozed out of the trailer park darkness. Old people mostly. Old people in boxer shorts and pink puffy bathrobes and an odd assortment of ill-fitting pajamas. Old people who couldn't find anything to say to each other. But their heads shook. As a police officer wrote furiously on a clipboard. And for a moment Martha thought the whole thing was staged. A movie. A bad movie, she thought as she climbed in.

But that odd statement. The only words spoken by anyone in the car as they drove back to the Ocean Palm Inn. Before the couple in the front seat embraced and totally ignored Martha as they went into Seymour's room and undressed.

Martha couldn't keep from smiling though now, as she floated in the pool.

As those two macabre bodies reunited, collapsing together like odd programmable aliens on sexual timers, and if Martha would have been there, she could have heard the only thing spoken between these two reunited lovers that night.

Stephanie, in a choking, croaking whisper, practically spit into Seymour's stunned ear, "You better fuck me like you mean it tonight, See Nothing."

But that wasn't what was said in the car. That wasn't what Martha heard and would have in her head for many years afterwards.

As soon as the girl climbed into the car back at the accident scene her head went hard to the window. She looked so sad. And still nothing was said.

And then as they waited for the light to change on A1A, as Martha contemplated saying something. Anything! The girl's head shot sideways from the window and her beautiful green eyes glowed luminescent and frightening in the darkness.

"Fuck me! "she said. "Charley Younger better not freak out and thaw his mother out."

That is what she said.

Exactly.

Martha, her smile frozen and stiff, closed her eyes and gently bent her knees and moved quietly across the pool towards the deep end.

God's Failure

Pablo was awake but his new friend was sleeping soundly, mouth wide open, in between him and his aunt as the bus pulled into a *parador turistico*, a big overlook where when they got out and stretched, they could look down and see a deep, deep canyon with a trickling river at the bottom and his aunt muttered how beautiful it all was. She had been here once before in her lifetime. It was farther north and they were getting closer to America. She didn't want to go to America. She wanted God to take her and Pablo back home.

Pablo didn't necessarily want to go back home just yet. He was with his pretty aunt and now he had a friend and now they were running. They were laughing as they ran and they played tag with anyone who wanted to and the *patróns* didn't seem to mind. There was nowhere to run off to and the *patróns* had papers to look at and phone calls to make. They drank cans of *cerveza* as they stood next to their guns.

Pablo and his friend ran and ran and stopped only to get their own can of *gascoda* that the *patróns* said they could have. They were 50 miles from the American border someone said.

Just for no good reason a *patrón* stuck out his foot and tripped the running *mongolista*.

Pablo stopped. He watched his new friend scuff her head and her hand hard on the ground. She didn't cry. She almost cried as she stared at the spidery blood spot now on her palm. But she didn't. She wiped her palm on her clothes as she got to her feet. And off she ran.

Pablo didn't run. He stood rigidly, coldly staring at the *patrón* who tripped his friend. Pablo would kill him if he had something to kill him with.

The mean *patrón* finally saw Pablo staring at him. The *patrón* moved closer.

But Pablo didn't move. His eyes were burning and he was trembling with anger.

The mean ugly *patrón* spit something at him. *Los Fallos de dios*! God's failure. Move on!

Finally, after a spell, Pablo took off running again.

Ferlinghetti

Forget The Sun Glow Pier for a while, forget that piddly little pier in the old people's part of town and go back up the road to where the tourists hang out. This is the one he was talking about. This was the famous pier, the longest pier, the biggest pier. It was the Coney Island of Florida. With Ferris wheels and tilt-a-whirls and scary ski lifts way out over the water and pink flamingos in the gift shops. And now there was a bungee jump ride that sent you flying higher than the highest building. Screaming.

He stood on a street corner just across the street from this pier. This famous pier. He was rather tall and heavy and his clothes were soiled and his tennis shoes old and he had gray hair that stuck to his face and head thick and gnarly like it had been badly pasted on him. But don't call him a homeless person. He wasn't a homeless person. This earth was his home and these dirty clothes were his home and this cup of coffee that beautiful girl over there bought him was his home and God strike him with death if he wouldn't still be able to procreate into her beautiful body enough times to fill a small pond inland with trailers parked around it.

Yes, it was true, home is where the heart is but a man's dick will take up residence anywhere. That's why he lost one home. But everywhere was his home. Destroy everything. Ferlinghetti. Fuck Ferlinghetti. No, don't fuck Ferlinghetti. That's what he would want. There was no Coney Island of the Mind. It was a Coney Island of his dick. His John Henry and fame and fucking and the reinvention of Walt Whitman fell short. One Vaseline-coated asshole short.

(Yes, out of the corner of his tired blue eyes he saw her laugh and make a note.)

And there was one easy way to end War. Take all the Republicans for a ride out over the great Atlantic and make them eat ballerina slippers until they called the whole thing off. How could that *not* work?

He pointed at the beautiful girl who bought him another cup of coffee. She was smiling. She had perfect teeth. Her smile set his world on fire. How many men would give up everything and sleep under a drawbridge and wash off every morning in a river and gag on his own smell occasionally for an audience of a beautiful girl every Wednesday at 5 o'clock?

Well, maybe not that many, but he would. Yes, he would and he has been beaten by others and beat others but there was beauty every Wednesday, and every other night in his dreams there under that concrete drawbridge beside two other schizophrenic smelly human beings without souls.

Without fear.

Without a place to shit.

Thank you and I must be going.

Black Comanche

"In the hour of our discontent, when the world has taken on strange discolorations."

That was how it started. *Black Comanche*. The great undiscovered novel written by a homeless person in Daytona Beach and faxed to a publisher he found on the Internet after sneaking into an office late one evening and that one line and his famous bio caused such a buzz in the Big Literary Apple Maggie's boss couldn't contain himself. He took Maggie into a broom closet, unzipped his front zipper and then the side zipper of her little slinky black business skirt, pushed aside a pretty pink thong and tiny mini-pad and fucked her like he meant it (Men rarely meant it, Stephanie would tell Maggie later on this novel, and she would agree of course).

That blurry faxed one line query had come from a homeless person who had once won worldwide acclaim as a Pulitzer-Prize winning Vietnam Veteran. There was an article about him in the *Times* and it got him tenure and a trophy wife. Until he raped a student. Then he became nothing for the longest time and now everyone was looking for him. Or were *they*?

Maggie let her boss fuck her because she had been trying to fuck him ever since she moved out of the Midwest and took a job as a copy editor for this publisher. She had a degree in Rhetoric and Composition from Eastern Illinois University. Her favorite writer, naturally, was Jane Austen.

Maggie moved to New York in hopes of getting her own novel published. When she decided to write it.

And New York fit her nicely. She didn't need a car and she had found a job in the evening making salads in an Italian Bistro to help pay for her little studio apartment and since she was as cute and fresh as a little Midwestern button and really enjoyed sex she didn't have any trouble finding a boyfriend. But the one she found and kept for a while was a vain little bastard who thought he was so much smarter than she was. And he didn't like Jane Austen. He said Austen was beloved for her consistently insecure women who talked a good game but always fell for the same puerile rich men that all women fall for.

And then one late evening after handcuffs and sweat and wall pounding he lit a cigarette, flicked at the remote and told her she needed a boob job.

Maggie never returned his phone calls or text messages after that and of course he gave up rather easily. The fucker.

But she did get that boob job. It was an incredibly undetectable augmentation that left her with absolutely no sensation in her nipples.

"Oopsy!" The Indian Doctor said to her while she sat on white crinkly paper about a month later. Out the Indian Doctor's office window was a beautiful view of Times Square. In his thick, consonant spitting Indian accent he said, "Sometimes something like that happens."

Something like that happens? Oopsy? Maggie wanted to kill him right there in his office. Now she looked like Barbie and had the same, cold, unfeeling breasts exactly.

Something like that happens? Maggie had nipples that could light whole streets when sucked in high school and college and man and boy sucked away, as if by such vigorous and powerful sucking those breasts would inflate to some appropriate size. They never did, but now there was plenty and they were perfect and they might as well be carry-on baggage.

"Oopsy," Maggie said, as she thought of that stupid Indian doctor as her boss stared annoyed at his period bloody penis before he tucked it inside these pretty ridiculous neon red silk boxer shorts in that broom closet that first time.

"Good choice of colors this morning, though." Maggie chimed in with.

Then, of course, they fucked all the time. In her Brooklyn apartment and his New Jersey beach front home. When his wife wasn't there, of course. This went on for over a year and two promotions and Maggie was very close to getting a job as an assistant editor when it all changed. Her boss lover went as hard and empty and lifeless as her nipples. He gave her an assignment to get her out of his life and out of New York.

His wife, a comely solidly-built Italian woman who was indeed an Editor, was pregnant for the first time in their twenty-two year marriage. It made the *New Yorker*.

Now Maggie found herself sipping stale coffee in tourist beach-front hell listening to a homeless person who might or might not be the author of *Black Comanche*.

She stared at a glimpse of the great and mighty Atlantic through a sliver in the tacky concrete of these old ugly buildings. If she looked the other way she could see motorcycles, leather shops, and people who looked like carnival workers.

She was staying in a condo just up the road in Ormond Beach that had a kidney-shaped pool that only old people sat around. It was a timeshare owned by Mr. Famous Editor. They had never been able to sell it and now they had forgotten about it. Maggie cleaned and cleaned it for over two days. Dust, American dust lay everywhere and the microwave wouldn't work. There were silk sheets in one of the two bedrooms. The bastard.

Maggie found herself lonely and sad and angry and if she did not come back with the *Black Comanche* manuscript she might as well change the flight back to New York to her parent's home in Naperville, Illinois. She might anyway. He was a prick and she was stupid. Stupid about men and stupid about New York and God was she lonely. She was smoking again even. Marlboro Reds, for God's sake. And drinking alone. And crying.

Maggie saw no easy way out of this one. This would be a long dark decline that, regardless, would not end well. She just knew it.

A Minor Good Thing

There under the drawbridge he had read a romance novel he dug out of the trash yesterday and what a treat. He found a working light bulb and a book on the same day in the same block and a cop, can you believe it? A cop spliced a hot wire for him to hook the lamp up to. The cop didn't say a word. He just shook his head that cop did and off he drove and if anyone tried to steal this lamp this dagger of glass in his coat would slice their jugular. It was the power of reading he believed in. If he just had some ink now he could finish it. Finish it all. He had the notebooks and they were a little yellowed and stiff from the salty air but his pen was poised and ready and the structure had solidified in his head and what a beautiful boat easing down the Halifax. Little yellow lights inside the small rectangular cabin and inside they surely sipped nice whiskey, single-barrel whiskey like he used to drink and they talked about how nice it all was and he bet she felt so good inside and in that yellow light her tan lines identified the great lost continent of lustful intentions and that's where they were sailing now, as it drifted down the great Halifax, the glistening wide Halifax and if only he hadn't held that lovely young girl down that cold wintry evening, hadn't forced her trembling thin legs apart and drove on deep into the ruination of his existence and it is right here on page 194 of this derelict paperback that thousands upon millions of sad lonely housewives read day after day in these nasty romance novels where the heroine always comes back to marry the man who violated her and just why is that little tubular female mechanism given the sanctity to be associated with the word violate? Why not just call it an inconvenience of the flesh?

Would she come back to marry him? Yes, indeed. In point of fact when he was let out of prison she did try to contact him. She wrote him a curious note on spiral notebook paper. It smelled of perfume. No, it didn't. But it did say she didn't want to kill him anymore.

A minor good thing perhaps.

In the opposite direction another boat burst down the Halifax suddenly noisy and bouncing. Sloppy foamy waves lapped against concrete.

With his finger he wrote this on the last page of the romance novel of life:

I will go to sleep now dreaming of ink

One Other Time

Out the open deck door and across A1A was an empty beach of pure orange sand and the Atlantic was murky tonight, active and cloudy and not a soul on the beach and her notebook was open and attached to a modern blue plastic clipboard. Maggie had arranged her expensive gel pens just so and the foundation for the alchemy she wanted to take place was punctuated by a Jack and Club Soda as she listened to Death Cab for Cutie on her iPhone and fought an emptiness she could not recall ever having felt before in her life.

Except one other time. An ugly time she would probably write about sometime but not this time.

That time Maggie was huddled in a closet, a big closet filled with women's shoes and expensive women's clothes she wasn't even interested in. Maggie was crying and covering her ears.

Oh, he probably thought about her watching it all. His wife coming home unexpectedly and Maggie was stark naked in a corner of that big closet as husband and wife made love on the bed, Maggie's little summer stack of panties and shorts and tank top pushed far under the bed and did she goddamn know what was at stake if they were caught together? Did she goddamn know?

So Maggie, crying, staggered naked into this cedar-lined collection of shoes and clothes and belts and cried through it all, ears tightly covered, scared, but more empty, and it was raining over the Atlantic now. The drink was the only thing good.

And he was right. His wife did what she always did after sex. She went into the large bathroom to take her makeup off and shower and prepare for bed and there was x-amount of time to get the hell out.

Maggie cried stupidly all the way back to her apartment in the back of a cab and it was raining when she stepped out and this very same cell phone vibrated and then played Death Cab of Cutie and it was the only thing ironic to smile about as she stood on that broken New York concrete in the rain in love with a horrible man.

Maggie took a sip of her drink. She wouldn't write a word of it. This was all a perfectly romantic setup and she knew for a fact the great writers all had an addiction to real ink and real paper as the first step in the process but writers, she knew, chose to be alone, and she didn't want to be alone so by God after this drink she was going out.

The Return

Crabby Joe's was packed tonight. It was the one restaurant inside the Sunglow pier several miles down from that famous Daytona Pier. This pier was the last pier before Ponce Inlet and at the end of it, under bright lights, minimal fishermen stood by their rod and reels and more bright lights lit the gift shop and restaurant in the middle of the pier. It was overflowing with people tonight. Waitresses in tight shorts and blue shirts hauled trays of fried seafood and clear plastic pitchers of beer to everyone from college students to families on vacation and then the ever-present retirees were everywhere also. Those bad tippers were always there. The old fucks.

But it was almost time. Word had spread and every Saturday Night at 9 o'clock sharp usually was when that beautiful bartender came on duty, made her appearance, wiggled her long, thin fingers and flashed her drop-dead smile. Then she would put out her cigarette, tie her hair back so it wouldn't get in the way, and then stand beside the six liquor bottles already lined up for her on the bar. Everything was ready.

She never said a word to anyone. She didn't have to. She was the star. She did put out her Dolphin-shaped tip jar however. Always.

The place went quiet. People who knew shushed newcomers up. They pointed.

Everyone waited.

Collective gasps sounded out when the first bottle shot high into the air over the bar. Then scattered clapping started as the second liquor bottle joined the first bottle high in the air.

It wasn't long before all six bottles were flying high over that bar and the bartender's long thin yet swan-like arms were blurring almost with this incredible act of juggling six liquor bottles. Pounding electronic music had begun in perfect rhythm and all the waitresses had put down their pitchers and trays and were dancing. Hips were swaying, arms flying. Everyone began to dance as they watched. Even the old people bobbed their heads as children jumped and clapped.

Stephanie had returned.

Lawrenceville, Illinois

Down along the Embarrass River (and that's pronounced Am-Bro, bro) and along the Indiana/Illinois border in Southern Illinois was the town of Lawrenceville. It was a dying old town with dying old houses with an old dying Town Square and almost everything there had seen better times. Time when oil wasn't deregulated out of the state and there were jobs for people and the houses were painted and the men from the coal mines filled the bars and they had the number one high school basketball team in the country but now the houses all needed painting and went unsold and the people who still lived there just kept getting older.

But this kept the nursing homes open and busy and alive. Like the one on a hill there on the west edge of town. The one that was shaped like a light brick L. The one that, at first glance, was so austere and washed out as to appear downright military. It faced the west and overlooked a huge expanse of freshly-mowed dull-green nothingness. As an afterthought it seemed like, a few years ago, a couple trees were planted in this nothingness and out of an embarrassed loneliness, those trees weren't more than a few feet tall even now. Small concrete patios with cheap sliding glass doors lined the outer walls of this nursing home.

An incongruously young man sat frozen in a wheelchair on one of these patios. Beside him in a chair sat a thin young female nursing assistant in a flowery tunic and dull-white pants. She wore dirty blue deck shoes and bobby socks. She smoked long thin cigarettes and had a four-inch dragon tattooed in that area between your shoulder and your neck. She also had her pussy pierced if we could have seen that.

The crippled blind young man could not move in the wheelchair. The young woman sighed. She said she was looking forward to seeing the Arch again. She had to go there soon. She had to be in St. Louis shortly. But she liked Chicago better.

She held her cigarette up to his lips. He took a quick puff.

"My family always went to Chicago," she said. "I had an aunt that lived in Elkhart, Indiana. She used to work in a factory that made trailers. Mobile Homes. She got lung cancer from the glue fumes and died. She said before she died the glue hit you just like model car glue and it made them all high sometimes." She smiled but he couldn't see her smile.

"Goddamn," the young man said. He had movement above his chest. He could move his arms. Everything else down below he couldn't feel. His name was Tony.

"I know," the nursing assistant said. Her name was Nancy. "It knocked a bunch of them down and they all died before it got to court."

Tony nodded.

"My sister ran off with this Illinois Power guy and she wasn't with him two years and he got colon cancer from thirty years of fixing those transformers. They were full of PCBs for insulation. His clothes had so many PCBs in them you could wash them a hundred times and couldn't get it out. It stuck in his guts like that too. All fifteen guys he worked with, they all died of the same thing. Some of them got together and hired this lawyer and he got with the Electric Company lawyers and you know what they said?"

Nancy shrugged.

"They said they would all be dead by the time it got to court. And they were. Nobody got a cent."

Nancy picked at her broken pinkie fingernail with her tooth, said "Fucking corporations."

For a few minutes they didn't say anything. A few birds chirped somewhere. It was a warm day. And humid. A solitary car, filled with two old people, made its way down the only road between the nursing home and a huge empty flat field.

Tony took a sip from a white foam cup of water. "So it was hard and everything," he said. Nancy had to think a minute about what he was talking about. Then she laughed. He was talking about last night. When she worked third shift for somebody. After eleven. When she got on top of Tony.

"Yes."

Tony sort of smiled. "That's how Christopher Reeve's old lady did it. She said on TV."

Nancy laughed again. "Yep."

"And you got me to shoot a load?"

"I did."

Tony let out a phlegm-rattled laugh and like it always did it made him cough hard and deep. Nancy gave him another drink of water. She wiped his chin and neck.

"And you," he coughed. "You cried like a baby on top of me. Why'd you do that?"

Nancy stared out over the vast expanse of nothing in the nursing home yard. She lit another cigarette. She shrugged.

"I don't know." She looked squarely at Tony's face. "It felt good."

She smiled. "And you couldn't feel a thing."

They didn't say anything else for a long time. It was close to lunch. Tony, behind his sporty, silver-rimmed sunglasses may have fallen asleep.

Then he spoke. "I want to see my son. I want to get a hug, I mean. From my son. I want to get back to Granite City somehow. I need to talk to that executor or whatever the fuck she was called." He coughed again.

"Nancy?"

"What?"

"Are there clouds in the sky?"

Nancy looked around the sky.

"Not a single one," she said.

Tony smiled. "I knew that. Goddamn it, I knew that."

Nancy tossed her cigarette into the grass, unlocked the wheelchair and started wheeling Tony inside. It was lunch time.

Ants

It was her fault. Her father would say this and so would her mother and her ex-lover and the man she had an affair with. They would all agree that it was Maggie's fault that at this moment she was penned against a bumper in near total ocean darkness as a young handsome Mexican fondled her cold hard breasts and pressed his swollen-half-hard, wart-infested penis against her stomach, and it was that barmaid, that juggling barmaid who earlier yelled in her ear through the music and drunken noise that while that Mexie looked hot he was diseased and might even kill her if he got her alone but Maggie kept drinking even though that busy popular drop-dead gorgeous barmaid who juggled whiskey bottles cut her off and sent her on her way to a cab. And she almost made it to the cab.

Maggie had never heard the term Mexie before. She was learning things right and left here in Daytona Beach and when that barmaid explained what the term meant she thought it pretty racist actually. Mexie was a blue-collar slang term for the fucking Mexicans pouring into America like ants and Maggie's nose almost touched the tiny thin nose of the barmaid. Then Maggie eased her finger under Stephanie's beautiful chin and slipped her a New York tongue, which Stephanie took for only a second or two, and then pulled away from her with an irresistible drop-dead smile and that Mexie was there smiling and the drunken Maggie forgot the things Stephanie told her and he first slammed her so hard face down on the hood of his ugly tacky car it gave her a bloody nose. Maggie was so drunk she couldn't get the curse words out. He turned her there on the hood to look at those fine breasts. He wanted a better look at those big store-bought American breasts on this skinny American bitch.

He tried to stand her up. He tried to push her little expensive American skirt up. He tried to get her silky white thong off. There were just too many fucking things to do.

Then he got pulled back off his feet by his shirt collar. He let out a string of Mexican curses. The bouncer threw him into the sand. Stephanie's knee was in his throat. He flailed but not for long. Her knee pushed the breath and the strength right out of him.

The bouncer dragged him away.

That was all Maggie remembered.

Her Glock

"Oh fuck," said Nancy as she pushed Tony backwards into the backseat of her old Taurus. The awkward way she did this caused Tony to yell out fuck also. He felt his shoulder and a bump on his head. Jesus Christ.

He asked her again where they were going. They were going to Granite City to see his kid Jerry. And she knew someone there too. And besides, she had a singing gig there she had to show up for. It was an annual thing.

"Jeremiah," Tony said. "You call him anything but Jeremiah, Steph will kick your ass."

Nancy stopped looking to see if she had broken his leg getting him into the backseat and then stared very coldly at Tony.

"Nobody is going to kick my ass," she said. She adjusted his sunglasses on his blind blue eyes.

"I'm just sayin'." He asked if they were taking his wheelchair. He needed his wheelchair.

"Relax." She started the car and then looked at her hair in the rear-view mirror. It looked like a rat's nest. She needed a new perm. She would kill for a new perm. A light bulb went off as her face went blank as a bird's. Then she reached between her legs and there it was under her seat. Her chest pushing hard against the steering wheel, she got a hold of it. Tony moved his head. He asked her if she was alright. Yes, she was just fine. She moved the Glock back and forth in her hand right in front of his face. She checked the magazine. Tony heard this.

"What the hell you doing?"

"Money," Nancy said. "I need money to get us to Granite City."

Tony seemed to be thinking about this for a moment. He said they don't have to go nowhere. He let out a cough. "I'll get there sooner or later."

He felt the car moving. He tried to hold onto something. He felt only fabric. He found the edge of one seat.

"I'll get you there," Nancy said through the noisy hole in the muffler. "Because I think you love me."

"What?" Tony said.

Nancy knew where she was going. When people knew where they were going they had a much better chance of getting there. She knew where her uncle lived. He just drove by a few minutes ago and light bulbs were flashing and sparking in her head like crazy. Her uncle had a big conversion van with a wheelchair and a wet bar and an LCD television. It wasn't even two years old. Then he got mad and pushed her aunt down a staircase and told everybody in the family he did it and just what the goddamn hell were they going to do about it? No one did anything about it.

Nancy was going to do something about it.

She parked a block away. Tony asked her where she was going. She looked at him and then turned and held the gun just inches from his nose. She asked him something odd. She asked him if he could smell the money.

"What?" His neck hurt. Man, she hurt his neck when she put him in the car. She opened the car door. He would be fine. "Goddamn my neck hurts something fierce."

Diamonds

The little old lady at the table with Maggie shivered. She shivered just thinking about how cold it was in that freezer Charley Younger and Jeremiah put her in.

"It saved my life though," she said. Maggie just stared at her. She looked so gray. Her hair, her eyes, her skin. She had never seen an old person so, well, gray looking. She tried not to stare.

The old lady said she was from Kentucky and sure enough, like everyone from those parts she was prone to exaggeration now and again but the Lord strike her dead if her special child hadn't put her in a deep freezer for so long she probably would be dead.

Maggie's eyes wandered out the trailer window where a retarded guy was working in the tiny yard. She could catch a glimpse of the river also. A sailboat floated in the river.

"Are those real diamonds?"

Maggie suddenly realized how bad her head hurt. She couldn't remember such a headache. And her nose. It was so sore. She did see where the old lady was staring. They were real diamonds on her watch. A graduation present from her parents. Not big diamonds.

"Big enough," the old lady said. "Are you pregnant?"

Maggie froze.

"You look pregnant."

Uncle Tyler

Nancy shot the little dog first. She hated that dog. Nancy would come over with her period and all that scraggly ugly thin mutt would do was try to hump her leg. That wet little pecker on her leg made her sick. Uncle Tyler would just grin. It made her sick. She shot the dog through the throat and it died instantly. His name was Buster. The dog hit the wall with a stupid little thump and died right there.

She wanted to wake her uncle up. How the hell could he be so sound asleep so fast? He just got home! The place was so dirty. Her aunt at least tried to keep it clean and ever since he killed her Buster shit everywhere. And her uncle never changed the cage with that stupid little yellow bird in it either. The whole place smelled.

Nancy plugged her uncle twice in the chest and the bullets just seemed to collapse into his fatness and silently vanish, even though she heard one thud into the wall behind the old ugly leather recliner. His eyes moved but they never opened. She wanted them to open to see her but that didn't happen.

Nancy watched blood bloom thick through her uncle's yellowed white t-shirt. She knew where he kept money. She had to dig into his pants pockets for his keys and she didn't think it creepy or anything but, as always, such proximity to him made her think of him holding her forehead to that fat ugly belly as he made her suck his ugly dick. She almost threw up. The fucker. She just wished he would have been awake. She unlocked the silver box in the bedroom closet and there was more money in there than she thought there would be. She stuffed it into all her pockets.

Out in the van Tony was anxious.

"You around, Nancy? I got one sore neck I will tell you that."

Breech

"He was born worse than breech," the old gray lady said about her special child, Charley Younger, who now stood out the window in the yard, with his twisted hands trying to clean out an old metal water spout with a rag.

The old lady twisted her old little hands up like she was twisting open a jar. Her mouth was twisted up also. Maggie's eyes were getting wider.

"You have a birth like that you feel it." The old lady took a sip of coffee. It was horrible coffee. Instant. Maggie had never had a cup of instant coffee in her life. Still she was on her second cup. Why the barmaid brought her here she had no clue. The old lady stared out at her son. Her son who was retarded and was born worse than breech and he had a disease only a handful of people in the world had.

"Are you friends with . . . ?" Maggie had forgotten the name.

"Stephanie?"

"Yes."

The old lady gently crossed her hands on the table.

"She's a saint, child."

Light

The satellite radio in the van blared the blues. Nancy loved the blues. Did he like the blues?

"What?" Tony said. He sat right up front in the van. He faced the open road. The wheelchair was hydraulic and it was cushier than the one he had in the nursing home.

"I thank you again. I like what you're doing. I ain't been a nice guy really. Especially to Steph. I was a stud. I fucked anything I could. She worked hard. We both love Jeremiah though."

Nancy eased the window down and let ashes blow out the window. She was happy. It felt good at the moment. She bobbed a bit right and left as she drove.

"You know, girl, I think God's in charge of this. I do."

Nancy looked hard at him. She turned the radio down. She told him to call her Nancy. She was no girl.

"Nancy," he said. Tony's head swiveled oddly around. He paused as he stared strange and bent out the window. "I'm getting something back. There's something bright some around the edges. I think. I think when I get to Jeremiah I will see him. I do."

Nancy honked the horn. This startled Tony. Then he smiled. There was no traffic on Highway 51.

"Was Stephanie beautiful?" Nancy asked.

Tony jerked his head around. "Most beautiful girl I ever met. Her smile was like a movie. No tits, long legs, and a smile that would kill you."

Nancy laughed. Stephanie did try to kill him. Stephanie shot Tony in the forehead twice.

Tony smiled. "Well, I know. She ran somewhere. I bet she ran off with her teacher. That fucker. She liked him too much. Maybe she planned to run off with him and kill me."

"You think?"

He shook his head. "Not really. She just has a temper. I was watching a porn movie and jacking off. I don't think she liked that."

Nancy let out a laugh.

"Not after I got caught with a 14 year old. You'd probably try to kill me, too."

Nancy stopped smiling. Yes, she would. She might anyway, she said.

"What?"

"Nothing."

"God says you treat someone one way they'd treat you that way too. I'm a new man when I get my wiring back. That's what they said the head shots did to me. Messed up my wiring. When I see again God will point me right and I will go there. I will find Jerusalem and Jeremiah right at the same time."

Nancy turned the radio back up.

"Amen," she said.

"Amen," Tony said.

Mr. Ugly

Even through the headache the Halifax looked amazing. It looked better even than Pier 17 down by the Brooklyn Bridge where she was told to meet Mr. Ugly for a drink every so often. Every so often when he couldn't be without her. And he would just stare at her as Maggie talked and she would stop and say, "It's me. Stop just staring at me. I'm not dead."

"I missed you," he would say, sad and nervous. But it was his choice. He chose to stay with his money and reputation and wife and it was her who had to make salads at the Bistro and her day job and her nights by the phone with popcorn and bourbon.

Maggie sighed and took a sip of strong coffee. She didn't believe this old lady. This weird old lady who said that retarded guy and some black guy named Jeremiah, who was dead now, put her in a deep freeze. For over a year! And then when she was thawed out she coughed twice, shuddered, and her cancer was gone. Jesus Christ she had to get out of Florida. How can you miss someone as badly as he missed her and not give up some things to be with her? Just a few things. He didn't love his wife. Maggie stared into her bad, brown faded instant coffee.

She asked the old lady why she was brought here exactly.

"Why, I think Stephanie had to be somewhere. You want to go to the Flea Market with Charley and me?"

Judgment Day

It wasn't much of a rest park. It was off the interstate on a side highway and all it had was one picnic table, a tree, and a rusty garbage can. Empty beer cans were scattered around the trash can like dead metal birds. Behind the rest park was a large barren grassy area with nothing on it. Trees formed a crooked path back behind the empty grassy area. There was a river there but you couldn't see it from where they sat. Just the trees lining it.

Nancy sat on the picnic table threading ten pound test nylon fishing string through a brand new cane pole. Her grandfather used to take her fishing at Carlyle Lake and they used cane poles. Everybody else was using rod and reels but they had cane poles and there was nothing like seeing a red and white bobber go under and then pull in a fish. They only caught small fish that usually weren't as big as her hand. She liked her grandfather for the most part but one time he beat her with a willow branch because she lied to him. It hurt but it embarrassed her even more. She was eleven and he pulled her shorts down and pounded.

Tony sat in his wheelchair and was trying all the time to see more around the edges. He stopped twisting his head comically. He asked her what she lied to him about.

Nancy stopped stringing. She said she didn't remember.

This was a much fancier cane pole than she had ever seen. The metal eyes you strung the string through were big and shiny gold. It even had a cute little black spool on the end for the string. Nancy liked everything about this new cane pole.

Just twenty minutes ago she parked the van outside Jerry's Fishing Place and walked in, shot Jerry dead, took all his money out of his cash register, stole this cane pole, and filled a nice green metal tackle box with all this fishing stuff. She even put a white foam container of night crawlers in the refrigerator in the van.

"I don't hold anything against Stephanie. I don't. I mean I never pressed charges or anything. Hell, I never really said officially it was Stephanie who did it. They started looking for her when she just up and left. Jeremiah cried every night for weeks. Did I tell you the night Jeremiah was born I fucked her sister?"

Nancy stopped threading nylon fishing string. "Bad boy," she said. She went back to stringing.

"Damn, my shoulder's sore."

"It will be okay. You're a big, bad boy."

"I know they always say it but you never know what you had until it's gone."

Nancy blew smoke high above her, looked around. She honestly couldn't remember ever having anything really. Most men were just like him. She asked Tony if he liked to fish.

"Hell, yes. My dad had a pontoon boat on Lake Kincaid and we went fishing every weekend. He'd drink whiskey as the sun went down. When I got to high school I took friends out there all the time."

Nancy got up and stretched. It was a nice empty day and she'd already killed two men. Two men she hated. Jerry from the bait shop didn't like her drunken mouth late one night so he pinned Nancy against a wall outside Packer's Pub and raped her. And he didn't rape her with just his dick. He shoved a thick Barlow knife handle into her repeatedly and then knocked her down and when she tried to get up he knocked her down again and said if she ever told anyone he would open this very same knife and finish her. Her and her fucking mouth.

Nancy finished him. She read somewhere that we create our own Judgment Day. She said this out loud.

"What?"

She asked Tony if he ever fished with a cane pole.

"Get outta here," he said. No way. His Dad had two hundred dollar Garcia rod and reels and there was this depth gauge on the pontoon boat. His old man won fishing tournaments here to Michigan.

Nancy rocked her head back and forth and rolled her eyes. La-dee-damn da! She sat back down. She stuck her tongue out, squinted, and eased the nylon string through the final end hole of the fanciest cane pole she had ever seen.

After the success of this endeavor she flicked her silver tongue ring off the top of her front teeth and patted her brand new modernized cane pole. It was a cane pole from the 40th Century.

"I'm hungry," she said. "You hungry, Stud?"

Yes, he was hungry, he supposed. He never got as hungry as he used to, but he was hungry.

Thank You

So they piled into an old faded yellow car and Maggie had to drive. Charley Younger could drive an automatic but Stephanie took the car with the automatic so all they had was this old stick shift car. The old lady sat in the back and once again told Maggie how cold cold cold it was all that time in that freezer. Maggie took a deep breath. Charley Younger rested his head on the window. He'd cut himself and had one rolled up hand in a paper towel. Who was this girl exactly? Where was Stephanie? Jeremiah had been dead two hundred and forty one days, the retarded guy said. Did she know how to drive a stick?

Of course she did. Maggie drove a stick her whole life. She was raised on a stick. An old Volkswagen stick and just how far down A1A did they have to go? She killed the engine. The clutch was absolutely shot in this car. She started it back up. North was up. They had to go north. Charley Younger had to be back at work at five. There was a pretty young Korean hostess who would smile at him and thank him politely for clearing a table and Stephanie was probably gone for a week. She sometimes left for a week and no one had Stephanie's legs. Her legs were famous now in the only island trailer park in the entire world and Charley Younger tried not to miss her because she gave back all the money. They were now six blocks from Route 92. Turn there and go all the way to Interstate 95. Did anyone have a cigarette? The girl asked. Charley Younger's heavy eyes went to this pretty girl. Maybe in the glove box. Yes. Stephanie kept a pack of cigarettes and a lighter in there.

Thank you, she said.

9:35

And there along that little lake just on the edge of Granite City Seymour Belmo talked so fast and nervous and after they fed the ducks they sat on a park bench and he was squirming. He nervously weirdly gently touched her belly, brushed her belly button ring and a young Stephanie knew she had a great stomach and a great tan and it all took his breath away and this amused her more than anything and it more than anything nudged her curiosity so she asked him what he was feeling. What he felt about her, please. Just tell her why he was with her now even though she was only seventeen and he was well into his thirties and her teacher and all. I don't know, he said, I don't know. She was just fresh, he guessed. And electric. Electric? And it was such a great day, a pretty lake he had never been to and he loved days like these. September was his favorite month, the colors were so vivid and diverse and the leaves had this wonderful glossy finish and then death followed in October. Barren dying October.

She laughed. She was slumping intentionally in the park bench. She tugged at her seductive little blouse, tried to pull it over her taunt tiny stomach. It wouldn't stretch that far. She understood nothing right then, would understand nothing really until that Chicago hotel room when Seymour would nervously penetrate her and then roll over and moan. It wasn't right. But of course she felt good. So did he. And they had talked all the way up on the train that they wouldn't do anything but she pulled her panties out from under her nightie there in that hotel room and put them neatly on a chair in the semi-dark and that was all it took. She knew that would be all it took. Seymour wasn't much different than any other man except for his silliness. She loved how silly he was. That's why she got on top of him and breathed deeply into his mouth and told him to fuck her. She was on the pill now and just for him and there on the black red rectangular LCD clock the dial read 9:35 as he slid tight and hard inside her and she said that would be the time for all time that they would think of each other.

9:35.

Each and every time it was 9:35 remember being inside her and think of her and she would think of him at 9:35 until they could no longer think. Her lips and tongue slammed into his.

Stephanie leaned over the bow of this beautiful new boat named after her as of last week and there on the dial of her diamond-studded watch it was 9:35. Her white bikini bathing suit was almost dry. She didn't want to be out in the middle of the Halifax this morning. Didn't want to sleep anymore with this beautiful handsome ugly man who wore her as some trophy around his Florida sports friends. 9:35 and Seymour probably was oblivious to it.

She felt a touch sick. She wanted to be with Charley Younger and his resurrected mother at the flea market. She didn't want to be here. Just across the water was the trailer park. The island trailer park and all she had to do was dive in and swim there . . . .

Stephanie absently patted down the thick blister Band-Aid that hid a razor cut on her left forearm. Stephanie had gotten into a fight this morning. She walked up alongside a cute little Mexie housekeeper who had just made her a screwdriver and who was also fucking her boyfriend occasionally and Stephanie smacked her up side the face and right into the pool where that housekeeper with the big brown gorgeous eyes and big round breasts fell.

Stephanie, her long legs parted and her hip out in total attitude pointed her long finger at that little Mexican wench struggling in the deep end of the water and said as long as she was sleeping with Mike you whore bitch better stay the fuck away from him or her two little Mexie kids would be without their fucking mother. She glared and swung around, hair flying, and walked towards the French doors going inside and the crowd of Mexies inside looked frightened and then terrified. Stephanie stopped walking. Why the looks on their faces?

Stephanie swung around just in time to block the housekeeper's hand from coming right across her throat. They both tumbled hard to the damp concrete writhing together. Normally that razor blade cleaned grime from the corners of walls but this time it was meant for this stupid *puta* but Stephanie only got it across the forearm and it was a deep cut but she was too livid to bleed. They rolled on the concrete together and the Mexie got a hold of her hair and Stephanie kept swinging like a mad woman with a free hand at the face of this bitch. Stephanie struck finally and gave her two Granite City punches to the face and then doubled her over there on the hard concrete with an unbelievable stomach punch with her knee that left her immobile and unable to breathe. No one had any idea how strong Stephanie was. Even though the Mexie seemed to give in Stephanie slammed her head hard twice upon the concrete and finally calmed down and stood up. The bitch had got Stephanie's bikini bottom out of whack. Stephanie snapped it back into place and adjusted her top.

Asombroso the Mexies inside the house all muttered and hurried off to do their chores and the beaten one could hardly sit up. The skin had broken on one side of the housekeeper's face and she was bleeding pretty good. No one came to help her. Stephanie was still in the house.

Asombroso.

RC Cola

The van stopped screeching brakes and then came back weaving in reverse to pick up the hitchhiker there along route 51 heading east. The hitchhiker jumped back scared goddamn it was like it was trying to hit him. He was a dirty young wind-burnt scruffy-headed hitchhiker. Tony was yelling all the way as it scared him these sudden noises and movements. The sound of brakes. Goddamn. What the hell was happening?

Nancy just wanted to give a boy a ride. She unlocked the side door and it swung open and in he hopped. He smelled bad good and wasn't that ugly but man his tennis shoes were shot.

He was only fifteen. He was almost at his grandmother's grave just up the road. He would stand over her grave because of something he had to get her to forgive him for and then he planned to work his way up to Minnesota or out as far as Portland and work in the logging industry like his cousin was doing right now. They paid his cousin almost forty grand a year and he could get himself a big truck for that.

"I can live on forty grand good," he said. His name was Robert not Robbie and did they need any Oxycontin? He had a bagful he stole from his sister after they got in a fight and he beat the shit out of her and left apartment 14, Lincoln Estates, Cairo, Illinois. Did he kill her? His sister. No, he didn't think she'd die but he left her hurting. She might have been pregnant, the dumb drug-addled bitch. He smirked as he rummaged around in his bag. She weren't pregnant no more, he figured.

The boy hitchhiker got picked up first by a fat trucker with Goth tattoos who threatened to kill him if he didn't suck his dick.

Silence.

"Did you suck his dick?" Tony asked.

Nope. He didn't. He just leaned against the window as they went through Superman's hometown, Metropolis, and fuck he would have jumped out at the four way stop but the guy said he was just kidding. He wasn't really like that he was just cranked up on caffeine tablets and some leftover crank. He was so over his driving logs a trooper would take his keys right there on the spot. He had watermelons from Florida in the back that he was hauling up to Wheaton, Illinois. He was late because he stayed at a titty bar in Nashville too long.

Tony stared into the blackness. Tony couldn't swallow all of a sudden. Tony came from people who wouldn't pick up a hitchhiker.

Harris

Nancy, for some reason, scared him. He swallowed finally. He felt dead anyway. Tony came from people who had some money anyway and went to college and wouldn't pick up a fucking hitchhiker with a bag of Oxycontin who just beat up his pregnant sister. Nancy was trailer trash and goddamn he missed Stephanie. Even more than he missed Jeremiah. That was weird but it was true. But you know, that's what separates one class of people from another. Whether they will pick up a goddamn hitchhiker or not. Don't pick up fucking hitchhikers!

Nancy, her eyes hidden behind sunglasses offered Robert a soda from the little refrigerator in the van. She knew it was loaded with RC Cola. In the rear view mirror, Nancy watched the boy remove a can, smirk, than pull out two more cans and put them in his bag.

"I love RC Cola," Robert said.

"Who, in southern Illinois, don't love RC Cola?" Nancy said.

Homesick

The Daytona Beach Flea Market wasn't like the flea market in Brooklyn where the cacophony of people, all races and sizes and dispositions, poured onto the sprawling concrete with their flowers and fruits and blankets and cheap watches and belt buckles and pottery. No, this flea market had all that but it was in rectangular aluminum sided buildings out on the edge of nowhere and the people inside looked half disinterested and half frightened by all these summer tourists and there was no breeze and the heat was dry and oppressive. Maggie parked where she was instructed to park and they walked past old people smoking cigarettes on a park bench next to a Mexican girl with a yo-yo.

Heavy suffocating dirty heat hit her face as they entered. T-shirts were three for ten dollars. Dried-out sunburnt people with tattoos sat lifeless behind stacks of t-shirts and trucker hats and cheap sunglasses. They wouldn't look you in the eye. What a place.

Maggie had no use for this place. She stopped dead in her tracks at a stand selling magnetic bracelets. Charley Younger and his mother had already branched off in search of the fruit and vegetable stands. The skinhead young man working this stand eyed Maggie, stared at her breasts, smiled. Maggie sighed and decided right then and there she would never be able return to New York. Never find the author of *Black Comanche*. She had a big red New York scarlet letter tattooed on her pussy. She bought a magnetic bracelet and then a cherry snow cone. A Chinese couple in a booth that sold necklaces made out of ugly ocean shells stared blankly at her. They gave her chills. Maggie got so homesick all of a sudden she felt dizzy. It was almost an indefinable homesickness. She wanted to go back to New York and yet she wanted her father and her mother and that feeling in her backyard there in Glen Ellyn when her uncle was grilling and her mother was laughing her big Chicago loud laugh. And the heat and humidity there left them all happily glazed with a Midwestern coating of pure joy and they were all warm with family, giddy with each other's presence.

Fuck this place. Fuck Daytona and these scary weird people.

This was hell. Maggie wanted to go home. She bumped into a fat old lady in pink baggy shorts and yellow blouse who turned just slightly to glare at her.

"Excuse me," Maggie said. The old lady said nothing, turned and picked up a trinket. Maggie had to find somewhere to sit down.

Radford Lanier

Was his name and now he was a gravedigger and on Saturdays he delivered brown eggs to regulars in Old Shawneetown, Illinois, the town with the first bank ever built in the Land of Lincoln. Those eggs came in square blue cardboard cartons and were stacked neatly in a trunk of a Ford Tempo that had, after over twenty years, only 45,000 miles on it and by God, if that skinny little woman didn't plug that boy in the back of his head with a gun and it reminded him of some movie he saw one time at the movie house in Carmi. She just walked up to that boy and plugged him. Like it was nothing. He was praying and talking all at the same time. She asked him, Radford heard her ask him, if he was right with God. That's what she said to him.

Was he right with God? Radford was right with God. His Edith was gone, two years now, and he was apart from her too long as it was, so yes, he was right with God, by God, but that boy said he didn't care about God. He wouldn't turn around and look at that woman with the gun. He just stared down at his grandmother's grave. It was her he wanted to be right with. He took money from her and she didn't have much really. He told that woman with the gun he beat his grandmother up that particular day and she died not too long after that. He didn't regret beating her or killing her, she was just another old lady really, but for some reason he wanted to be right with her right now.

So that woman raised that gun up and shot that boy right in the back of his head and Radford flinched and then that boy fell so slow and easy and strange it was, it was weird. Radford exhaled so hard he was certain the woman heard him. He leaned against the tree. He didn't care if the woman heard him or saw him. He even let out a cough. A lazy, insignificant cough and she heard it, he knew she heard it, and he knew she saw him, but she didn't even stare or glare or anything.

That boy wasn't right with God and that was a problem for that woman with the gun. After she fired the gun and the gun went to her side she just stood there rigid for the longest time and then she let out a strange song. Radford reached into his overalls for his Prince Albert tobacco and rolling papers. He wanted his hands to stop shaking. He had heard that song before. Somewhere he did. It was in a strange tongue.

"Oh death oh death how can it be . . ."

"Oh earth and worms both have their claim . . ."

It gave him chills. He started rolling a cigarette.

Singularity

"In the hour of our discontent, when the world has taken on strange discolorations, the last lost Apostle of the Apocalypse will step out from the wicked shadows of Singularity and, let's think about this now . . . well, the first thing he will do is start dancing."

The homeless man, in front of a makeshift podium deep in the rectangular pre-fab labyrinth of the Daytona Beach Flea Market, catty corner from the fruit stand and close to a booth that sold incense and five dollar sunglasses, was preaching. It was his preach day. He had walked all the way from his home under the drawbridge over the Halifax River and now he was preaching. His hat had seven dollars in it already. He continued his sermon.

"It's a problem he has. He gets nervous and all and his feet start moving, and then his shoulders start bobbing and pretty soon he is doing this two-step kind of thing.

"But when he settles down, when he has stifled the cries of derisive diversion, when the chaos of the world has diverted people from its horrors, its injustices, and sold part and parcel the global concept of Singularity to first the literati and then people even dumber than the literati, politicians, then he will stop his little dance steps and then he will . . .

". . . head straight for the bathroom. (Pause) Let's face it, after a millennium, you, like any old codger, would still have bladder problems."

(Several people milling around listening smiled.)

"Yes! The last lost apostle of the Apocalypse will emerge from the pristine and over-engineered machinery of the modern age, that distributed system of virtual messiahs of Singularity, and plug himself into this mass distributed global network of moral and intellectual deception and, frankly, I hope he doesn't start touching himself. This, in all honesty, is another issue he will have after a more or less incontinent millennium. It's an inchoate lack of regard for his surroundings."

(Several people had lost interest.)

"Yes, in the hour of our discontent, when the world has taken on strange discolorations, the last lost apostle of the Apocalypse will finally explain the path."

Someone from New Zealand dropped an American dollar into the man's hat.

The Confession

Nancy bent the rear-view mirror of the van so that she could see her face and then gently ran her pinkie over her dry and cracking lips. She needed some ChapStick. Did Mr. Blind Man have any ChapStick?

Tony didn't have any ChapStick but he swore there was now light around the edges. There was. Maybe a shadow? Maybe not. He was tired. What happened to the boy? Where was the boy?

She stopped feeling her lips. Right where he should be, Nancy said.

"I bet, when you get your eyes back, I am prettier than Stephanie." She said this as she turned the key to start the van.

"I think not," Tony said, still swiveling his head to find the light. Nancy stopped turning the key. Her eyes eased over to look at him.

Nancy took a deep breath. It stung her lips to exhale. She needed ChapStick bad. "Tony." She put her cigarette out and fluffed her hair up. She turned around in the big van seat to face him better. She had something to tell him. She had something very important to tell him. She had something to get off her chest.

"I have to confess something to you," Nancy said. It seemed like she had a moment when it was hard to swallow.

Tony was looking somewhere else. Like blind people often do. "What?" he said, staring askance out the passenger's window.

Nancy wiggled excitedly in the seat, and cleared her throat. Then she realized she still had the gun under her butt. She removed it and put it under the seat and got back into position to confess something to Tony.

Nancy, her hands outstretched a bit like she was about to play an imaginary piano hanging in the air in front of her . . . began to sing.

It was in an odd voice, light and airy and, as Tony noticed, in a foreign language. Yet it was so melodic, strange, and beautiful. He had never heard such a voice. He thought for a moment she had put in a CD.

Nancy sang the whole song, all three verses. She sang for maybe five minutes. Then the song died quietly away as her lungs went empty and her voice faded into a whisper. She took a deep breath, filled her lungs back up with air.

She asked him if he liked it. Tony nodded. He liked it. It was beautiful. Nancy started the van.

She told Tony as the van pulled out of gravel and onto pavement that she was the last remaining Gaelic singer born in America today.

The very last one. Of her generation.

"Well, goddamn," Tony said. "What was that song about?"

Nancy reached to adjust the rear-view mirror. She gathered everything she needed to have another cigarette. She steered with her knee.

"Destructive fairies," she said.

Grilled Cheese and American Pie

Out that corner floor to ceiling sealed window, twenty floors up, he could just as easily leap. This thing that started in Seymour's stomach, started when they started watching this childish movie, this R-rated movie called *American Pie*, about eating pussy and jacking off in a towel and such, this thing in his stomach grew even larger when he ordered champagne and a lobster pasta brought up to the room and what did she like on the laminated, uber-fancy room service menu?

Grilled cheese and French fries.

Seymour blinked. He blinked twice.

"That's what I would like," she said, head tilting to the side as she combed out her long straight blond hair in this fancy Chicago Hilton hotel room. Her jeans were fashionably torn at the knees and fit her so tight and so low a thin layer of her nicely brown, nicely bare belly eased itself electric out of the front of those jeans.

Grilled cheese. What had he done? Seymour felt so nauseous he couldn't swallow. He wanted to quit teaching anyway. That's what he decided on the train. As Stephanie stared wide-eyed out the window he thought about how he could easily move out to his farm he inherited and work the fields and stare at wide swaths of Midwestern flatness and enjoy every minute. Alone. A friend of the family worked that farm now. He would work that farm soon. Maybe.

Stephanie ruffled out her hair, let out a big laugh at a bad adolescent joke on American Pie, and then carefully tore another swath off the plain toasted white bread and melted cheese sandwich.

He didn't touch his lobster pasta. The salad was so tiny it looked like it had been dropped on the floor and only partially put back on the square white plate. The bread was stale. Stephanie loved the movie and continued to pick very carefully at the grilled cheese sandwich and French fries. He drank the champagne but she said it smelled funny and drank an 8 dollar Coke from the refrigerator instead. He wanted to leap out the window. Yes, he did. She caught him looking at her once. "Don't try anything," she deadpanned. Then she smiled and got right back into the bad movie people her age loved. She filled her mouth with grilled cheese.

Don't try anything had been a running joke between them. She would secretly come with Seymour to Chicago and nothing was to happen between them and even though they did some heavy petting in a car once it would all remain innocent between them because it was just too weird him being so old and her being seventeen and it was all his fault anyway. He always made up excuses to talk to her and then he kissed her one night and sent her zooming, she said.

Zooming.

Seymour still couldn't breathe very well. He stared out the window down Michigan Avenue at ant-sized cars zooming silently in both directions. As a black haired young man in American Pie not unlike Seymour had been at that age stared at a tall thin blonde's pussy. Stephanie was chuckling.

A Weird Day

Comfort at last. Charley Younger wiggled comfortably into the lifeguard chair, crossed his legs, and stared mesmerized and utterly at peace at the shimmering slivers of indigo and orange and gray just above the ocean water line. It was his time of day. The sun was almost completely somewhere else and the wind had died and the ocean roar was now just a nicely calming hum and he was the only one who existed at this very moment. He was relaxed finally and away from Stephanie and her newfound friend, Maggie, who was hysterical earlier as she drove home from the flea market yelling and screaming about how that homeless person could have saved her life if those ugly people hadn't stopped her from chasing him and the world was a shithole when you think about it etc. etc. It made his mother nervous. She wrung her hands in the back.

"Why, Honey, I don't know what to tell you," his mother said. Charley Younger looked back at his mother when she said this. Oddly enough, they both knew that homeless person. They sometimes, through the church, delivered food and other stuff to him underneath the Silver Beach drawbridge. They liked him even. He was always polite and appreciative and remembered their names. His name, Charley Younger remembered, always changed. The last time they saw him he told them his name was Rosco. And before that Bill. They had no idea he was some famous writer or teacher or whatever Maggie said he was. He just always made his mother laugh and Charley Younger didn't hear his mother laugh very much. It took him back to his youth when she laughed like that quite often.

Charley Younger, his bent hands folded comfortably over his thigh, got so relaxed in his special spot in the universe he may have fallen asleep for awhile. It was good to be here. It had been a weird day.

Earlier, there was Stephanie sitting in that tiny white bikini smoking a cigarette when that girl, Maggie, got them home from the flea market. Stephanie's arm was cut pretty good. Charley Younger fixed it up better. She was so pale and red-eyed and coughing up water and smiling weakly as Stephanie said she swam all across the Halifax and truly thought she was going to die at one point. Charley Younger looked at her cigarettes. Stephanie must have stopped with the patches and yes, she had. They made her heart race and she thought she was going to die from a heart attack every time she put one on so she would rather smoke. Thank you.

Maggie took a cigarette and collapsed in a chair on the patio and it was uncomfortable for them all for a while. His mother went inside. Charley Younger piddled around and got to hear it all.

Maggie started spilling her guts finally after Stephanie asked her what was up and then they all heard the story about the book. His mother's ear, he was sure, was glued to the open kitchen window.

He heard the whole story of the great unpublished book and an evil man Maggie had been sleeping with who owned the condo up in Ormond Beach and Maggie went from laughing one minute to crying the next as she told Stephanie everything and Stephanie, like she always did, never said much, as she talked less than anyone Charley Younger knew, and it made him for some reason recall the time all three of them, Charley Younger, his mother, and Stephanie were watching American Idol and Stephanie fell asleep and he stared at her. It wasn't nice to stare but his mother was asleep in her chair also and he wasn't bothering anyone so he paid close attention to a mole behind Stephanie's ear. He would trace this mole with his droopy eyes and then trace the rest of her body, especially her long beautiful perfect legs. He would trace especially the little dolphin tattoo on her left ankle. He would trace and retrace all of her over and over as if he were preparing to paint her on a canvas someday. He would do this until his eyes hurt or he got tired or she woke up. Eventually he fell asleep also, the traces he made working as some strange lullaby.

But it was Saturday evening now and it had been an odd day. Maggie and Stephanie were getting to know each other and they, Charley Younger could tell, liked each other. Charley Younger, earlier, just kept pulling up weeds sprouting in the small crabgrass yard. He couldn't believe Stephanie had jumped off a boat and swam here. Stephanie was the only one he knew who could do such a thing. Charley Younger, actually, had no idea what to think of Maggie. She liked to talk. Stephanie brought them out beers and Maggie just kept talking.

Nettie, Charley Younger's mother, kept wringing her hands inside. Finally she decided to do what old ladies from the south always did, regardless of the time of day, when staring into the face of calamity or stress of any kind.

Nettie decided to cook a big meal. Nettie had a chicken cut up that was going to be fried that night anyway but that wouldn't be enough so she opened six pounds of pork chops they had bought yesterday but hadn't put in the freezer yet and she had plenty of fresh green beans and new potatoes they had just gotten at the Flea Market.

It was 2:30 in the afternoon. So? Nettie got out the Crisco tin and set it on the counter and for a moment she went back to a time during the Great Depression when the tins of lard ran out and they would pour off the fat of fried bacon every morning and fry everything with that for supper. Nothing fried in bacon fat ever suffered.

Nettie put newspaper on the kitchen counter and tore the plastic wrapper off the pork chops. Those two girls out there were crazy as bed bugs and skinny as rails. They needed food.

Charley Younger jumped, startled as he sat in the lifeguard station. A couple, black and gray silhouettes in the approaching darkness, hand in hand, ambled his way along the beach. He sat up straight, made noises, and tried to act as if he meant what he was doing. They didn't pay him no mind. They walked on by, oblivious to the fact they had intruded on Charley Younger. He took a deep breath when they passed, wiped drivel from one corner of his mouth and once again settled into his corner of the universe.

More Light

The path was so well-worn through the thick old trees and the black gray dirt was so packed flat it was shiny like glass but so cool and soft underneath her tiny bare feet it almost tickled. Nothing moved in the small brown pond. The small brown pond on the outskirts of a small Illinois town called Woodland. Nancy was maybe four then. Her uncle had his finger up to his mouth. She had to be quiet. Fish could hear you. She smiled at this. She looked down at the little bitty sunfish lying dead in the grass beside them. She saw no ears on it. This made her uncle laugh and surely the fish heard this. She sat down next to him and next to a small green metal tackle box and a white foam container of red worms. Crappie liked red worms better than night crawlers. Catfish liked night crawlers. They were fishing for crappie and blue gill sunfish in this little pond. They both stared out at two red and white plastic bobbers not moving one bit in the pond just off the bank in front of them. Little Nancy's heart was pounding so loud in her chest there was no doubt those earless fish could hear that. It was one happy dream from her past that had boiled up and so vivid because she wasn't sleeping very heavily when Tony's screams woke her up she thought she might be having a heart attack.

Then she realized where she was. She cursed. This place wasn't any place like that magical place of her youth, her pure and simple youth when nothing bad had ever happened to her and no one hurt her to the bone and the world was a place of beauty absolute without sickness deep in your bowels that never went away. What the fuck was he yelling about? No, this was an open, noisy ugly lake without fish. Without beauty. The bobber rocked disoriented in the uneven ripples of clear sterile water. No, and what a great dream mister cripple blew away. Shut up!

But Tony wouldn't shut up.

He had got his eyes back.

Just like that. He had been asleep too. And the earth moved. Swear to God. They were right along the New Madrid Fault, correct, and tremors happened all the time but it was more than that, goddamn it. He had been asleep too and then the earth shook violently, violently enough to rattle his wheel chair there along that ugly sterile lake, and it was a piss ant lake, bare and open like the spread legs of a Sauget stripper. Tony's eyes were back and there was a big blue sky and over there was a beautiful beat-up dead sailboat docked and over there a solitary rundown trailer was empty with graffiti painted on it and the wind was causing little white caps across this wonderful beautiful lake and there wasn't a cloud one, well, maybe one little one far out there but son of a bitch he could see again and by God, was that feeling in his leg? No. Yes! It was! It was all coming back and he was coming back and where was that goddamn Nursing Home Assistant? Where was goddamn Nancy? Fuck! He swatted at a fly on his leg. He felt that bug on his leg! Can you believe that? He felt it. Nancy!

Nancy was in the back in the van. She heard him. She heard every word. He woke her up and she lost her place in her nice little dream and it would probably never come back again. She went to the front seat of the van as Tony yelled and yelled and yelled and now she was carefully applying eyeliner and then dusted up her makeup and then decided on a dull-red lipstick that always accentuated her big blue eyes, her Kate Moss eyes, one man she fucked once told her. She paused. Tony got delirious. He was laughing and pounding on his wheelchair and yelling and then broke into what he guessed was funny or ironic or something. Now he was yelling out the song, "Feelings!" It made Nancy frown.

Nancy sighed as she checked herself out in the rear view mirror. Come to think about it, she needed to get some feeling back herself.

She carefully reloaded her Glock and put it down the front of her jeans.

The Celtic Killers

Were in town! They were getting out of a limo right downtown in front of the Millennium Hotel right there along the great and mighty Mississippi in the brickyard town of Saint Louis. A freckle-faced Irish lass named Pasty (long a) Breathless stepped out last, flashing a pair of green panties that bloomed incandescent between two solidly cute short legs as her overly short dull red skirt slipped way too far up. She smiled at the black limo driver who watched it all through shiny black sunglasses. She stretched and looked around and then patted down her shirt. It was her first trip to St. Louis. She played the Irish fiddle. A violin, actually. No, St. Louis was no New York where they played the night before. She stared down the mostly empty street. If New York was the city that never sleeps, St. Louis was the city of frequent naps, Pasty's lover and lead guitarist, Bradley Downs, told her this morning. And he didn't stop there. St. Louis was a dirty tired excuse of a river town, much like Cardiff back in jolly ol' England, another town whose days slipped languidly away into nowhere. St. Louis was a place urban sprawl had ripped apart leaving only dirt and blood and everything was dead or dying in downtown St. Louis. And now even the great institution of American Beer, Budweiser, was bought out by Belgians. Only corporations of evil existed in St. Louis, Bradley said. Boeing made bombs and Monsanto, the creator of the ugliest most devastatingly murderous pesticide called PCBs, was now engineering Nazi corn for the world. And you know the irony of it all, Pasty? Pasty wonder thighs, and suction lips? Pasty my temporary love? (What? she had said) St. Louis was over ridden by Catholics. Hard core Catholics, upper, lower, middle class Catholics, Catholics in huge vehicles with those metal fish on the back who trucked their kids off to private Catholic schools where they routinely chanted "McCain! Not Hussein!" and "Kill Barack!" all because they would kill kill kill anyone who wasn't Pro-Life! (That makes sense) And you know what the irony of that is? (I'm not really listening, Pasty said, lighting a cigarette.) The whole state of Missouri from the KKK ruled boot heel to the very toppy tip was brimming with millions of evangelicals and Catholics and who was the highest paid Catholic employee in the entire state? (Do I care?)

Rick Majerus. The head basketball coach of the seminal Catholic university, St. Louis University. Millions of dollars paid to him to lead the great men who would set an example for Catholic sports greatness throughout the heathen liberal nation.

Rick Majerus took over the team and promptly attended a Hillary Clinton rally. (Cool.) He was quoted as saying, "You know, I kind of think it's a woman's choice, you know?"

Did they fire him? No way. Rick Majerus is a great man. Superior to those self-righteous Catholics. The priest section of the new St. Louis University basketball arena grew exponentially! If he could bring success to a piss ant Catholic joke of a basketball program, he could support the killing of as many fetuses as he liked.

Amen.

And why did Bradley Downs, lead guitarist for the third most popular Irish Punk band in the land (After the Dropkick Murphys and Flogging Molly. Never mind the Pogues . . .), care or know so much about the city that took frequent naps? And why was he ranting like this in that beautiful high-rise hotel across the street from ground-zero in the city that never sleeps after a sold-out concert? After some extremely penetrating and a bit painful anal action with Pasty as they stared at the massive cargo ship from Brazil that was easing itself through the New York Bay?

Because Bradley was from St. Louis. He was abused by a priest there. Right in a parish in St. Louis, that priest's soft pale chubby hands, eased apart his ass cheeks, gave it to him up the arse right over the holy book, turned to page one, and all Bradley could remember besides the pain for the longest time was the gold flecks of holy book glitter that came from the edge of that massive foul-smelling book as he clung to it.

Yes, the fastest guitarist and chief song writer of the Celtic Killers, was born and raised until that unholy penetration, born and raised in the confines of south St. Louis, and then off the family went to Ireland, where the taxes were low and the Catholic head count even lower. Yes, after that, St. Louis to the Downs family, became a caustic ugly horrible memory.

"So," Pasty said, rubbing a bit more jelly on her sore little bottom, as they drank straight from a bottle of expensive Irish whiskey, "Why are we returning again?"

Bradley's intensely beautiful brown eyes glazed as he stared out the glass façade and into the New York Bay.

"Nancy."

Nancy?

Yes, Nancy. Nancy across the distant sea. Nancy who floated ethereally, translucently, ghostly into the Fox Theater that hot summer's night three years ago. Floated unseen in a fog of fairy dust, her beautiful white dress billowing all around her lithe, almost shapely body. And right at that moment in time when the mostly out of town crowd of mohawked and tattooed punkers were screaming their loudest as Bradley had just mutilated and shattered the stem of his second Stratocaster . . .

Something sucked the air out of that gorgeous old Theater. The plug had been pulled somehow. The crowd abruptly stopped screaming, yelling, leaping. All fists went down.

Nancy was in the house.

Nancy.

Nancy eased her hand delicately, deliberately, seductively out in front of her and the thousands of girls and mostly boy drug-addled, drunken punkers had their breath mysteriously sucked out of them. A chill filled the smoky air. A real chill. Honest to God.

Utter silence.

Nancy, the greatest of all American Gaelic singers opened her wide pouty perfectly black-painted lips and murdered them all. Dead.

Dead as Irish punker door nails.

Each and every one of them died. Destroyed, annihilated by the most heavenly angelic lilt of a voice to ever saturate that old building. Each and every heart was pulled gently and completely from their fashionably defiant, nipple-pierced and needle-painted chests.

They understood nary a word of her pitch-perfect hypnotic song.

But when it ended they knew one thing.

They all wanted to fuck Nancy.

Pasty had heard this story several times before. (And it varied slightly each time and depended upon the quantity of Irish whiskey Bradley consumed.)

"But will she return again tonight?"

Bradley smiled. Of course Nancy would return. At precisely ten o'clock her voice would ease itself over the manic Fox punker crowd and begin its beautiful Gaelic magic.

Yes, she would. It was more than magic. It was more than fate. It was more than anything earthly. It was, fecking *unearthly*.

It was Nancy. It was the voice and body of the last great American Gaelic singer in America today.

That is what Bradley told her in New York.

Now Pasty looked out across the mighty muddy Mississippi as a stiff mid-western breeze hiked her flimsy skirt a bit too high up her thigh. Pasty was six months new to the Celtic Killers and two months new to sleeping with the angry crazy Bradley Downs. He had said many outrageous things. But this was one he kept repeating since leaving Dublin.

Nancy was on the bill and would make her appearance. Fecking truth, Bradley said.

Pasty Breathless (real name Sarah McDougal) would only believe it when it happened.

Sinking

When Stephanie jumped off that boat, when she decided she didn't want to be where she was, she knew as soon as she hit the surprisingly warm water that there was a good chance she wouldn't make it across the Halifax. The strength of the current surprised her. She wasn't a particularly good swimmer, anyway. She just wanted away from that boat and that sick man who was standing next to the small bar on the boat fondling himself in front of that young Mexican girl who had brought him a drink. His third drink already. The girl looked so frightened. She didn't care about his dick. She cared about making some money and probably sharing that money with the rest of her family and she would even suck his dick to keep this job and that probably would happen next and this wasn't a life Stephanie felt good about so she jumped in.

She tried to swim to the other side but it seemed like the other side was now farther away from where she jumped in. Her boyfriend hadn't seen her jump. He wasn't her boyfriend anymore. She stopped swimming and drifted as she removed the big diamond earrings from her lobes and let them sink in the water.

Stephanie went back to swimming. She didn't care if she couldn't make it to the other side. She missed her son all of a sudden and at least if she didn't make it to the other side that ever present feeling in the bottom of her stomach of always wanting to go back home and get her son would go away.

Why Stephanie hadn't gone home again she didn't know. She was as tough as any woman she knew and tougher than most but she was paralyzed when it came to going home and getting her son. She would go on with her life here in Daytona like nothing was wrong and then suddenly out of the blue she would have to go throw up because she missed her son so much.

But little Jeremiah had forgotten her now. She was sure of this. Fuck. Stephanie stopped swimming. It was a perfect time to stop swimming. And she did.

Stephanie let her eyes blur as she also let herself drift with the mighty current.

Stephanie began to sink, her arms losing all strength as she thought about her son and how she bet he had forgotten all about her.

Ormond Beach

From where they sat in the orange sand up from Daytona where the trash shops and strip joints were replaced by colorful condos filled with old ladies driving big Fords and Mercurys years and years after their husbands had died were coming back from the Publix grocery store with their soup packets and instant coffee, Stephanie and Maggie, thigh to thigh, knee to knee, shoulder to shoulder, chins resting almost identically on a knee, the orange sand and dark gray blue sky, the steady quiet roar of the Atlantic was better than even the orgasms they just exchanged quietly and reverently between each other.

Stephanie was staring south. There was no one on this beach. It was a smaller beach with deep orange sand that felt softer between her long toes. She had never been here before. Her first visit to Florida was almost a year ago and still she had never gone back for her son yet. Yet. The state probably had him now. After her mother beat him probably. Her eyes grew wet and cloudy and heavy.

"We came to Florida every year and ate at the same places and swam in the same pool and that was okay and fun but I hated the drive," Maggie said. "God, it took forever to get through Georgia." She rubbed her fingers softly over Stephanie's knee to knock off sand and of course she enjoyed fucking Stephanie. Maggie would fuck a hot girl any day of the week and had done so all her sexual life. She liked men more probably but not that much more.

Stephanie stared way out to sea. Way out past the spot of a boat, past the thick and dying sky. Stephanie stared so far out her eyes began to burn. Then she blinked. There was no reason to stay around here anymore. No reason to toss liquor bottles in the air for tips. No reason to fuck bad men just for comfort. Yes, she would cross A1A and shower in the yellow and green painted condo with Maggie. Yes, she would, one more time at least, suck and bite and kiss every last drop of salty slightly bitter juice from between Maggie's pretty little legs. And she would allow the same to be done to her, because, regardless, there was no one like a woman who knew how to fully please another woman, and then she would sneak out from between those ridiculously soft and tacky red satin sheets some old man bought for the place and there past midnight, under a glowing huge full moon, as she sat on the heavily painted concrete condo ledge, light a cigarette, stare at the kidney shaped condo pool and think about Seymour. Think about the poetry she used to write about him, think about his silly dry wit and sarcasm, and then think about her son and think about everything really and mainly just how far she was from Granite City at this very moment.

Psalm 23:4

Tony must have fallen asleep. He was so excited and he had his life back now, most of it anyway, and yelling like he was doing, yelling for Nancy that dumb nursing assistant, he must have gotten so tired that he just passed out for awhile.

He was startled awake. Nancy was right up in his face. He could smell perfume. She had her makeup on perfect. Tony had not seen a woman with her makeup on for a very long time. The blue sky was gone and there was a thin red and orange ribbon of a sunset there on the other side of the lake. The white caps were gone and the lake was as shiny and quiet as glass. A couple ducks floated aimlessly, hardly moving, just in front of them. A huge ass skeleton-looking full moon hung in the sky right next to the huge silver earring Nancy had on. Tony was digging everything. He had his vision back. He stared finally at her eyes. My God. She had beautiful eyes. Well fuck, she *was* as beautiful as Stephanie. Maybe even more beautiful. He blinked. He could see! She wasn't quite as beautiful as Stephanie really. Stephanie had that beautiful mouth, those razor thin lips that parted into that deadly ass smile.

"I will be a changed man," Tony said.

"Am I?"

"What?"

"Am I more beautiful than Stephanie?"

Nancy was making him a little out of breath. It was the first time in how long since he could feel his penis. His mouth went wide open and she squeezed him just right. She was rubbing over the tip like she was about to pull a trigger.

Regardless, Tony wasn't born yesterday.

"Twice as beautiful," he groaned.

Down her head went. He was lying of course. She knew immediately when a man was lying but she was granting him one last request (even though he hadn't actually made the request and certainly had no idea it was his last).

Those two ducks, startled, splattered across the quiet lake when Tony finally exulted so loudly he may have ruptured a blood vessel in his eye.

Hotel Drawbridge

It all fell into place. It's funny how things work. Earlier, just over a pop tart and coffee, Stephanie casually told Maggie where the manuscript was. The manuscript Maggie had been looking for every single day she spent in Daytona. When Maggie first told Stephanie about the manuscript it didn't register at first. Now it did. Stephanie had seen it quite sometime ago. It was in a corner of Hotel Drawbridge, as Stephanie called it. She had gone there with Charley Younger and his mother with a canceled order of twelve egg rolls and fifteen Chinese hot wings. And some leftover rice.

There were three homeless men living there. Rosco and two of his friends. While Charley Younger's mother divvied up the food Rosco showed Stephanie a manuscript with a front page that had written on it in big blue crayon: BLACK COMANCHE.

Rosco told Stephanie, after he was dead, it would win a Pulitzer Prize. Then Stephanie asked him what a Pulitzer Prize was exactly. She kind of knew she thought.

Rosco paused. "I don't know," he said.

Stephanie asked him what the manuscript was about. Rosco, after he returned from taking a piss in the Halifax, told her it was about what all award-winning novels since the beginning of all novel writing were about.

And that was? Stephanie asked.

"Hateful people who eventually turn things around."

Stephanie thought about this but not for very long.

He read Stephanie the opening line to his future posthumous Pulitzer Prize winning novel. In fact, Stephanie hadn't forgotten that opening sentence that homeless person read to her.

"*In the hour of our discontent, when the world has taken on strange discolorations*," Stephanie recited.

After first explaining to Stephanie that it wasn't a sentence, but a fragment, Maggie went berserk. Everything rattled on the table as she bolted to her feet. She grabbed her car keys. Maggie knew where that bridge was.

"Be careful," Stephanie said, sipping her coffee. Maggie didn't hear her.

She was already out the door.

Jimmy

Nancy sat up so slowly in the bed inside her now dead uncle's van you wouldn't even have known her temples were throbbing and her heart was pounding so hard in her chest she could hear it. Out the tilt-out back window the face on the moon was huge and leering at her. Out that window the sky was an opaque black. A weird black. As black as her heart. She had wet the bed. Nancy always wet the bed.

Just down from the van at the end of a wide slanting concrete boat ramp was an overturned wheelchair that was mostly in the water. One of its exposed spoked wheels spun slightly.

Earlier, Nancy just let Tony roll down that concrete ramp. It surprised him and if he hadn't been so angry and yelling and cursing the bitch who just gave him head he might have been able to stop himself from rolling on into the water. Instead Tony kept running his mouth and pointing his finger and kicking his newly discovered legs and somehow got one foot caught in the wheel and the whole wheelchair flipped straight forward right there at the water's edge and down his head went.

That was how it ended for Tony.

Nancy took a breath finally. She hated being awake. It had been another good dream.

Nancy was chasing a little boy named Jimmy and it was first grade all over again and she finally cornered Jimmy down concrete steps that lead to the basement of Stockland Grade School and she stopped him from running back up the steps and then grabbed both of his cheeks and planted a huge wet kiss on his mouth.

Then she let him go. He didn't react like the two boys she had done that to before. He didn't ask for more and try to hit her or spit in her face.

Jimmy just stood there quietly and even though he might have been trying not to, he was smiling.

Disneyland

It was breezy under Hotel Drawbridge this morning as old yellowed newspapers rattled in the wind and somewhere down Main Street Daytona Beach a police siren wailed. White caps the size of plates rippled across the Halifax.

There were genuine tears in Maggie's eyes. Rosco's eyes were genuinely blood shot. He held a Daffy Duck Disneyland mug. He towered over the little girl. His bloodshot eyes widened. He surprised himself but he remembered her from the flea market where she had tried to kill him. She sure seemed a lot bigger when she tried to kill him. He asked her if she was going to try to kill him again.

"No," she said. Maggie tried to contain her emotions this time. She wouldn't try to hurt him. She could tell, even though she was barely five foot tall and he was probably closer to six foot four, he was cringing a bit. But Maggie was having trouble talking. She kept choking up. The prospect of having the *Black Comanche* manuscript and her getting her life back and returning to New York and those Brooklyn bagels and lattes with whiny insensitive, overly sensitive men who were all very close to massive success, Oh Lord, Maggie missed it all.

"I—" Maggie was finally able to speak. "I just want you to get the success your novel deserves. I- I think it could win a Pulitzer. I do."

This made Rosco go catatonic momentarily. Then, in a surprisingly sharp tone, he said, "Without ever having read it?" The tone panicked and startled Maggie.

"Reputation!" She said. "Your reputation. You, well, you have quite the reputation."

Rosco slowly turned to look out across the Halifax. He was an aging homeless person who heard voices and often spoke back to these voices and had once been disgraced when he had raped one of his students twenty years ago. Not to mention the fact that he would occasionally take his penis out and show it to tourists.

The concept of a reputation somehow eluded him.

So when Sage, his newest homeless tenant in Hotel Drawbridge, stepped up behind Maggie and buried a steak knife into her lower back and twisted it, Rosco just went about his business.

Rosco, as Maggie lay dying, finished his coffee and took a dump in the Halifax and headed down to his Flea Market pulpit.

Four Cheerleaders and an iPod

That's what ended most all of it for Seymour Belmo. Don't laugh. It could happen to you. He was a history teacher one minute and the next he was standing outside his bottomed-out Jetta a quarter of a mile from a tin-roofed little house deep in southern Illinois. He wasn't sure about this. He felt a touch lonely and even more, he felt more than a little bit afraid.

He had also been a girl's volleyball coach. That's how he met Stephanie. She was a very good volleyball player, the best he had ever coached, and before he knew it he was showing her how to play better defense and the next he was going down on her like his tongue was drilling for sexual oil.

Then she graduated and after awhile he came to his senses and told her it was over and that was that for awhile and then he saw her again when he was in Florida one time and Stephanie ran away from him that time and he drove all over Daytona looking for her and then he came home and tried to make things work with his wife, but that wasn't going too well and then came the four cheerleaders and an iPod. (As Maggie's boob doctor said earlier in this novel, Oopsy).

The tin roof had some dull silver in it as he remembered but now that roof was totally brown with rust.

Seymour hadn't been back to this particular old farmhouse for a long time. Maybe once with Stephanie on a road trip but the last time he was here in his childhood was 1982. That's when his Uncle Bud died. Uncle Bud left the farm to his father.

Then Seymour inherited this farm in 1987 when his father died. At first, Seymour planned to just sell the small plot of earth in southern Illinois. But it had been his uncle's so for some reason he kept the farm and now he was going to live on this farm with a barn, a chicken coup, and even a pigpen. He wouldn't raise pigs however.

Oddly enough, the chickens were still there. They moved slowly, deliberately all around the back of the fenced in farmhouse. They made guttural little chicken noises when he approached. He smiled. He had gotten here finally. The tiny little yard with the big catalpa tree was freshly mowed and there was still a wooden bench swing hanging from rusty chain links.

The house looked smaller than he remembered. Of course it did.

That one time, a couple years ago, when he was driving around with

Stephanie and he drove here and they sat on that porch swing, Stephanie said she would live here if he wanted her to. She could raise chickens and have children and all that.

And all that.

To think that Seymour was trying to get her out of his life then.

That day the door was locked and he had left the keys at home and they could only look in the windows. A farmer named Roger lived down the gravel road from here and he took care of everything. He farmed the 150 acres his Uncle Bud used to farm and every day he fed the chickens and he had taken over the chicken route and he even oiled the tractors and machine tools just like Uncle Bud did. Robert collected the money from the egg route and got the money from the corn and beans he grew and for $250 a month he kept this house working because someday Seymour would move in.

Since 1987 Seymour sent this farmer $250.00 a month and he did all of that and he even kept coal in the coal box in both the kitchen and the living room. You never knew when Seymour would finally show.

Seymour was finally here.

The little farmhouse had a coal stove in the kitchen and another one in the living room. They were blue-black metal round shapely coal stoves with little spiral metal handles attached to the square front openings you put big chunks of coal in. That's how the house stayed warm in the winter. An open square tin box set beside each coal stove and they had large chunks of coal, about the size of a softball in them. These coal stoves looked like the ones Seymour used to see in old Bugs Bunny cartoons.

The floor in the house was a wood floor covered with vinyl. The vinyl was very thin cheap vinyl in the living room that had a dull black pattern on it of a horse and buggy. Like an 18th century buggy. The vinyl was more upscale in the kitchen. It was white and black checkered vinyl that felt cushier. Not a lot more cushy but a little cushier.

Walking around inside for the first time in a long time it suddenly came to Seymour that there was no indoor toilet. He walked into the room in the back off the kitchen and opened the door and there, across the chicken yard, and through a small gate, was the outhouse.

Yikes.

There were still wooden 2 by 4s laid out longwise to walk on so you wouldn't have to step on the chicken shit when you had to go to the bathroom. Seymour opened the door and walked down old wooden steps, four of them, and onto the wooden 2 by 4s, opened the gate, and then opened the creaky soft wood door of the outhouse and pissed for the first time in a long time in this outhouse. There was a fresh roll of toilet paper in the outhouse.

Evidently Roger kept the outhouse working also. The outhouse smelled of lime and mold. It was a smell Seymour remembered vividly from his childhood. His aunt and uncle, back in the seventies, were the last people in his family to not have indoor plumbing.

His Uncle Bud had put up some sort of wallpaper inside the outhouse that was now very faded and peeling. It was white and red with inlaid brown barns as the pattern.

Seymour looked out the glass window on the left side of the outhouse (if you were standing up pissing) and there was his Uncle Bud's small pond in the distance. The pond was still there. Of course it was. It was maybe a two-acre pond and his uncle had built a levy around the edge of the pond and one time he had asked his uncle if he could fish in it and his uncle smiled. There were no fish in this pond. And that was all that was said.

On his way back to the house Seymour stepped off the wood and looked around. Outside the tool shed behind the house was the yellow machine he used to push field corn on that carried the hard, brittle yellow field corn up into the silo. It was very rusty and the black rubber tires were flat. The machine sat inside an overhang off of the tool shed. The door to the tool shed had a padlock on it. He knew where the key was in the kitchen. He smiled.

Seymour remembered many things from his long stays with his Aunt Edith and Uncle Bud and it surprised him how vivid and strong his memories were.

Then suddenly his eyes got heavy as he looked at the tool shed. His aunt and uncle were long dead and four cheerleaders and an iPod had put Seymour here and he frankly would have liked to have gotten here a different way but so it goes and if there was a lonelier moment in his life he could not remember it.

Coma Girl

From the hospital an ambulance took Maggie to a nursing home in less than eight hours. The hospital had no ID and she was attacked by an unknown homeless person and the police filed their report and blew out of there and they didn't really care about her anyway so Maggie lay in a coma in a room for four hours without any attention from anyone.

Welcome to the Florida Health Care System.

An orderly came in finally and looked all around and then touched Maggie's breast and yes it was fake. Even though coma girl was on oxygen he lit a cigarette and stood in the window and tried to remember where he parked. He was staring out at the parking lot. He got off work in a couple of hours and he planned to go down to the Inlet Harbor and drink a few beers and listen to a band his uncle played in.

The orderly was twenty-five years old and he had tattoos all over his body. Among others, he had a snake on the left side of his neck and a swastika on each shoulder. One time while he was sleeping with a girl she asked him if he was a Neo-Nazi. "A what?" He said. "Never mind," she said.

His name was Walter.

When they decided to send Maggie to a nursing home where they fully expected her to die in a few days and that nursing home stood to make a few thousand government dollars because of this, Walter called a friend of his and said a real cutie was coming.

"Okay," the phone said to him. He flipped the phone shut and went on a break to the third floor where there was an empty waiting room and he could smoke and watch TV. He thought for a moment about the pretty girl who came in with coma girl and then told the front desk person she would be back soon. She had to leave but she would get back as soon as she could, she said. And she might even be able to tell them what her friend's last name was. She didn't know her friend's last name. Her condo might have it though, she kept saying. She was very upset by what happened to her friend. He knew her from somewhere. Somewhere around town. Then it hit Walter.

The whiskey bottle-juggling barmaid! Yes!

Walter smiled at this. The pretty barmaid who could juggle would come back soon and she would be very surprised that since coma girl had no ID and no one knew her from Adam that everyone would pretend that coma girl hadn't even been here. They would look at each other and shrug and not say anything to the girl. It would really piss this girl off.

Walter almost wanted to tell her that her friend had been assigned to a nursing home to die but he didn't because then he would lose his job. He needed his job. He was addicted to very expensive painkillers.

But frankly, it happened more than a few times at this hospital. It was a relatively new hospital. Out in the main lobby of this hospital was a huge picture of Jeb Bush, Governor of Florida, standing in dirt with a lot of other people in suits cutting a ribbon. They were smiling real big.

The pretty barmaid would come back and she wouldn't even have the girl's last name and she would go berserk practically when every one acted like coma girl didn't exist.

This too had happened before. And more than once.

The pretty girl would have to be escorted out by a security guard and a burly orderly named Sam and Walter would have to help also. All the way out Walter would want to tell this girl what really happened but he needed his job.

"Coma girl," Walter said rather inconsequentially. He kept his cigarette in his mouth and scrunched up his eyes from the smoke as he flipped through the channels on the TV.

Music

Before Seymour decided to go to the farm he inherited and shortly after his ex-wife took all of his CDs out onto the front lawn, poured gasoline over them, and burned them all, he rented a trailer in a trailer park just down the road from the nice ranch home he had to give to his ex-wife. His wife had a very good excuse to do this because he loved music and there was that four cheerleaders and an iPod thing.

It was a small trailer with thin brown carpeting and some cheap furniture and a strange old electric oven that had these spiral burners that were warped and swelling up like some bad art project. A metal coffee pot barely stayed on a burner. It wanted to slide off.

Seymour drank instant coffee now. He used to drink Starbucks coffee. His wife had bought this big-ass coffee maker that you poured beans in fresh in the morning and then pressed a button and loudly, it ground the beans and fresh coffee followed. He bet it annoyed her new lover in the morning too. His wife had been sleeping with both Seymour and her lover before the cheerleaders and the iPod thing but she still took great pleasure in piling all his CDs up and burning them. This had to do more with some emails his wife found between Seymour and Stephanie a couple of years ago on an old computer. His wife, correctly, believed that Seymour still loved Stephanie, a young white trash tramp from Granite City.

The four cheerleaders and an iPod were a great excuse for her to burn all his music.

A couple neighbors, while Seymour watched from inside his Jetta in the street, clapped. They, like everyone else, believed Seymour was a pervert and was getting what he deserved.

They didn't know that his wife was sleeping with someone else.

Seymour, that afternoon, drove off very slowly and sadly.

It was at that moment, as he caught whiffs of smoke from his burning CDs, Seymour realized more than ever that if there was any justification for staying on this planet, it involved the existence of music.

Sunday Morning

Driving Sunday morning down A1A you could see Daytona Beach without its makeup on. All the dull, once-bright colors outlining the concrete buildings held sea salt and dirt and no one walked around and if it wasn't for the loose newspaper fliers for the titty bars flying around, the streets would be completely empty, outside of a meandering local going after some cigarettes. Stephanie was oblivious to it all. It was time to go after her son. She shouldn't be worrying about a girl she just met, just had sex with, but she felt guilty.

She shouldn't have told Maggie about that homeless guy. Maggie was more lost than she was and that was saying plenty and she hated guilt. It was something Stephanie hated feeling worse than any other emotion and now she had the guilt of her son and if Maggie was dead she just might not be able to live with herself for that either. She wanted to cry but she lit another cigarette instead and turned up the radio. Maggie lost so much blood. That's why she went into a coma, they said. They didn't know if she would be all right or not. She was alive, they told her.

Stephanie turned off at Dunlawton Avenue and headed towards Route 1 and shortly she would be at the Catholic Church where she planned to wait for Charley Younger and his mother to get out of mass and maybe go to breakfast with them at the IHOP. They would like that and so would she and they had a calming effect on Stephanie and someday, someday soon she would break free of her paralysis and just pull the trigger and go get her son.

Ridgway, Illinois

"Sir?" The bank teller didn't hear Seymour say exactly how much he wanted to take out of his savings account and put into a checking account. It looks like he hadn't taken any out of this account in twenty years. But his social security number matched. Her name tag said she was Rhonda. She was thin and pale and her long blond hair was pinned back in a simple pony tail and she wore a yellow old sweatshirt and her fingernails were painted black and she had a whole bunch of tattoos all over her body but you could see only the name of her son, Jimmy, on the top of her right hand. She was twenty-eight years old. "How much did you say you wanted to take out?"

Seymour had drifted off. There was a fish tank about the size of two suitcases in the tiny lobby and this seemed out of place in a bank but then Ridgway, Illinois only had eight hundred people in it. And when he came into this bank Rhonda was the first and only person he saw. He didn't know where every one else was. He heard someone sneeze somewhere. He told Rhonda he was born in Eldorado, Illinois, which was maybe twelve miles away from here. She said she had an uncle who lived in Eldorado.

"Five thousand dollars, I guess," Seymour said.

"New in town?"

"Yes."

She almost smiled. So he wanted this put in a checking account. She could do that. She had him fill out some paperwork. She stopped in the middle of it all and asked him if he was running from something.

Seymour thought about this. "Yes," he said.

Rhonda didn't wear any makeup outside of a little eyeliner and her lips were small and her nose was about the smallest nose he had ever seen on a woman. She was almost cute. Her eyes were gray. Seymour stared at the fish tank again. It only had maybe eight fish in it.

She counted out the four hundred in cash he also wanted. She was running from something too, she said. He stopped looking at the fish tank. He asked her what she was running from.

"You!" Rhonda said, as she slapped the final twenty onto the dull beige bank counter. Then she laughed and it was a quick sharp laugh that reminded him of Stephanie.

Threes

Tragedy happens in threes, Stephanie was always told. The sun bleached the yellow side of the Our Lady of the Lourdes Catholic Church in Daytona Beach Shores so severely it looked orange this morning. The rotating lights of the Emergency Rescue Vehicle didn't help any either. And as soon as she drove up she knew it had to be Charley Younger or his mother. Or it had to be his mother, rather. There just was something not right about all that. Unthawing her and her coming back to life and all.

And Stephanie was right.

Charley Younger was sitting on the steps. They were attending to his mother inside and most everyone had left the mass without taking communion. Amen. Stephanie sat down beside Charley Younger and he hardly noticed her but he did finally and then he muttered something and he was probably more stunned than sad at the moment but he had a piece of wood in each hand and this meant he was very upset.

His mother died right beside him. It was the part of the mass where everybody was supposed to stand up and greet all the people around them and say, "Peace be with you" and Charley Younger absolutely hated this part and that is why they always sat in the back row because that meant the fewest people needed to touch his thumbless and disfigured hands. His mother didn't get up this time.

She was dead as a doornail this time. She died with her eyes open. She was smiling a little. Just a little.

Charley Younger awkwardly reached up to touch her forehead and instead hit her pretty good on the temple and she fell right over stiff on the pew. Oops.

Stephanie sighed and her whole body shook. Did she say anything? Any last words or anything?

Charley Younger lifted his head a bit. He thought about it. Yes, his mother had said something.

"Is it cold in here?" his mother said.

Stephanie turned her head away.

Just One Thing

"I figure," Seymour stopped talking for a moment to stare out the window. God, what a sight. There were so many stars and they were so close to the ground everything was lit up like a parking lot. But it was a barnyard. The chickens were sleeping. There would be heavy morning dew. This was his home now.

"What were you gonna say?" It was the woman from the bank. Rhonda. When he took her clothes off and the moonlight came through the window and lit up her body it took his breath away. She had a lot of tattoos. (Took his breath away with a little fear, actually.)

But he fucked her anyway. He made her come but he couldn't but he didn't tell her that. It's not hard for a man to fake it really.

He continued. "I figure if I can just do one good thing. Nothing major or anything maybe just something small. You have to shoot for these things, you know."

Rhonda was relishing in the feather bed. It was the biggest, thickest feather bed she had ever slept in. She didn't have any clothes on and she was even thinner than she looked with her clothes on and she had two six-inch blue teardrops on each thigh. One for each man who did her wrong. When she told Seymour this she kissed him and said there was a place right over her pussy for his big blue teardrop.

"I wouldn't go that far," Seymour said.

"Well," Rhonda said later, as he stared out the window, "I'm not the best place to start." She thought about it. Seymour wasn't sure what she was talking about.

"I'm married, I got a son, I've been in jail for possession, and I once slept with two men at once." She laughed her laugh and asked if she could smoke in here. She could. She sat up and lit a cigarette. He liked her right away because she wasn't embarrassed. Stephanie was never embarrassed either. Embarrassment killed so many things. And she smoked too.

"I got a few years left. If I could just do that one thing right I will be all right," Seymour said again.

Rhonda blew smoke in the air and settled even more into the feather bed and stared at his butt. "What are you planning?"

Seymour didn't say anything. He just turned and got back in bed and Rhonda put her cigarette out and they started playing around again and he turned her over and she liked when a man did this without asking and then he fucked her very slowly and gently from behind and then he came inside of her finally.

She went to sleep after that but Seymour just stared at the ceiling and then occasionally at the blue dark light out the window where his past and his present had finally merged. God, it was so bright out there tonight. The window glowed as if black lit.

It was quiet and for the moment simple here in his uncle's feather bed that smelled old and musty but felt so good so all Seymour had to do now was figure out that one good thing that he decided he only would have to do just once. His eyelids finally got heavy.

It would come to him.

The Pageant

Was already full tonight and the punkers joined the twenty something normal people who just liked Irish Punk okay? And there were a hand full of music fans who thought Flogging Molly was a god with gray hair and the local media of course was out in force (All three of them here in St. Louis) and of course Beetle Bob was hanging out in front like he was important or something and then there were the people pulling up in yellow cabs staying in downtown hotels who came from Chicago mostly, where Irish punk was really god, who knew the Celtic Killers, and probably knew even more about the myth of Nancy, the Gaelic singer who was supposed to appear out of the dark pot smoke filled blandness of the Pageant and make her third appearance and kill them all with her lilting voice and ethereal presence and just how did they get her to hover over the crowd like she did before? And those glowing blue eyes and my god fuck seriously, not a single picture took had anything but a blur in it. No kidding. Bradley showed Pasty one. And how could St. Louis forget? *The Post-Dispatch* didn't have a single article about it. They didn't remember anything. The Celtic who? This was the third year Nancy and the Celtic Killers have come a-singin and not even the fans remembered? They were buying Flogging Molly t-shirts and bags by the gazillion and there Pasty stood in her Ramones t-shirt behind small piles of Celtic Killers t-shirts and buttons and CDs and not a buyer one and occasionally Pasty would yell out "Nancy's a-comin!" in a fake Irish accent (She came from Liverpool) and only one or two would look a bit askance at her so there it stood. She didn't believe the boy in the band, who liked mainly to stretch out her anus, was telling the truth. It had to be a lie Bradley was telling her. The bass player said it was true through his cockney mumbles and the drummer was constantly drenched in an opium stupor and he went ape-like in his description of the coming Nancy appearance and this just left Pasty feeling even more alienated from the band and hell, was this why she spent four years at the London School of Music— to be led astray by a band of lunatic punk rockers?

Suddenly a young girl burst out of nowhere upon the folding table. Pasty almost bit through her tongue ring she was so surprised.

The girl leaned close. She was maybe fifteen. She wore cheap fifteen year old perfume. When she spoke she revealed she was English. Probably in the middle part of lower England, Pasty surmised. Her eyes said she was stunned a bit and frightened.

"Did ya say Nancy was a comin' here tonight?"

"I did."

The girl put her hand over her mouth. There was genuine pleasurable fear in those green eyes of hers. Her fingernails were alternating green and red. She said thanks. Pasty asked her if she wanted a t-shirt. The girl shook her head and was gone.

Eggs

When Seymour woke up he thought he was a child again. There was the smell of bacon frying and he was in his uncle's feather bed and the sun was coming through in full force and his heart was pounding in his chest like a jackhammer. And he had a hard on. He climbed out of bed slowly.

Rhonda had gotten up two hours earlier and already driven into Ridgway for some bacon and biscuits and other stuff and carefully eased skinny legs into the chicken coop and pulled out six big brown eggs. She stood with her back to Seymour in faded designer jeans and a black faded Ozzy t-shirt. Her ass was no bigger than an Ostrich egg. She had her long blond hair in a ponytail tucked through the back of some Trucking Company's baseball cap. She was waiting to flip the eggs. She found some Crisco under the kitchen sink and there wasn't a damn thing wrong with it. The old sixties or even fifties table with red rubber stoppers at the bottom of chrome legs was set with plain white China and dull silverware that had black handles. There was coffee waiting for him in a small plain white cup. She had even picked some wild flowers from along the barbed wire fence and they were sticking out of an old tin pot.

Seymour thought for a moment that he had died. Yes, died, and as soon as Rhonda turned around her face would be a skeleton's face with red glowing eyes. He sat down and startled her but at least she looked okay. She had a nice smile.

Shortly they had breakfast together and Rhonda could do this because her husband took her son Jimmy to Evansville every month or so for the weekend so that the in-laws could see Jimmy and he could go out partying with his high school friends. She hadn't slept with her husband in over a year after he came back from Evansville with the crabs.

Seymour broke the most yellow yoke he had seen in years and then asked Rhonda why she stayed with her husband. Rhonda cut into her eggs. They were hard. She shrugged. They loved Jimmy. They went their own way. There weren't many options in this area.

Seymour thought about this. It was hard to fathom. Rhonda had to be at the Bank at 1:00. She got off at 5:00. Rhonda said there was a guy out there collecting the eggs for the Saturday delivery. They weren't delivered to her apartment but occasionally she stopped him and asked if he had any extras. This was the first time she knew what farm he got those eggs from. He charged $1.75 a dozen. Seymour knew the guy.

His name was Roger, Seymour said. "I know Roger," Rhonda said. "I don't think he lives far from here. How do you know him?" Seymour wrote a check every month to Roger Beechum to take care of the farm for Seymour. Roger farmed the land and delivered eggs and kept, as it seems, everything on Seymour's farm in good shape in exchange for farming this Southern Illinois farmland Seymour owned. It wasn't until recently Seymour realized he kept chickens here. Or perhaps Roger told him some years ago but he didn't remember. Seymour had just gone about his life in O'Fallon, Missouri near the big city of St. Louis and then he got his life changed by four cheerleaders and an iPod.

"What?" Rhonda said.

No Good Reason

Charley Younger was in denial, Stephanie could tell. He picked weeds out of the crabgrass trailer park lawn when they got home. She lit a cigarette and stood staring through the trailers at a sailboat in the distance on the Halifax. It was quiet this morning. It was always quiet on Sundays. He would miss his mother. Stephanie fought back bursting into tears. She asked him if he wanted to go to IHOP for breakfast. He spotted one of his mother's flowerpots next to the trailer that was crooked. He straightened it. Not really. He wasn't hungry. His voice, as always, was monotone and dull. His mother was gone and Jeremiah was gone and there would be no good reason for Stephanie to stay around. He took a long hard labored breath. Spittle gathered at the corner of his mouth.

He wiped it away with the back of his curled up hand. Stephanie was in full-blown tears now. It just hadn't been a good day so far. Something startled both of them.

On the little concrete patio of the trailer next to Charley Younger's, in a top hat, white boxer shorts, a striking black gold-tipped cane, and wearing gold tap dancing shoes, their old neighbor man turned on an ancient crank 78-rpm record player and began to dance.

Charley Younger stopped pouting and Stephanie stopped crying as they just watched.

The old man began to dance.

The old man could do a pretty good two-step.

Dogtown!

That beautifully old, caustically historical slice of the St. Louis landscape was built out of bricks. Yes, bricks. Brick by brick. Ten turn of the century Dogtown brick plants built St. Louis into the brick capital of the world, more brick homes than anywhere in America right there in St. Louis, brick by brick, and now the Bosnian and Croats were migrating into these old brick homes. In droves.

Some with pale skin and paler hair and washed out tiny android looking eyes and others who were so darkly olive-skinned with those deep rich brown eyes, yes, they all were dotting the Dogtown landscape with such density as to force out even the black people. The black people were heading farther south, mother fuck, those strange-talking white and Arab people with their chickens and bonfires in the alleys, goddamn, they were the scariest white Arab people on this planet and if the Hood tried to shake down their meat store they would just roll up their bloody aprons and come at you with a fucking hatchet. They survived a 90s revolution, *Cetnik,* you Cerbian asshole, and no goddamn skinny baggy pants *Majmune jedan,* you fucking ape, was gonna shake them down and if you flashed a gun? They would just yell, *Jebaću ti Boga!* I will fuck your God! and that hatchet would hit you in the chest. It happened. Right there one street from the Hill.

Yes, but they were good hard-working people. They filled the English as a Second Language classes down in Arnold and they washed dishes better than the Mexies even in the fancy restaurants downtown and they knew how to make a small business work. They didn't whine about taxes like the *Kurvo* whore white Republicans did, instead they started meager and built up their shoe repair stores and coffee shops and bakeries and prepared their children for the great American Dream that they weren't actually convinced completely of yet, but they were alive and their mothers and wives and sisters had a little less fear of being raped in Dogtown than the rape camps many of the mothers had come out of.

So when Pasty lit a cigarette and sat in the window sill of the apartment overlooking this brick by brick wonderland of old tiny shops on this dead end Dogtown street and stared fascinated at three chickens, a brown, black, and white one, ambling nervously about, three stories down, she just smiled bemusedly as this young Bosnian girl who sat next to her in nothing but blue panties told her all this. Her name was

Fred. She didn't weigh more than eighty-five pounds and her face was so tiny and pale and her hair so stringy, she looked more like a east end heroin addict than a de facto historian of this marvelously wonderful neighborhood. Fred tapped ashes from a joint into a dull green ashtray that looked like a hollowed out hand grenade.

"Did it happen?" Pasty asked in a dull voice.

Fred nodded existentially. Of course it happened. They both knew what happened last night. The house lights came on right smack dab in the middle of "Black Friday Rules" and then commenced to blow out one by one (and this didn't happen last year) as a huge cold icy breeze swept across everyone in the pitch black darkness of the Pageant and then Nancy appeared. Just a speck in the upper right and then she expanded into a full blown beautiful apparition on some invisible platform and you would have expected every one of those Irish Punk fans to burst into cheers or something but swear to God no one could utter a solitary sound.

Nancy was in the house.

Right in the middle of the Flogging Molly set.

And Nancy it was. It did happen.

And Nancy did sing the most beautiful Gaelic song about killing and sacrificing your brother for the cause or country or something like that. Pasty, who was backstage and had come on stage, wasn't that well versed in Gaelic, but she caught some of it.

Woman Slaughter

There were chickens not that far away in southern Illinois too. On Seymour's farm. He opened the creaky wood and metal fence door and walked into the barnyard and Roger was concentrating so hard on measuring out the chicken feed he hardly acknowledged Seymour. When he completed that however Roger took off his big work glove and shook Seymour's hand. It was good to see him. He figured, someday Seymour would come back. He took off both gloves. Seymour looked at the barn. It didn't look any different. A little more weathered, but not that different.

Seymour had returned a couple years ago on a road trip with Stephanie and they had made love back behind the barn. He remembered her snug pink blouse underneath overalls and those translucent Victoria's Secret soft silky underwear. Stephanie had sat in the swing on the front porch and it was just too odd. He had left his key at home so they couldn't go inside. He told her about no indoor plumbing. She just shrugged. To be with him and have chickens and everything else. No, indoor plumbing wouldn't bother her. Not at all.

And he was certain it wouldn't. He had to do that one good thing.

"Now I have to tell you something, Mr. Belmo." Roger tapped out a cigarette. Lit it. He was a big, burly man. With a scraggly beard and a big gut. His overalls fit him pretty snugly. He was probably over six foot. Roger said back in the 90s he let this place slip for a couple years ago.

Seymour wasn't listening really. He was still watching Stephanie on the porch.

"I was in prison for a couple years."

Seymour looked at Roger. Roger shrugged. Roger said he had killed his wife. Seymour froze.

Roger lit his cigarette, tossed the match into the dirt. But it was an accident, more or less. Behind all that beard he may have smiled.

She had passed out dead in the driveway right behind his F-150. Usually after a night of carousing she made it to the living room at least and once only the front yard but this time only the driveway and thump. It was still dark that morning and Roger drove right over her.

Seymour put his hands in his pockets.

"She was a looker," Roger said. "Loved her more than anything. She just, uh, had issues." Roger made a gesture like drinking a glass of beer.

He had his brother take care of the place for a while but he was a pretty big fuck up himself so for a while things just went to hell.

"I apologize for that," Roger said. Roger looked around. It was all back to normal now.

Seymour didn't know what to say. He looked around. Things looked all right now. Oh, yeah. Roger got out and got everything back up to snuff. It didn't take him that long really.

"One thing you wouldn't believe though," Roger said. "Someone took care of those damn chickens. They were exactly as I left them. Meandering around in the yard here. Fat and sassy as hell. I still to this very day have no idea who took care of the chickens. Chickens don't take care of themselves. At least I don't think they do."

Seymour nodded.

"I got two years for involuntary manslaughter." Roger chuckled, then deadpanned, "Woman slaughter." He offered Seymour a cigarette. Seymour didn't smoke. "I reckon I would a got off completely. Two of those jurors in Carmi were from Ridgway. They knew all about Sarah's issues."

Seymour kept nodding and thought about running.

Roger was half-smiling. He had pretty good teeth except most were missing from the right side of his mouth.

"But I don't think that jury liked I just sat there in my truck in the driveway with my headlights on her for awhile. I just stared at her. I told this to the jury. I don't know why I told this to the jury. I was just being honest. I don't know why I just stared at her. Hell, I knew she was dead. And then I just drove on to work." He was full smiling now. He stopped smiling. He missed her every day. Every single goddamn day of this life.

Seymour didn't know what to say and frankly wasn't so certain Roger wasn't just fucking with him. But he did say something finally.

"I bet," Seymour said.

At the IHOP

Sunday morning and the IHOP was full of tourists and old people and locals alike. There was something of a wait and Doc Garrelts stood inside in the air conditioning and Stephanie stood outside smoking and Charley Younger stayed home. He went to bed. His mother was dead and so was he and there wasn't any point in doing anything besides sleeping so that's what he did.

It was awkward at first but Doc Garrelts was up for IHOP and so was Stephanie, she supposed. They sat next to three small kids and their parents in the smoking section and he ordered as big of a breakfast as he could find on the menu. Doc Garrelts had never been inside an IHOP actually. He hadn't gone out to eat in fact since his wife died way back when and she wouldn't dare eat at a place like this and man this girl was pretty messed up. She wouldn't talk at first and then Doc told her smoking would stunt her growth and they both laughed and she started talking and wouldn't shut up. He listened. Doc was a great listener. He always had been. Stephanie pretty much randomly told him everything.

"Damn," he waved and smiled at the waitress for more coffee. The waitress was older like him and tired and she gave him a he-could-just wait-a-goddamn-minute look. This girl Stephanie killed her husband and left her child and things just snowballed after that and she ended up half dependent on a retard and vice-versa really and then what happened this morning with Maggie and Charley Younger's mother dying and Jesus Christ. Her eyes were wrinkled and wet and this made him sad so in between it all he said he fucking called his old house back in Illinois just to hear it ring and hopefully his dead wife would answer. He smiled oddly when he said this. As if trying to tell a taller story. Really? She said.

That's so sad. She continued to fight back tears. Doc Garrelts shrugged. Uh, more like crazy, he said and bared big partially yellowed but straight teeth and she laughed out loud.

The tired old waitress brought him more coffee and asked if she was all right, hon.

"I'm fine," Stephanie said. She was from Illinois too, for Christ's sake, and on she went. She had to stop being paralyzed and stupid and just go get her son and damn if the state didn't have him by now and then a wave of tears came and she set her cigarette down and got up and went to the bathroom.

Doc Garrelts looked around. This was the best morning he had had since coming to Florida. He sighed a deep sigh of contentment. Then sneezed. His white coffee cup rattled. He had paid cash for his little white trailer. He had to put his house back in Illinois up for sale. His dead wife would never answer the phone and if she did it would only mean one thing. He made a face at the smallest of the children. The kid was wobbly in a wooden booster chair. Perhaps the ugliest kid in the world smiled big and then laughed.

Doc's food came. Fuck a duck. He had never seen so much food on a plate before. And it was all mixed together like someone had already eaten it and then put it back on the plate. The waitress asked him if she could get him anything else. No, this looked really good. He dug in.

Her Gun

Fred pulled on a pair of cutoff sweat pants and asked Pasty if she knew where the boys were. The boys in the band. Pasty thought Fred knew. Neither of them knew where the boys in the Celtic Killers were. Downstairs? Did the party start downstairs? Fred paused. Yeah, she guessed it did. This was her apartment and the roadie's brother owned the apartment downstairs and they both kind of jumped when someone stirred in the piles of comforters and blankets on the bed.

Nancy stuck her head up out of the blankets. They both gasped. That had been very good pot and even better ecstasy and Pasty thought that girl who floated in late looked like the Nancy chick but maybe not. Nancy smiled. When she smiled Pasty knew it was THE Nancy. Oh, my, gosh.

Pasty and Fred both eased toward the bed. In awe more than anything.

"How'd you do that?" Pasty said. Then asked Fred if that was really *her*. Yeah, she thought so. Fred tugged her underwear out of her crack.

Nancy looked around like maybe this place was brand new. Then her eyes landed on Pasty. Those eyes took Pasty's breath from her. It was her. It was the apparition floating above everyone last night. No doubt about that. Then Nancy started patting down all the thick blankets and even thicker comforter. She lifted up one corner, let it fall down.

"Looking for something?" Fred said. Her accent was European.

Nancy smiled. "My gun."

The two surprised girls looked at each other. Then they laughed. Her gun.

"Uh, weren't you the one with well, Bradley, kinda late last night?" Pasty said.

Nancy nodded as her hand froze on a spot. She found it. She found her gun.

"They're downstairs," Fred said.

Nancy nodded. "Yes, they are. I killed them."

They had to get going, Pasty said. They had a show in Louisville tonight. Killed them?

They both laughed again. Nancy asked if anyone had a cigarette.

Fred had to clean this place up. Both places now probably. She asked Nancy why she killed them. This made Pasty laugh as she walked over to her purse and rummaged for some cigarettes. She found some. Now where was her lighter?

"Well," Nancy said. She was staring at a naked lady watercolor on the wall. She asked Fred if she did that. Yes, Fred did. It surprised her Nancy would know this. Fred was a struggling artist actually. When she lived in Bosnia she painted graffiti on the sides of government buildings. Under the bed were several others. She liked only this one at the moment.

"And just why did you kill them?" Pasty asked, still a bit amused Nancy said this as she lit a cigarette for Nancy. Nancy took a big puff and then smiled her really captivating smile.

"No one messes with my pooper."

Both Pasty and Fred froze.

St. Augustine

The Castillo de San Marcos fort in St. Augustine, Florida, the oldest city in America, was built by the Spanish in 1694. While St. Augustine was established by the Spanish in 1565, it took them a hundred years, nine wooden forts, and fifty or so assaults from the French and British to realize they needed to build a better fort. So, while it took those clever, if not a bit slow on the take, Spaniards to do it, they finally built the Castillo de San Marcos out of a limestone- like substance made of seashells. This substance was virtually indestructible but it took them twenty-three years and by the time it was built the Spanish Empire, which was still just a lackey for the Catholic Church, was rapidly declining, and well, when the 18th Century rolled around, even though the Spanish had a nice, indestructible fort to fend off British cannon balls, they were still overtaken by the British and not by cannon balls but by something that always got those crazy world Empires every time-A Treaty. So the Spaniards left town and the English quickly renamed it the boring and silly name of Fort St. Mark.

"Interesting," Charley Younger quietly said to the resident historian, Doc Garrelts, who was telling him all of this.

This castle was also made famous during the American Civil War when Florida seceded from the Union, and all the Union soldiers left the fort except for one soldier who belligerently refused to leave behind this strategic and quite handsome fort to the Confederate army unless he was given one very important thing: a receipt.

The Confederate Soldiers just stood around looking at each other. A receipt? One raised a musket to shoot this crazy Northerner and his ridiculous demand. A Confederate General from the Big Sur motioned down the musket. He called for a receipt to be written.

The Confederate soldiers talked among themselves. A receipt? Really?

They decided to write one for this crazy ass Northerner. A receipt was written.

The Union soldier left with it and shortly thereafter became a successful litigation lawyer in Cincinnati.

And . . . the . . . home . . . of . . . the . . . brave . . .

The Confederate Army took Fort Mark without firing a shot. Not one shot, Doc Garrelts said.

Charley Younger struggled to look at the writing on the wall of the most famous fort in the oldest city in America. Did it really say all of that on the wall?

Doc Garrelts shrugged. Well, it didn't have all those details but he was pretty close. He loved this fort. He knew its history well. He had been here many times over the years. His wife, when she was alive, liked to take pictures of him straddling a cannon. Charley Younger smiled. He was hungry. They hadn't eaten since they left Daytona.

Doc Garrelts sighed. He knew a great deli in downtown Augusta he hoped was still there.

He pointed at Stephanie lying on her back on a concrete park bench holding her bandaged and broken nose. Beside the bench Maggie had her sunglasses on in her wheelchair. She wanted to try and walk a little farther today. She thought she could do it. She was almost back to normal, she kept telling them.

Doc Garrelts sighed again. What had he taken on?

The Right Thing

She floated away, yes, she floated away, she lifted her arms and she floated away . . . . This song by Husker Du kept rolling through Stephanie's skull as she stared up at the blistering sun. She was flat on her back on the beach and the thick soft sand was hot.

She didn't care.

Beside her was her dead boyfriend on a surfboard. His body was wrapped in a pink flamingo blanket. Behind her was peach colored concrete. Daytona Beach Shores, this morning, was fairly empty. Which was, when she thought about it, a good thing. Her nose hurt and her cheek stung. Her boyfriend had broken her nose. She had come home from the hospital where she threw a fit about Maggie and right when she opened the door to Charley Younger's trailer her boyfriend was standing there and he doe-cocked her right as she took one step in.

Stephanie fell backwards and then lost her footing and not only was her nose broke but one side of her pretty face got sliced open pretty good in the fall off the short steps onto the concrete patio and probably she wouldn't be quite as pretty ever again but she didn't care. The hot sand felt so good against the back of her head. Not far from her an old lady with a metal detector scanned the sand. She wore gaudy yellow shorts and a pink and yellow blouse dotted with daisies. The skin underneath her thin tanned arms looked like burnt cheese. She reminded Stephanie of her mother and one quiet time, the tire factory looming dull and ominous back behind their yard there in Granite City, her mother planted a rose bush and Stephanie laughed because it seemed so out of place there among all the ugliness of the factory across the street and all the garbage strewn in that backyard but maybe her mother had done the right thing.

Stephanie fanned her arms in the sand and stared directly at the sun. She fanned her legs. Sand went quietly everywhere, slowly.

Her mother, unlike her daughter, always strived, except for once when she dumped her newborn baby daughter in a trash can at the holiday dance, to do the right thing. Stephanie stopped fanning. She sat up and perhaps it startled the old lady with the metal detector.

Stephanie hoped there was still time for her to do the right thing. She looked out to sea. Doc told her to wait right here and he would go get his boat. Then they would bury her dead boyfriend out to sea and that would be the end of it because their trailer park was just that, and CSI never came there. It wasn't worth it. This even made Charley Younger smile. And he was the one who killed her boyfriend.

While her boyfriend pounded and kicked away at Stephanie there on the patio for leaving him just like that you lousy tramp bitch, jumping off his quarter million dollar boat, goddamn it, no she couldn't just up and leave him like that. He was important, goddamn it and he would sure enough just almost kill her and then Stephanie Cunt girl would feel it for a very long fucking time.

Charley Younger killed him in a rather cliched and comic fashion. With a cast iron skillet. He couldn't hold it by its handle because of his thumbless hands but with both his hands together he plowed the angry dude in the base of his skull with the stem of that cast iron skillet and down he went. Something popped in the back of the guy's neck.

Dead.

Charley Younger, evidently, packed quite a wallop when he wanted to. Or he got lucky where he hit. He stood quite awhile over him, skillet in hands.

Stephanie wanted a cigarette but she didn't have any. She asked the old lady if she was having any luck.

"Not at all," the old lady with the metal detector said. She stared a moment at the lump on the surfboard. It might just as well have been a dead jellyfish.

Then the old lady ambled off, her metal detector moving methodically yet randomly in front of her.

Cigarettes

After Seymour got kicked out of his house and kicked out as a high school history teacher because of four cheerleaders and an iPod, he took his one remaining friend up on moving into a trailer in a very small 32 lot trailer park that had nine child molesters in it according to Google. He paused as he looked at his laptop. Ten now. He almost smiled. He didn't really want to move into the trailer but it was a nice gesture from a friend and frankly he was the only friend he still had now so Seymour moved in for a while until he got his finances squared away and he could move out to his farm.

If in fact he did have a farm. Sometimes he thought he had only manufactured his Aunt Edith and Uncle Bud's farm in his imagination to keep him going through all this but he hoped not. He needed that farm and all the possibilities it had for him to put some semblance of a life back together.

He missed Stephanie suddenly. He missed her moving gently under him as he sucked in her hot breath when they made love. Oh, well.

He was startled by someone knocking on his door. He let in a maybe sixteen year old girl. He didn't remember seeing her anywhere in his high school but this was a different district anyway probably. She wanted to borrow some matches. He didn't think he had any. But he looked around in the kitchen anyway. She stood slumped a bit and bored and looked around herself. While he rummaged in the kitchen drawers she asked him if she could bum any cigarettes while she was at it. He stopped rummaging and looked at her. She had a slight faraway smile on her face. Seymour didn't smoke.

The girl absently lifted her black faded AC/DC T-shirt and toyed with a tiny skull and crossbones belly button ring. She was still looking around. Her jeans were so low-slung he was convinced she had to have shaven to allow so much skin.

"Sorry," Seymour said. "No matches."

She scrunched up her mouth oddly. She said she would give him a blow-job for cigarette money.

"What?"

She said she was kind of a regular for that kind of thing around here. She didn't have any money usually and she liked to smoke.

Seymour asked her if she wanted to join him for lunch. He wasn't interested in getting a blow-job from this girl. He was hungry though.

Sure enough, she said.

They would order out for pizza and a big bottle of Pepsi for her and Seymour would drink beer and they would sit out on the broken concrete patio in old cheap plastic white chairs and have lunch.

Her name was Libby. She lived with her father, and her mother lived in Crystal City with some black guy, and she didn't watch TV much so she didn't know Seymour was the perv who lost his teaching job until her dad told her. But then her dad was a perv too. So was about everyone in this trailer park. She talked and Seymour listened. She had a date with a boy named Neil who lived down the road and had just gotten out of jail for breaking and entering.

"We're going to Florida as soon as we get some money saved. He's the best roofer around if he can stay sober and shit like that." She got tired of pouring into the little plastic glass Seymour gave her and instead lifted up the 64-ounce bottle of Pepsi straight. It was still a little cold.

"You married?"

Not anymore, Seymour said.

"I bet she was pretty, huh? You're kinda pretty." She laughed and she had very bad teeth for a young girl.

When Libby left she said she would stop by every once in awhile for a free lunch or matches or something.

Seymour just sat there. This is where he was now. He looked around. A few trailers down there was aluminum foil on all the windows of a very old trailer with rusted edges. Across the street a tired, thin man without teeth of any kind, sat in a broken webbed lawn chair with a huge brown bottle of beer beside him. Libby waved at this man as she walked by. He gave her a tired wave back.

The Sirens of Dogtown

There was no doubt in the minds of the five black detectives standing around on this dead end street in Dogtown that a drug deal had gone bad. One of the detectives wore an old 40s brown hat and a rumpled trench coat. He looked funny. He was the chief detective. They all wore gold six-hundred-dollar badges. They were St. Louis's finest.

It was the Mexicans, it looked like to one of the detectives. Three headshots and the white boys were all fucked up at the time and the Mexicans walked in and blew them away. A Yugoslavian owned this complex. They spent all their money on booze, the dumbasses, and then they couldn't pay their drug bill and sure enough these Eastern European pricks ran the people of color out but you just don't mess with the fucking Mexicans. Yep, the fucking Mexicans walked in and shot those white boys dead. Those white boys should have stayed downtown after their little rock show at the Pageant.

There was a loud clang over their heads and all five of the detectives jumped and one even almost went for his gun. But instead they looked up on the metal stairs and on up the white mini-skirt of one Gaelic singing serial killer named Nancy. She had on orange panties. Orange panties so tight her vagina lips were smiling at him like a snake, he would say later. Her long legs were pearly white and she had the biggest most infectious smile on her face. She said "Oops," and then picked up the Glock she had dropped on the stairs as her and two other attractive mini-skirted young women were climbing out a window and trying to sneak away down the metal stairs.

Not a single detective noticed the gun. Not one. They were enticed by the snake.

There were three pairs of legs and three panties flashing that made it all more distracting. Detective work was hard. All three girls got in Nancy's van and off they went. The van did a U-Turn at the end of the dead end Street. A pretty hand flew out in a wave.

The detectives just stood there. Someone would have to write this up. Dogtown gave all of them the heebie-jeebies and Harris you're the newest one on the force so you have to fucking write this up and just say the fucking Mexicans did it.

"Okay," Harris said, pretending he was writing something down. "The fucking Mexicans did it."

So it would be reported, on the sixth page of the *St. Louis Post-*

Dispatch. It wasn't an important event in an important neighborhood, that a drug deal allegedly went bad and all the male members of the visiting Irish punk band, The Celtic Killers, were killed by a band of Mexican cartel drug dealers. They didn't even report there was one surviving member . . .

Years later, as word spread like molasses in this Bosnian, Croat, Yugoslavian neighborhood, those three young women would become the legend called the Sirens of Dogtown . . .

Clayton After a Murder

And shortly after that there the Sirens of Dogtown sat, sprawled out lazy on a Clayton Street, sipping Chai Tea frosties that Sunday morning, as indifferent to what had happened as three Cheshire cats after a bunny kill. Well, almost. Pasty was still more than a little scared of Nancy. Fred stared off towards the fancy tall buildings of Clayton. The rich skyline of American excess. This wasn't Dogtown. This wasn't U-City where her boyfriend lived. This was the rich part of St. Louis, Fred told them. Old money supporting a new class of bourgeois young people who had their nails painted by old Korean women in shops right next to Vietnamese restaurants and on through into this fancy little street eatery a tall, tanned young blond girl in skin tight black pants and a see-through white blouse stood behind a cherry wood podium holding fancy brown glossy menus and on through there past fancy white clothed tables three Mexicans could be seen briefly when the shiny metal door of the kitchen opened. One Mexican was maniacally preparing crepes and another one was scraping leftovers off plates as another rapidly washed nice white china plates and bowls. Clayton. The center of St. Louis politics. The center of St. Louis old money.

Nancy had never had a Chai Tea frosty. It was good. Suddenly Pasty couldn't stop herself from shuddering. So Nancy just up and shot all her band mates dead. Just like that. Fuck.

"Yes, I did."

Fred thought about this. Such stuff happened all the time now in Dogtown. Well, maybe not three at once like that. Her cousin, Sam, with a barbecue fork, killed a black man who tried to rape her. The fork ended up right through his heart and tore into his lungs. The black man was so surprised that this little Bosnian woman named Sam could bury it so far on just the first stab, he backed up startled and then fell over on his back and she was on him instantly and deeper the fork went. He died pretty quick.

The whole family gathered around the dying black man and stood and watched him die there on the small wooden deck next to a charcoal grill. It was an hour before anyone called the police.

Fred stared at a tiny asterisk tattooed on Pasty's thumb. Pasty got it in New Orleans on tour.

"Those same detectives didn't even write anything down. They just nodded and left. My cousin kept crying and rattling off in Bosnian."

Fred smiled. "She's a drama queen. They all looked confused." She asked Pasty why an asterisk. It was black and about the size of a dime. After her favorite writer, Kurt Vonnegut, Pasty said. And in honor of all the men she had ever met who had ever asked her for a blow-job in the business of rock and roll. Nancy laughed. She didn't know why she laughed. Nancy had no idea why an asterisk would stand for this. But it was funny. She bummed another cigarette off Fred.

The Sirens of Dogtown worked on their Chai Tea frosties and smoked and quietly stared off in all directions like they were posing for a Renoir painting.

Pasty jumped suddenly as if shot. Her cell phone was vibrating in her pocket. She took it out and it was her manager.

Pasty stared around at the clean empty street and at all the tall new American buildings in this part of St. Louis. Yes. She wanted to get back to Ireland right away. As soon as possible.

"Like right now," she said under her breath.

Someday

Seymour stepped off the wooden steps and into thin sparse grass and for a moment stared off into the almost endless waves of knee high wheat in southern Illinois when he found himself in the living room of his rented trailer again. Perhaps he would never get to his farm. It seemed very far away right now. He was holding one of the only possessions he was allowed to keep by his ex-wife. His cell phone. He was holding it in his lap like it was a piece of dead wood. He was expecting a call but not expecting it too much. He had applied for a job with the O'Fallon Environmental Waste department. They had told him they might call him back for a job helping them dump old appliances into a big hole out on the edge of town. This seemed like a reasonable job for a convicted felon child molester on probation. Even if he did have two degrees in history.

Out the dirty trailer window he could see through an ugly line of weeds and happenstance little trees in the back of a big new house in a new subdivision. A dog barked at something in the backyard.

At one time he and his wife, if they planned to stay together, had wanted to upgrade their house. His wife wanted a very big executive style home with five bedrooms and four bathrooms and they would each have their own office. Why? Seymour asked her.

She looked as if she had to think about this some. "Because." she said.

After he eased his penis inside Stephanie there behind the barn that one day they took a road trip to the farm he hoped to move into someday, after he slowly fucked her and she came and cried like she did sometimes, and he came finally too and they lay side by side staring up at a sky blue sky back behind an old barn, Stephanie said she wanted to live here with Seymour more than anything ever period. Seymour watched a very thick cloud move very slowly across the sky.

"Someday," Seymour said, finally.

"Someday," Stephanie echoed.

Julians

Was a restaurant just up the road right on A1A in Ormand Beach that looked on the outside something like a Swiss Chalet yet curiously enough had dark Hawaiian décor on the inside. The old people loved it. It looked a little long in the tooth if you looked close enough but it had been around for over thirty years and was considered an institution and at night, when it was the busiest, it was so dark inside you didn't notice anyway. The house specialty was prime rib and it was hit and miss depending upon how busy the night before was but they all three ordered it anyway. Along with some strong drinks.

Stephanie had two big band aids on her cheek and Charley Younger had buried those wooden pieces so deep in his palms Stephanie had to shred a t-shirt to wrap his hands up with. The only one in a halfway good mood was Doc Garrelts. (After his third whiskey sour, anyway.)

He proposed a toast. "Now that wasn't so hard, now was it?" They all clinked glasses. Doc was referring to hauling Stephanie's dead boyfriend out to sea, tying three old boat anchors to the body and throwing it overboard. And then moments later waving meekly at a passing Coast Guard vessel. The vessel stopped to look more at Stephanie than anything else. One of them yelled out that they were a bit far out to sea, weren't they? Behind the wooded steering wheel Doc shrugged, tipped his floppy bamboo hat at them and smiled real big and friendly like. He said they were heading in now. Charley Younger was peeing his pants on a pine bench under the top deck of Doc's boat and Stephanie was stretched out posing on the bow like a love-struck sailor maiden. The Coast Guard vessel eased away and then the engines kicked in and it sped away and faded around the Ponce Inlet Jetty.

Doc and Stephanie slapped palms high-five as Charley Younger just put his head against the boat wall and wanted desperately to go home. Just straight home.

Their prime ribs came and a Frank Sinatra song came through the old speakers and they all dove in like nothing had happened.

Fireflies

When total blackness settled over the farm the whole grassy area between the house and the barn was awash in yellow twinkling bio-luminescence like nothing Seymour could ever remember seeing. Fireflies so thick and heavy in one place left him staring dumbly in the swing. Rhonda sat beside him holding his hand in her lap and humming slightly some song he didn't recognize. She evidently had planned to spend the night with him and this stirred Seymour up some but his head was still buzzing with just as much bio-luminescence as the barn yard was. It was remarkable actually to have thousands of fireflies in such a small expanse of grass. But it made sense. Fireflies were just flying predatory beetles who feasted on earthworms and other insects. Fireflies were sparse in subdivisions and trailer parks because there wasn't as much food. The fertile land, the chicken shit pasture, these fireflies had it made. Seymour twiddled with Rhonda's little thumb. She had small thin fingers.

Earlier in the evening they had walked in the gray pre-darkness back behind the farm where the pond was and Seymour suddenly remembered why the pond existed. There were all these small inverted mud cones of all sizes all along the edges of the pond. His Uncle raised crawfish in this pond. They would use a net and seine for these crawfish and then put them in metal buckets and go fishing. His aunt and uncle would never eat crawfish as they did elsewhere. In southern Illinois crawfish were only used for bait in the little and big Wabash Rivers. They wouldn't even think about eating them. As he looked at the upside down cones the crawfish made and then across the gray expanse of the field and then at Rhonda who stood gingerly rubbing her big toe against one of the compacted mounds of mud the crawfish made, he thought of a corpse bride. She was so gray and her blonde hair in this grayness of gray was now gray and the sky was a darker gray and it was so gray everywhere it was almost black lit gray or dull neon gray or something. It was surreal him being here. The row of trees behind the pond was coal black. Regardless of how nice Rhonda was being to him, Seymour felt so alone it felt like several bricks had been put in his stomach and they were forcing all his other organs to slowly suffocate him. He would get over this perhaps. Or perhaps not. This was his new life and his life as a teacher was over now and his wife was sleeping with another man and Stephanie was an even farther away memory.

This probably wasn't the impressionistic life Seymour had asked for but this was all his now and this was all he had.

"That's a lot of fucking fireflies," he said.

She laughed.

"Yes, it is."

What Happened

There in the darkness in the distance a boat drifted slowly where Stephanie dove into the water and Stephanie first thought it might be her boyfriend's boat but that couldn't be. He was dead now. Her and Doc sat on a park bench down near Doc's boat dock having an after dinner drink. There were very few lights still on in the only island trailer park in the universe. Charley Younger was home now and no doubt had gone to bed.

There was a nice breeze but it was a sticky, warm breeze. This view of the Halifax was nowhere near as romantic as some of the other views but this is where Doc would sit and occasionally he would dial his old phone number and never did his wife answer. He laughed. On the other side of the Halifax River from here you could see the neon sign of Aunt Catfish's restaurant and down from there were old houses and dull lighting from what looked more like shacks than the nice houses. They weren't really shacks probably but they were old. Doc made them whiskey sours. Stephanie liked whiskey sours especially with Jack and Doc loaded them up with four cherries a piece. She sat with her knees pulled up and he liked her long thin legs. Who didn't? This was one of the better evenings he had had in a long time, regardless of the body they had to dispose of. Stephanie asked if he had any children.

Doc had three kids and they were all grown now and one was a doctor like him in Phoenix and another was a teacher in New Zealand and his only daughter lived in Illinois and he didn't really keep in touch with any of his kids now and hadn't really after his wife died. She was the glue and he was just something else stuck to that glue and when she died everyone just fell somewhere not close to each other.

"It didn't help that they thought I went crazy after their mother died."

Stephanie lit another cigarette. Did he go crazy?

"Pretty much, yeah."

She asked him what he did. He just cried all the time, really. He retired from being a doctor and cried all the fucking time and wouldn't get rid of the house or do anything his kids wanted him to do so they just said fuck it and went their own way. His teacher son in New Zealand, if he wasn't in New Zealand, probably would have helped him some and he got along with this son really well and he liked him but he had two kids of his own and a pretty wife and they had lives in New Zealand.

His son sent him a picture back from New Zealand of goats crossing a road. Okay, to that.

Stephanie thought about this. She puffed several times on the cigarette and it was a peaceful evening here in the dark staring across the river. Two pelicans slept on posts on the dock. She asked him about his daughter. She was more curious about his daughter really. She wasn't interested in his sons.

"She never liked me. It's strange how it's easy to love someone because you're supposed to love them, you know? And she loves me, tells me this every time I talk to her but she doesn't like me." He laughed. "I don't think I like her either."

This seemed strange to Stephanie. Why didn't he like her? He didn't know. He tried for the longest time through high school and college to like his daughter but she was the most self-absorbed person in the whole family. It was always about Trish. Trish was always nice to him at the end of each month when her graduate stipend was gone and that was the only time really and it was always about how horrible it was for Trish when her mother died too and besides, she married some thirty-year old live at home government employee and became some psycho neo-conservative Catholic who thinks your position on abortion somehow qualifies you to make decisions about war and the economy and shit like that.

Stephanie stared at the ground. His daughter was a tender spot. She didn't like her dad either.

"And she didn't even let me give her away."

What?

"She didn't. Trish wouldn't even give me the pleasure of handing her off to a bland dull government employed momma's boy." Doc laughed and Stephanie felt the pain in that laugh. His daughter said it was what a lot of people were doing nowadays, walking each other up the aisle, in a sign of holy unity or some crap like that.

Stephanie let out a laugh she couldn't hold back. She hated her father really and he was mentally abusive her whole life and still he gave Stephanie away. He walked her up the aisle and he was pretty drunk even then. It still made her cry.

Doc just shook her head. He asked Stephanie if she knew anyone who didn't let their father give them away in their wedding. She thought about it. No, she didn't. One of her friend's though thought about it because she liked her stepfather better and thought that might be the best way to handle things.

"What happened?"

"You can't disrespect your real father."

Doc nodded. He was getting tired but suddenly Stephanie started talking about how she had to get her son back now. How after all that had happened here recently she now knew what she had to do. Did she tell Doc that she has tried to kill herself at least four times in her life?

"Jesus Christ."

"It's something I wrestle with."

Doc looked away. "Evidently," he said.

And did she tell him about Maggie? How she wished she knew what happened to Maggie? She told Doc about Maggie and what had happened and this got her all upset all over again and then Doc said out of the blue,

"Uh, hold on here. I think I might know where they took her."

Historic Soulard Market

Down on Carroll Street in the Soulard District of St. Louis that particular morning was stuffed with people, all kinds of people, buying peaches and watermelons and corn and the vendors were scamming people right and left, if they didn't remember you from the week before then you got half rotten, bug eaten peaches in your brown paper bag instead of the perfect ones you couldn't pick on display. You were just a tourist to the Mexican mob that ran most of the fruit vendors now anyway, who handpicked a nice older white woman to boss the other Mexies around in front of the nice white and black crowd of sweaty tourists and yuppie locals walking up from the rehabbed condos and apartments in the Historic Soulard section of south St. Louis, the oldest Market west of the Mississippi the sign said (at least two miles west of the Mississippi) and it was run by the same people who didn't pay for any of the fruit actually, they just shot and killed the redneck independent drivers of semi's running the Argentina onions and bananas up from Florida, then had them driven to here in south St. Louis every week and fuck, man, twenty-five million illegal immigrants now in the great and wonderful US of A couldn't be wrong. It was the greatest of all countries for people who slept on dirt floors and had a relative's throat slit right in front the whole family if they didn't pay them the weekly two hundred pesos, $1.45, for selling their marble dolphins on that Tijuana side street and look at those two fresh faced tanned yuppie boys with their tanned and yappy yuppie wives—they were eying sexy beautiful Fred like she had just flopped out of the ice cooler where they sold fresh fish (ha, fresh fish in St. Louis—like finding a Hawaiian luau in an Eskimo Hut), but oh did Fred look every bit the eastern European vamp that morning. In her little white skirt that came just inches below her portal into the new world and her thin pale bare legs and pale stomach with her showcase little bellybutton ring and yellow skin tight stretchy t-shirt cut off just below her little perky breasts and the obligatory overdone blue eye makeup and pink lipstick. She propped up some of her shoulder-length pale blond hair with hairspray and then let the rest just fall fashionably where it may. She looked straight off a street corner catty corner to a Ukraine Holiday Inn and the wives of those two lecherous clean-shaven tanned boys were her same age but they were prematurely heavy, sailor bobbed seventy-dollar haircuts and pedicured and manicured and just a touch of blue eye makeup, enough to distinguish them from no one, and in college those deep tans hid the onslaught of overeating and too many Starbucks Chocolate Mochas, and did it matter really? They would move out into the suburbs shortly anyway, when the romance of Historic Soulard had fallen to an onslaught of children and promotions and did one of them smile lasciviously at her, point and say something to the other? Fucking American pig, with just a slip of paper and her cell phone number Fred could send him spiraling through a couple years of business trips to New York and San Diego and of course she would leave him alone when she got bored with him. But her dirty little secret was she really badly needed the money to get back to Sarajevo to see her sick mother.

And Nancy looked as good. She fit perfectly into one of Fred's minuscule jean skirts and my god did they crash the night before. Nervous energy must have kicked in and then pulled suddenly out of them after they dropped Pasty off at the airport and then they got really fucked up on ecstasy and coke in the Flames disco there on Compton Avenue and Nancy didn't kill that little boy she left with for awhile, did she? Her pretty little nose just went up and Nancy sideswiped a light pole with that big-ass van on the way to Fred's apartment last night and the other six people in the two-bedroom apartment there in Dogtown were sound asleep when they snuck in. Fred was fried as fried could be. She still was in denial about Nancy. Nancy killer girl. She couldn't have. She was lying. Fred kissed the forehead of her three-year old sleeping niece and for just a brief moment she pulled back the musty smelling blanket on the little child to show Nancy in the moonlight the face of an angel, Fred said, and then they crawled into a same sleeping bag together, her and Nancy, and were shortly sleeping, but not before another brief moment when Nancy thought about pulling from her pocket the crinkled picture of the boy child she now considered her son, almost told Fred she planned to call him Jerry not Jeremiah when she had him for herself, but she didn't. She left the picture right where it was and just spooned around the little body of Fred and nestled her nose into the stale, sweaty head of this person she hardly knew, and went to sleep.

Emory L. Bennett, the most celebrated Korean War veteran in Florida history, won the Congressional Medal of Honor during the Korea war. When his company was attacked by two Korean/Chinese regiments, he and his buddies fought back these regiments for a time and then those slant-eyed sons of bitches got pissed and started over that ridge Kamikaze like where those boys were. And in droves. Emory's buddies started dropping like lead-riddled flies. They were ordered to retreat. They were highly outnumbered and it was just a matter of goddamn time. Those slant-eyes really wanted that hill so Emory and his handful of buddies were told to get out of Dodge but as soon as they would stop shooting and start retreating the wave of Korean Chinese sons of bitches would knock them down again and they wouldn't get very far.

Fuck, Emory L. Bennett, the nineteen-year-old Florida farm boy said. Enough of this shit. He took three M1 carbine rifles fully loaded with a chamber each of 30 ought 6 bullets. He wasn't going anywhere. Now get the fuck out of here, he said to his buddies. And he was smiling when he said it. Emory was always smiling. He was a big handsome curly headed farm boy built like Charlton Heston who smiled all the time regardless. Before anyone including his Sergeant could argue with him Emory lunged into a position just up the hill from his buddies and parked his ass there and started firing like a madman. He was the best marksman in his entire regiment. Not a single bullet he fired missed a slant-eye. His buddies were stunned at first and watched as several exploding thuds of smoke and fire entered Emory's body and exited and that just seemed to irritate Emory. He tossed one empty M1 down and started firing another.

His buddies got out of Dodge.

Emory L. Bennett died right there on that hill and a Congressional Medal of Honor came back to Volusia County Florida with his body.

There was an Emory L. Bennett statue and streets and viaducts all over Florida bore the name of Emory L. Bennett. What fame!

Why they named a nursing home after a celebrated war hero who died in his teens, Doc Garrelts would never know. Most people in Florida no longer even knew who Emory L. Bennett was. That was the fate of most heroes.

But that's where Doc figured Maggie would be. And she was.

Farmer

Seymour wiped sweat from his forehead and watched as Rhonda tugged at her son's little wrinkled t-shirt and pulled up his tiny rolled up blue jeans. He was as skinny as she was and was pretty much the spitting image of his mother. Then he took off running, trying to avoid the big out of control sticker bushes and deep dried ruts of the field. He was yelling or laughing or both. He wanted to see the pond. The Pond! There was a time when there was the same sort of magic in Seymour seeing this pond just as this little boy was feeling but now he was feeling it through Rhonda's son.

Rhonda had fallen for Seymour. She didn't say much about it but he could see it in her face when he came into the bank to ask her to come out and see him and when she looked a little disappointed that she had her son and when Seymour just said bring him too this shocked her he could tell and she tried not to look very tickled but she was and now her son was running and tripping and laughing towards a little rinky dink pond in the middle of nowhere southern Illinois.

Seymour wasn't sure what he felt for Rhonda. She made him very horny with her petite little responsive body writhing on top of and beneath him and the way she had helped him figure out how to successfully remove eggs from the chicken coop without spooking the chickens and even how to wire up his new phone line and Internet connection, she had been a great help to him but Seymour had some big scars to heal.

This was a big and fast change for him. He went from married history teacher to divorced unemployed registered sex offender for his four cheerleaders and an iPod episode, to a trailer park loner, to now a farmer. These transitions had left him somewhat hollow and frightened.

The thought of calling himself a farmer made him smile, though.

The Nursing Home

"Just, uh, just act like we are doing something normal," Doc said as Stephanie pushed the wheelchair with Maggie in it down the smelly, shit brown nursing home corridor. There were old people still-lives everywhere throughout the corridor. One old lady was tied into her wheelchair and bending straightforward talking firmly to her daughter about something. Her daughter was nowhere to be found. Another old man in a wheelchair looked quite happy to be there. He was smiling. He just smiled as they passed. Stephanie was so nervous she thought she might throw up. Another old man stood against a wooden railing asked seriously if someone could tell him where the Post Office was. This old man did make Doc stop. They all stopped. Charley Younger ran into Stephanie.

Doc smiled at the old man and pointed down the hallway. Right down there, he told the old man. The old man said thank you and started down the hallway. Doc shrugged and on they went.

How Doc knew Maggie would be there Stephanie had no clue. He said something about working briefly as an on-call Emergency Department doctor some years ago when he thought he would need to augment his retirement money and they wanted him to get in on a Republican scam to collect money from unidentified Daytona Beach tourists who had been in accidents. There was an abnormal number of tourists who were in accidents in Daytona Beach. He didn't participate however.

Doc gave two hundred dollars to this disgusting orderly who was nowhere to be seen when they wheeled Maggie out of the nursing home. Two nurses and this one young girl behind a desk, they all just looked somewhere else when they passed. They split the money probably.

Maggie could talk and all her extremities were moving but she wasn't exactly coherent. This left Stephanie in tears. Except for her perfect breasts she looked so sickly and emaciated. She hardly looked like the same person. Doc said she would be okay.

"Mainly just dehydration," Doc said. "She'll be fine," he said. "I think." When he said this Stephanie just starting bawling and this upset Charley Younger so he started cleaning.

Maggie would be okay. For the most part. She did indeed need to be hydrated and she had a bad bed sore on one side of her hip that Doc bandaged perfectly but then they were, within a few days, sitting out and talking.

A New Millennium

Granite City probably should have been named Faux Granite City way back when, back in the late 1850s, back when the Industrialized Germans moved into that fertile land across the Mississippi from St. Louis, and built those big factories that made those glass-covered iron utensils that people fell so in love with when they used them on their new German-engineered iron stoves. Nothing stuck to that glass that looked like granite. It would take a hundred years almost before aluminum and Pyrex and the like made better, cheaper utensils and pots than those Granite City factories. But by then something else replaced the granite in Granite City. Steel! Steel moved so fast into Granite City they needed to haul Mexicans in to keep the factories rolling out those massive sheets of steel. Not even the 10,000 or so Eastern Europeans that migrated there at the start of the 20th century were able to fill the labor shortage created by these perfectly running factories, so in came the truckloads of Mexicans. Ah, America! It was a glorious run Granite City had all through the late 1800s and on into about 1970. Faux Granite and real tin and real steel had brought the city up to a population of over 40,000 happy contented working class people. In the shadow of billowing gray black smoke stacks on one side of town and the mysterious Indian mounds of Cahokia on the other, blue collar prosperity was everywhere and then? The machineries of modern industry were brought down. Brought down by what would eventually bring down the American makers of everything from microwave ovens to televisions.

Imports.

Chinese and Canadian imports specifically. Steel flooded in from China and Canada at half the production price of those steel factories there in Granite City and down the city went. Just like that the city went dark.

But a few of the hardy people stayed. They still produced some steel and some tin and those factories limped along and after half the population moved on to where the work was, some people still bought those 60s houses built all around those soot-soaked enormous factories.

One such street was lined with these badly faded peach and red and blue painted Masonite sided 1200 square foot houses with the tiny concrete front porch and no basement with their window air-conditioners and rusty metal backyard fences that had too tall and too many weeds lining them. If there were one of these houses without some broken appliance in the back yard you would have to look hard to find it. Fifty years ago these houses, with their dark wood paneled living rooms and one bath olive-colored stools and sinks, were the signs of middle class success.

But it was a new millennium now and there were meth labs every fourth house and tattooed long-haired unemployed bikers tossing beer cans into the street mid afternoon. Most all of the good people had moved out.

But not Stephanie's mother. She had nowhere to go. She had just recently been diagnosed with mesothelioma due to working in the asbestos lined annealing rooms in the factory across the street for twenty-five years and just this last year, a year where she hadn't heard from her daughter Stephanie, her cataracts had gotten so bad she barely saw out pinholes really. And she wasn't even fifty. And on top of all that she had been diagnosed with severe agoraphobia. The same thing Paula Dean that obnoxious southern cook celebrity had. That's what they said she had. But this kept Stephanie's mother's disability check coming every month. And her younger daughter, Stephanie's sister, was there faithfully every other month or so. Now with her own little child. Another boy and wasn't life strange? She loses one little grandson and his mother too and presto another one comes along.

Stephanie's mother was out in the back yard holding the only grandson she had left. She smoked a cigarette and tried to comfort the little fella. His mother, Stephanie's sister should be back soon. She was downtown visiting an old friend playing pool and downing Jello shots at Daddy's Bar and Grill.

Two people Stephanie's mother couldn't quite identify because of her eyesight were inside totally trashing her living room. They were circling a 70s era dark coffee table in the middle of the living room like hurt angry lionesses. One's face was bleeding and the other had such deep scratch marks on her thigh, she was bleeding also. One had a rapidly swelling right eye where the other tried to gouge it out. But Stephanie's mother didn't know this. She didn't know that those two people had finally reached the end of a journey of some sort. She especially didn't know that one was her lost daughter, Stephanie, and the other was a Gaelic-singing serial killer named Nancy.

Stephanie's mother, holding her grandson, made funny faces to try and calm the kid down.

The Bipolar Bears

Daniel was bipolar. He had been diagnosed with this at a pretty young age when his mother discovered him on the hood of her Chevy Cobalt trying to smash his head methodically through the windshield.

"Daniel!"

She took Daniel to the doctor and they gave him medication and were always checking to see if he was suicidal.

Whenever his mother would ask Daniel if he had thoughts of suicide Daniel would smile and say, "Yes."

Daniel got pretty fat in high school, too. It may have been the medication and how it was messing up his thyroid or maybe it was because he liked to eat. Regardless, he had a cute round innocent face and when he wasn't trying to throw a chair through a window or choke to death a complete stranger in school, he was a pretty good student.

Daniel even had a girlfriend. Her name was Alice. She was fat too and cute like Daniel and while she wasn't necessarily bipolar she once tried to kill herself and when they were spotted in high school together they got the nickname the Bipolar Bears.

So it surprised no one that after Daniel ruined the career of a teacher, he tried to kill himself. It especially didn't surprise his mother or father or his girlfriend. They all asked the same question that many people ask about a bipolar person who tries to commit suicide:

"Did he forget to take his medicine?"

Nope. Daniel took his medicine.

After he ruined that teacher's life by snapping a digital photograph of four cheerleaders leaping around the desk of the history teacher, who was also the volley ball coach, as two of the cheerleaders exposed striking panty shots, and that history teacher was there standing amidst all four of the cheerleaders grabbing a big hard-on in his pants, after Daniel put this digital photograph for all the virtual world to see on Flickr and YouTube, and after that teacher lost everything he ever owned because of this Internet published photo, Daniel tried to kill himself.

Daniel took a .38 caliber handgun out from under his father's bed and asked his girlfriend to drive him out to Horseshoe Lake State Park. He said he wanted to be alone.

It was a beautiful warm sunny day and there were at least two dozen ducks and maybe fifteen Canadian Geese on the bank in an area called Oxbow lake where Daniel and his girlfriend often went to be alone and make out and stuff. It was a great place to catch crappie off the bank but they weren't in season but the half buried cypress trees across the way were beautiful certain times of the year. And they were beautiful right now. It was the time of year where you would often see snowy egrets and occasionally a blue heron. There on a log sticking up out of the water stood a blue heron. Daniel waved to Alice and then sat down on a nice open place overlooking the water. He put the gun between his legs. He didn't want to kill himself right at this minute. He waited until a mother and her two small children had left and it was just him and an old fisherman was on the other side of the lake. He didn't care if the old fisherman saw him kill himself. That was okay.

Then Daniel put the barrel of the gun in his mouth and pulled the trigger. The pop of the gun made the old fisherman jump.

The old fisherman sort of saw what happened, he told police. He was the one who called 911.

Daniel didn't die. He just blew the upper part of his mouth, most of his nasal cavity, and some of his brain away. One of the first things his girlfriend, Alice, would tell him afterwards was that a .38 caliber handgun wasn't the type of gun he should have used. He would have been far more successful at killing himself with a .45 caliber revolver. A .38 just wasn't enough to do the trick. Her dad and brother both said this.

Daniel also lost his right eye.

They put Daniel on life support and he was in a coma for well over a week.

They all kept asking the same thing: "Are you sure he took his medication?"

And many of his friends and family, after seeing the shape Daniel was in, wondered the same thing: Why didn't he just die?

But nope, Daniel didn't die. With his fellow bipolar bear soul mate beside him in the hospital room well over a week after his attempted suicide, Daniel came out of his coma and out of what was left of the corner of his mouth, he said,

"Hi."

Alice closed the Japanese Manga novel she was reading and smiled.

"Hi, yourself."

And then Daniel said a few more words that Alice had to think about before she realized what he was saying.

"My Spy little Eye Photoshop folder."

Yes, Alice knew what he was talking about. When they weren't being the Bipolar Bears, Alice and Daniel were both gifted graphic designers. Their artwork was very popular on the website DeviantArt. com where Alice's beautiful alien sunsets got thousands of hits and Daniel's dark Anime characters with the frighteningly unique eyes were viewed even more.

With each of them having ripped copies of the expensive Photoshop program with Bit Torrent, they spent all their computer time drawing pictures or modifying photographs.

So when Alice went home and opened the Photoshop folder Daniel told her to look at, she almost had a heart attack.

There was the infamous photo Daniel had taken with his cell phone of Mr. Belmo standing in the middle of four cheerleaders reaching into his jeans inappropriately, but this was the original. This wasn't the one Daniel touched up. No.

Not unless Mr. Belmo had a hard-on as wide and thin as a 1st Generation 15 gigabyte iPod, this was indeed the real photo. For a moment, for some odd reason, Alice tried to think if she had ever seen a boy with a square, rectangular penis . . .

No, Mr. Belmo, clearly startled by four cheerleaders leaping and screaming suddenly all around him, as he sat bored and almost asleep in study hall where he wasn't really supposed to be listening to MP3s, had not stood up and lasciviously grabbed his dick in front of these cheerleaders like everyone thought. (And Alice couldn't help but smile again as his hand grabbed the iPod right between the tanned legs and blue pantied crotch of the Principal's daughter.)

Mr. Belmo wasn't touching himself at all.

He was just trying to shut off his iPod.

He didn't even have a hard-on.

But Daniel sure did a good job of *touching* up the photo.

OMFG.

LOL.

Then Alice frowned. Mr. Belmo though lost his job and wife and everything over this touched-up photograph. He was even a registered sex offender now.

Alice's reflection was strange as it was super-imposed on the computer screen with the panty shots and bulging iPod in Mr. Belmo's jeans. She sighed.

"Dude," she said.

Pregnant

And all the while Alice was telling this to Mr. Belmo, after she had driven in her very own Chevy Cobalt to the trailer park everyone knew Mr. Belmo lived in, after she had knocked on his door and he answered the door in a black t-shirt and plaid lounge pants, after he let her in, got her a Coke, and they sat across from each other as she told him this story, after she told him she helped Daniel send the touched up photo to the principal and O'Fallon Police Chief, and after her voice stopped shaking and Alice was sounding almost normal, Mr. Belmo chimed in with something Alice would later find very odd.

"Well," he said. "Sometimes an iPod is just an iPod."

Alice slapped her large thighs hard. She was suddenly quite proud that she had been able to tell him the truth all by herself.

"He feels bad," she said, about Daniel. "He ruined your life."

Seymour paused for a time, as if he was pondering this. He wasn't really. It was hard not to look at this young girl's massive cleavage. Her sweater was way too small and pulled over her large chest and it looked like there might be a ripped seam at any time.

He shrugged finally. It didn't matter really. He was heading off to the life of a farmer. He laughed out loud and this startled Alice. She did indeed look a bit like the polar bear from the movie *The Polar Express*. So did Daniel. (Or at least he used to.)

Alice didn't know what to do next. Seymour could tell she wanted to leave all of a sudden.

"Well." Seymour said. "I appreciate this." They both stood up at the same time.

He still wanted to laugh for some reason. It really struck him funny how this all went down. He sighed deeply to keep from laughing.

Alice left. Seymour stood on the top step and watched her climb into her car. He waved awkwardly.

"Thanks!" he yelled out. She just looked at him funny and drove off.

So there you have it. The story of four cheerleaders and an iPod.

Seymour sat on an old green John Deere tractor that was manufactured in 1928 that his uncle had purchased in 1953 for 350 dollars. It was a rich green color as it had been repainted in 1975 and the large metal wheels were repainted a bright yellow back then too. Seymour, as a small child, had watched as his Uncle Bud methodically repainted this old tractor.

It was clouding up over the bottoms of southern Illinois. A couple of birds flew out of a thin row of trees lining the bean field Seymour stared across. The bottoms were so flat and treeless here in southern Illinois Seymour could see a large silo in the distance that was, to Seymour's eyes, the size of a pencil eraser.

Everything happens for a reason but not necessarily a good reason.

Now he was lonely again. Rhonda had left him this morning.

Not that she was necessarily with him. He thought maybe it freaked her out when he put his collection of Renoir prints all over the old farmhouse with the tin roof, plywood doors, and vinyl floors.

Oh, well.

The Bipolar Express had brought him here.

It began to rain. And then the rain got heavy and the rain seemed cool at first and then warm.

Rhonda, after Seymour had taken her thin legs and draped her ankles over his bare shoulders and then with her right hand she guided his penis inside of her and slowly methodically worked herself into what seemed like the most intense orgasm she had ever had with him, they collapsed together and Rhonda held him very tightly and cried afterwards and this surprised him.

"Did I feel different inside?"

Seymour thought about this as he stared at several tiny tips of chicken feathers that were making their way through the snowy white feather bed.

Now that he thought about it, yes, she did.

"I'm pregnant."

His heart almost stopped.

"I'm glad," Rhonda said. Then, "I can't see you anymore."

His heart did stop for a moment. Rhonda was pregnant and Larry her husband and her had a come-to-Jesus conversation and Larry promised to stop going to Evansville to fuck his girlfriend there and really he planned not to play around anymore and he just wanted to be a good father to his little boy and whatever his new kid was going to be and even though Seymour was good and creative at fucking it had to end so there.

Rhonda was so sorry, she said, biting on her bottom lip to keep it from moving.

Seymour was quiet for a while. He liked fucking her too. They didn't have much else in common. She was good at showing him how to do farm things. Rhonda started mildly rambling and said it was for the best because when Seymour got his head together he would start teaching or something again and being around people like he was and not like how Rhonda was and then the fucking like bunnies part of their life would be over and he would leave her for a twenty-year-old elementary school teacher.

So there.

It was for the best.

Even though it was Seymour's child.

"Yes, it's yours, Seymour," Rhonda said. She didn't know why Larry wasn't upset about this but he wasn't.

They planned to move into his grandmother's old Victorian house in Ridgway. Rhonda always wanted to move into that house. It needed painting badly but had hardwood floors in every room and a spiral staircase even. She could walk every day to work at the bank.

"I'm sorry," she said.

It was raining hard now. It made the John Deere glisten incandescent. Seymour closed his eyes and the rain sounded like the rustling of empty sheets as it struck the leaves of the beans in the field.

America

Fred's teeth were chattering so loudly in her head the sound echoed off the vinyl floor and dirty kitchen walls. Dishes and empty bowls and nasty pots were everywhere. A calendar of pictures from Kiev was dangling by one nail on a plaster wall. The small blue refrigerator had magnets all over it of St. Louis, the Arch, and skull and crossbones. She had told Nancy to bring her back here and now Nancy was being badly assaulted and hopefully killed in the other room. Fred had sent a text to a bad man named Memduh and told him to take care of Nancy. Nancy. Nancy evil killer girl.

But Fred couldn't stop thinking Jesus Christ Holy Mother of God amen this American killer girl was crazy just think about that Mexie at Soulard Market Fred could have handled fine when he took her out behind the counter to keep Fred from bitching so loudly that crooked wetback would have given Fred a ten spot probably after he felt her up but goddamn that bitch just walked up and plugged him in the head right there in broad daylight right next to his backed-in truck and the fucking people were everywhere but it was too goddamn noisy Fred figured because no one even looked up and fuck that bitch just shoved him back on his back into the truck and his body hit the steering wheel and off they ran and Nancy killer girl just had this weird smile on her face and Fred was freaking out and spazzing crazy and yelling in her language and off they drove with the killer girl just lighting a cigarette and calmly calmly calmly asking her where the fuck they should go and Fred was still spazzing and freaking goddamn stop killing people bitch, don't call me bitch fuck you gonna kill me too no fuck where can I drop your sorry foreign ass off so Fred climbed over the seat and a stiff smell of urine struck Nancy the girl peed her panties! The Bosnian tough girl peed her pink panties and she kept dropping her cell phone in the back as she rattled on in her dumb spitty language before she finally got through to somebody where she could go. That's when Fred tee'd Memduh.

Nancy drove on and it would be okay soon, Fred surmised as now she sat, teeth chattering like some satanic teletype machine. She would just have to fuck Memduh for awhile afterwards and goddamn he needed to hurry up, kill that crazy killer bitch Fred no longer wanted any goddamn part of. God, dead God, Nancy was crazy crazy crazy fucking crazy.

And Memduh, in an empty bedroom was taking care of Nancy. One of her eyes was black and swollen shut and blood was heavy in her mouth and her precious Nazi handgun was way over there against the wall and he punched her so hard so many times in the stomach and side she stopped clenching finally her legs and she wasn't so tough now. America didn't have tough women. They were soft and fat mostly but this one wasn't. She was a crazy cat American bitch with a nice tight American pussy that he would violate more than just right here right now in the great empty stupid Republic of Missouri and he was just about to finish her off for a while with his fists and then throw her in the closet for a while and come back but while he was inside her and he started to do this something happened. Her one good eye was fixed oddly on him and she swallowed enough blood to muster a smile. The *kuja bitch* was smiling! And Holy Mother of God Jesus Christ she was moving, fucking him back!

This was America. This was the America Memduh wanted all along. It was here on this dirty empty floor. He didn't need to plug Miss America here with his own Nazi gun he had set on the floor by her thigh, or pummel her any more with his fists.

This was the America of his dreams and he was almost about to make her come. He was! And so was he! OH MY LORD JESUS CHRIST!

Fred was in the other room. Fred froze.

Fred nearly jumped out her skin when the gun went off.

She stared at the wall. Finally that crazy bitch was dead, she thought.

Fred's teeth stopped chattering.

Memduh had taken care of that crazy killer girl and now it would be all right.

She thought.

The Violent Bear It Away

Down at the bottom of the mountain, Lookout Mountain Chattanooga, Tennessee, at least the bottom of some part of Lookout Mountain, on an overturned yellow plastic heavy duty milk crate of some kind the self-proclaimed Reverend Leonard South proclaimed how of course the violent bear it away and wasn't it obvious that out of destruction comes creation and here in the land of summer and the sad lazy God hating malcontents the beauty of God's eternal love could only be found by the sacrifices of the sinners, the whores, the illegals, the democrats, aristocrats, progressives, the cross-dressers, the transgressors, and on he went there on the edge of an old dirty strip mall where Doc and Charley Younger did up two loads of laundry for everyone just right there as dawn broke over the high horizon of dense thick dark green trees that covered this Tennessee mountain like some massive Chia pet.

Doc and Charley Younger sat inside the laundry-mat as Maggie and Stephanie's white and purple and yellow panties, tees, and thongs and their own tattered boxer shorts pounded wet and soapy against the bulbous thick glass of the washing machine.

They ate donuts from the donut shop next door where a quiet little blond girl barely in her teens with a five-inch black and red snake tattooed on her forearm and a pierced tongue put two jelly donuts and two regular donuts in a white paper sack and barely smiled when Doc poked a dollar in the paper tip cup. He asked her about the noisy little preacher standing on the crate outside.

He was the Mayor's son and he did this every Tuesday, the girl said. He walked all over town otherwise. He usually didn't bother anybody. Usually. Sometimes he would break something, the girl said. Yikes, Doc said.

Doc put clothes in a dryer and sat back down and Charley Younger had been good about applying the ointment Doc gave him to put on his bloody palms and they were finally healing correctly, Doc thought.

They ate their donuts and the Reverend Leonard South turned to face them and ranted on now about how all the dead fetuses of this world should unite and climb over the unbelievers and smother their children and their children's children.

They couldn't hear all of what he was saying. The washer and dryer were too loud.

Doc sighed.

"Sumbitch is crazy, ain't he?"

Charley Younger, as he carefully took apart a jelly-filled donut, nodded.

Alone

Nancy, tugging at the sore spot on her lip and wiping away the last of the caked blood from her chin, was driving on deep into southern Missouri, down route 44, down towards the Ozarks. It wasn't the direction she was supposed to be going in, and right then, she didn't know it and didn't even care. She just knew that at this point in her life she felt like she felt most all of her life—alone. There was again no one and nobody in her life and if and when she got little Jeremiah then maybe somewhere there was a nursing home where she could take care of old people and then pick little Jeremiah up at a day care center and go home and make him mac and cheese and color with him and the world could go to fucking hell but if you have that one someone life was always better.

Her swollen shut eye was too sore to see out of or even touch and damn he must have been close to 250 plus pounds and not an ounce of fat on him the fucking ugly animal. The bullet went in his temple so oddly Nancy expected something out the top somewhere but his head was hard. But he sure died instantly. It didn't matter.

The trees and the clean calm empty road it hit Nancy suddenly that she might be going in the wrong direction and this thought was a little amusing considering. If her father would have not been so difficult—he was always so argumentative. He killed her sister. Drove off a road dead drunk and ripped apart the passenger side when he hit a metal-poled sign after picking her up from school. Things might have been different. They both had such beautiful voices everybody said. Don't cry Nancy, don't cry as you drive. It stings too bad and there, backpack on, treading towards somewhere, a man-boy, wind burnt and it looked like he was talking to himself.

Nancy put on the brakes and eased the van off the side of the road.

A Miracle

If out there somewhere was a lower class, less gaudy, jazzier in a minimal kind of way Renoir-influenced artist they might have appreciated this morning poolside at the Hampton Inn there off interstate 75 just outside Chattanooga, Tennessee. Lookout Mountain from this vantage point looked less like a giant Chia Pet and more like the belly of some green teddy bear.

Beside the pool through a parking lot the fashionable light brown brick of the lobby had a big window and you could see inside where a heavy-set young Mexican girl in a brown Hampton Inn uniform emptied a large round stainless steel vat full of dull yellow chunky scrambled eggs into a square stainless steel container for the weary American travelers to pile onto their foam plates, along with fake sausage links that tasted like salty peppered newspaper fat and they all ate the hell out of that shit, it came with the room, along with ESPN and one free HBO channel, and clean sheets sometimes (Rao Kaza, the greasy Indian manager on duty, gave the three Mexie maids clear instructions to look for cum stains, boogers, blood, or excessive pubic hair, otherwise a swift brush and no changing of the sheets!)

But poolside, this early morning shortly after daybreak it was a painting.

The pool was a bright white box lined around the top edge in brilliant blue and the surrounding deck was a gray rock concrete that absorbed the heat. Over by the little round hot tub where children throughout the day would pee in because it was so hot and swirly, Charley Younger sat head titled back, his legs crossed stork-like and his mildly contorted body slumping comfortably in a white plastic chair, as he stared at the dense green trees of the mountain, this huge mountain. It was a big mountain.

On the other side of the pool, about half way towards the deep end Stephanie was stretched out in a flattened white plastic lounge chair on two white towels in a baggy white bikini and with that sad expression on her face, if she would have comically stretched her arms out into a T she would of looked like some female Christ parody lying there. She stared at nothing and had nothing but pain on her scarred pretty face and why shouldn't she? She was heading on deep into the unknown. Unknown what happened to her son and now her abusive boyfriend was dead and deep sinking into the weird ocean and she had already killed her husband, Tony, she thought. And here she was now.

Stephanie kept thinking about Seymour. This wasn't right but that's what she was thinking. People always cling to the past when things go south. As if by some magic it would all be made right and work out and all that. She knew the truth. She closed her eyes and tried to sleep.

And there that other girl was, a bandage the size of a pancake on her cute little hip Doc put there to cover the decubiti ulcer that was starting there, as she hadn't been turned very much in the nursing home the short time she was there, this girl was chattering on a cell phone like there was no tomorrow, as she paced back and forth along the deep end. She just kept talking and talking to this person then that person then her father and mother and her sister and yeah they were all a little worried but not quite as worried as she had thought. Maggie had always gone long periods of time not talking to anyone back home and LOL! She had the *Black Comanche* manuscript! Fucking yes! In its entirety and not one missing page! She told her mother. Three times just this phone call and now she was telling her mother again about Stephanie and the old guy and their retarded friend and it wouldn't be long before she was home. She planned to catch a plane in St. Louis. She still had to edit it. Well, actually she still had to read it. Maggie had only gotten through the first five pages but they were brilliant.

"The prose is incredible, Mother. I know it's not the kind of stuff you would read but there is not a misplaced word. The tone is perfect." Maggie paused to look at the phone, put it back to her ear.

"I'm not slamming your reading habits, Mother. Please. It's not even the kind of stuff I would read. It's uh—I don't know, muscular, chiseled prose. Sort of Cormac and Ernest but hip like Delillo and Pynchon. It's just ungodly perfect." Maggie frowned.

"Cormac McCarthy, Mother. You know that, uh, *Road* writer or whatever. You gave it to me. All those idiotic fragments and no parens—I got about ten pages—NO! this book isn't like that. I just meant . . ."

Maggie sighed, then, "What? No way. I can't let you read it before I send it to New York. I should have sent it already!" Maggie waved in the air with her free hand. "I'm out here in cowfuck America, Mother! I gotta send it soon. I can probably send it at the airport. I think Sonny thinks I already sent it! Mom, I gotta go potty. I'll call you back later."

Maggie nodded though before she hung up. Her mother said it was a miracle she found *Black Comanche*.

Yes, it was. Yes, it was a miracle, that after Stephanie followed Maggie to where she was stabbed and right before she got in the ambulance to go with Maggie to the hospital that day, she looked down and there the manuscript was. Right in a cut out cardboard box with a jar of peanut butter and crackers.

Stephanie picked it up.

A true miracle.

Lazy-ass America

Ridgway, Illinois, Popcorn Capitol of the World! (even though the last popcorn factory closed over ten years ago) was alive tonight. Not really, but the Silver Dollar Saloon had its old wooden door propped open and music from the jukebox was blaring mutedly out into the empty dark street and it was raining so gently on the cracked and buckling concrete, the two sounds together left Seymour with a feeling of uncomfortable reverie as he pissed on the side of the old bar like everyone else did when it was a Saturday night and the one bathroom inside was in use.

Inside Rhonda was slow dirty dancing with a pot-bellied bearded cousin of hers who was driving on a revoked license after getting his third DWI but goddamn you had to get to work somehow and this was just a few days before Rhonda would tell Seymour she couldn't see him anymore.

Seymour had never been to the Silver Dollar Saloon, or any of the two thousand other Silver Dollar Saloons spread across the great American continent and this particular one was an authentic one because it actually had silver dollars pounded into the old seasoned wooden bar and like everyone who came into this bar Seymour asked the barmaid, the old lady who actually owned the place, if anyone ever tried to pull one of those silver dollars out of that bar. The old lady, short and skinny and wrinkled, blew smoke high over the bar.

"Every goddamn week," she said. "Someone tries to pull one of them up." She laughed and her teeth were perfect and yellow. "And some have been trying for twenty years."

But they were pounded in the bar with a nail longer than your arm.

Seymour liked the old lady. This was his first trip here. He came with Rhonda, who was over there by the jukebox, tiny button hips swaying to a bad country song. She knew everyone of the twenty or so people here tonight. Rhonda probably knew everyone within fifty miles in any direction of the Silver Dollar Saloon, here in Ridgway, Illinois. He asked the old lady another stupid question. Was Ridgway really the Popcorn Capitol of the World? Like the sign over the bar said.

Of course it was. Along with five other towns in Illinois, she said. Popcorn, she said, was invented there next to the Cahokia Indian Mounds by a lazy Kickapoo Indian who fell asleep boiling maize over an open fire and when the water all boiled out of the pot the angry Indian gods blew those kernels right out of the pot and popcorn was invented.

"Wow," Seymour said.

"You sleeping with Rhonda?"

Seymour froze. The barmaid poured him a shot of whiskey to go with his 75-cent Pabst Blue Ribbon on tap. She was just asking. Rhonda and her went way back. She ran with Rhonda's mother. She was Rhonda's godmother.

Rhonda had turned her little body so her butt almost touched her cousin's crotch and was grinding, hands held as fists, legs bending, no expression except concentration on her face, and did her pot-bellied cousin love it. Both the barmaid and Seymour had turned to watch her. When Seymour turned back to the bar the barmaid's face was almost too close to his. He smelled her smoky breath and not so subtle perfume.

"You sucked down that catfish like I hadn't even put it in front of you," she said.

"It was good."

"Joe is the best goddamn fry cook I've had in the Silver Dollar in thirty years." She straightened up, and moved the ashtray closer to her. She needed a breather. The place was hopping.

"He's here on time, stays late when he has to, and if I run off to the lady's room or a quick one in the parking lot, he don't sneak no whiskey either."

Seymour thought about this. "That's good," he said.

"You want to meet Joe?"

Seymour looked around. Not particularly. She yelled out for Joe. But Joe had just dropped seven pounds of heavily breaded, lightly seasoned tilapia into the fryer. He didn't want to leave it. You had to move it around just right to adjust for the difference in temperature in this old fryer.

So Joe just stuck his head out and smiled real big in the doorway.

Joe was a Mexican. He wore a faded yellow Mexican Nationals Soccer t-shirt. Seymour smiled.

His real name was something like Joaquin but she couldn't say it right so she nicknamed him Joe.

She said she didn't care what color card he had, yellow, green, purple. She didn't care if he was legal, illegal, or a goddamn Martian. Joe came to work every day and she didn't have to worry the goddamn fish would be half done when the last guy got drunk and she had to take over for the asshole.

"And that yahoo was my nephew," she said. She lit another cigarette.

"I kid you not. I had a sign in the window for almost two months for a fry cook." She shook her head. "You know how long it takes to be a fry cook? About ten minutes. And that's if you're stupid. Not a goddamn person anywhere applied for the job. I got twenty people come in here bitching about no work every goddamn day and not a person wanted the fry cook job. No, it ain't quite minimum wage, but you get free food and drinks. You'd think I had cooties or something. Lazy ass America."

She pointed. And there on the other side of the road, across the train tracks, the Mexicans came on their stand up riding mowers to knock down the weeds for the State and for awhile they would get a little too close to her place when they sat and opened up their red and white plastic coolers and ate their lunches. This gave her the heebie-jeebies sometimes so she would walk out and glare them down once in awhile but they never made eye contact.

She laughed.

"Then one morning I unlocked the door and got the cash register all loaded and I went out to prop the door open and fuck I nearly jumped out of my skin.

"Joe was standing right there, his ball cap in his hand, head down like I'd just caught him stealing something. I just stared at him. He's a little dude. I figured I could take him if he tried anything and then he pointed. I didn't know what the hell he was pointing at. He pointed again. He wanted the fry cook job. He kept staring down at his ratty old tennis shoes."

She nodded.

"Best goddamn fry cook I ever had." She let out a big yell for Joe again, said he had new tennis shoes now!

There was a pause and then out came a not so big Mexican foot with a brand new Nike tennis shoe on it.

Seymour smiled. The foot went back inside.

"Any time they're mowing out there now Joe kinda goes on the downlow, you know?" She laughed. "Don't ask, don't tell." She put her cigarette out and went to pour some more drinks.

Rhonda had turned and had her palms open and was almost holding her cousin's cheeks as her tiny hips gyrated and moved up and down as she continued her very nice, gentle dirty dance. Seymour emptied his free shot.

The barmaid came over for one final comment about Joe.

"I wouldn't be surprised if he don't live with fifteen others just like him in some old barn outside of town and he digs a hole, takes a shit in it, and covers it over every time." She had a smug look on her face. "I don't care," she said. "I don't goddamn care. He's the best fry cook I ever had."

Then off she went with the drinks.

Women

It wasn't a big park. Maybe an acre. Ridgway wasn't a big town. The silver tin colored playground equipment was austere and rusty and the small black metal charcoal grills scattered minimally around the park were mostly bent or broken. But the trees were huge and not that close together and this made it a beautifully simple park in the middle of a flat empty Illinois landscape.

Seymour sat on a park bench with a Snickers bar and a diet Mountain Dew. He had left his farm and come into town for a strange reason.

He came into town to watch Rhonda get off work. He wanted to watch her walk down the steps like he did before when they were together. This only happened once and he wasn't sitting in front of the bank or anything this time. But from where he sat in the park across the street he could see her and she wouldn't be looking so she wouldn't see him probably. He smiled a painful smile and looked around. There was no one around. There were a line of small houses off to his right and directly behind him there was another row of small houses. No kids played in the street and no one sat out front of these houses. It was dead tranquil quiet.

Seymour thought for a moment that perhaps no one lived in these houses and there was no one alive anywhere and he was in some sort of purgatory.

When he and Stephanie were no longer together he drove all the way out to the farm he now lived on and leaned against the back door of the old barn and stared at the place where they had made love. He wrung his hands together that day and drove home sad.

He would do the same here.

Rhonda broke off their relationship and did it for all the right reasons and when he tried to hug her and kiss her goodbye that day she tensed up and this told him everything and this was how his life was going now that he was forty.

Rhonda was crying full blown that day and trying not to and going through a laundry list of things he had to remember to do like shut the gates so the chickens didn't get out and they were running low on feed and he could get Roger to help him lay down the carpeting they ordered. She had said she could do this. Okay, Rhonda said. If Seymour would leave the door unlocked she would lay the carpeting down for him as long as he didn't show up or anything. She could do that for him at least.

She sniffed and her eyes were so red and her shoulders so slumped. She thought of one last thing.

"And shortly that asparagus Roger planted will need picking so don't let the Mexicans scare you when you see them in the fields in your front yard. There's asparagus planted on both sides of the driveway all the way to the main road."

Seymour nodded. He wouldn't let the Mexicans scare him.

Rhonda opened the car door.

He liked how she was standing with one leg inside the car and the other stiff and showing off her butt.

She sighed very deeply and said very deliberately, "Bye Seymour."

He said bye too that day but it never got out of his throat.

Now he was alone and eating a Snickers bar and drinking a diet Mountain Dew and waiting for a glimpse of a woman who no longer wanted to see him again.

Stephanie, there in the parking lot of the Ocean Palm Inn over a year or so ago had tensed up like that too when he went to kiss her goodbye.

Yes, he did not have much luck with women.

Seymour smiled.

It was probably a good time to be without a woman.

Seymour nearly jumped out of the park bench when what he was waiting for happened. The door opened and out walked Rhonda. She was talking on her cell phone. She had on beige corduroy pants and a very nondescript old blue sweater and black flats. Her long blond hair was back in a plain ponytail. She stopped on the bottom step and kept talking on the cell phone and might have even looked his way but she looked right through him and then looked somewhere else. She kept talking.

A large shiny black pickup truck pulled up. It had dual wheels in the back. It must have been her husband. Rhonda opened the back door first and reached in and hugged her little boy and adjusted the car seat. She kissed him.

Then she got in the front seat.

The truck eased away on down the street.

Home

The big van pulled into the QT there on Interstate 44 fast and stopped suddenly on a side parking space. The driver rummaged around in the back and found something he could put hot water in and practically ran into the dirty bathroom to fill it up with hot water.

Nancy was hurting and she might even have a punctured lung so maybe he should drive her to a hospital but she wouldn't have any part of that.

He took care of her bleeding eye though with the first aid kit in the van like he was some doctor or something. He told her he had been a medic in Iraq until his head got scrambled by a roadside bomb. Then he got to come home early and for the longest time he walked around afraid something would blow up.

"I can't keep a job." He asked Nancy if she wanted anything at the QT. She told him to bring her back a sweet coffee of some kind. There was money stuck everywhere in the van. He had money. He didn't need her money.

He came back with coffee and two breakfast sausages but she didn't want even a little bite.

"If I have to do more than two things I forget them so even a goddamn job in a McDonald's I can't even fucking do for very long. Man, somebody beat the shit out of you."

Nancy was stretched out in the back and he sat in a captain's chair. She indeed was hurting and this guy wouldn't shut up.

In Iraq he got to this kid, a girl, real pretty like she was only she had a shaved head and she didn't look hurt at all she just looked uncomfortable and she even smiled a little when he got to her and then when he turned her on her side her fucking heart fell out her back. He wasn't shittin' her. That bomb blew everything away back there and when he lay her back she was blue as can be and deader than anyone he'd ever seen.

"That was about the worst thing I saw really. A leg blown off a guy but he lived." He chomped on the breakfast sausage.

"My disability check goes to my mom." He dug into his dirty jeans. He pulled out a plastic card. "There's usually money on it. Sometimes not." He shrugged. "I just wait."

Nancy sipped the coffee. It hurt bad to breathe. She asked him where he was going.

He laughed. "Anywhere this card is good." He coughed. He was eating the breakfast sandwich too goddamn fast. "Yourself?"

She eased her one good eye shut.

"Home," she said.

The Word

His name was Jay and he was driving the van now. He had no trouble driving. For the most part. When Jay got his license he drove three of his friends up to the stockyards there in south Chicago from his hometown of Mendosa, Indiana right on the lake. They had three bottles of cheap wine and started throwing rocks at some niggers who were also hanging out drinking and smoking there in the stockyards where the stench of pig and cow shit hung so thick in the air it would make you cough and on that first day, no, it was the second day of basic training in Fort Leonard Wood it would be the last time he would use the word nigger for a long time because six of them beat the shit out of him for using that word and no one helped him one bit, no, he couldn't do anything with a girl now so don't ask about that shit his plumbing didn't work after the brain rattling road side bomb. They gave him some shit like Viagra or something and it made him feel like sex or pissing or something but he would just tug and tug and it would stay as soft as it always was and yeah technically he was a virgin but that only bothered him sometimes. Not much.

They were heading back to St. Louis. Jay didn't care what direction they went in. He slept under the Arch last night and a black guy and his retarded girlfriend, in these old army green trench coats (man, did they smell bad) split with him a four pack of some energy drink they stole and that caffeine might well have been ecstasy as wound up as those two got. They got higher than fucking kites. It didn't hit him at all. Did she notice he didn't use the word nigger? That was a big black nigger with dreadlocks and a beard, man. The girl was a kid almost, and she wore these black broken glasses with one lens missing. Fuck.

Nancy didn't hear this. She was asleep now.

Sex Talk

It moved toward evening on the edge of Chattanooga. The mountains of trees looked gray moving towards black. The pool area at the Hampton Inn was clean and well lit. Doc and Charley Younger sat in plastic chairs poolside playing checkers and then when Doc found out Charley Younger could play chess he pulled out the plastic set the hotel provided and off they went.

Doc asked Charley Younger if he knew what a Queen's Gambit was. Charley Younger adjusted the piece of wood in his left bent palm.

"No," he said.

"Okay then," Doc said, and then he made his first move. Pawn to Queen Four.

Jeremiah taught Charley Younger how to play chess and they played it for months a few years ago and then never played it again. In the second bedroom back home there was a wooden box lined with green felt with a marble chess set from Mexico inside.

Nine floors up in room 935 (Stephanie asked for this room anytime a hotel had it) Maggie and Stephanie drank whiskey and Cokes out of clear plastic cups and watched TV.

Stephanie was glad Maggie's phone died. She was tired of hearing Maggie tell the same story over and over again and sometimes over again to the same people.

But it did distract her some from thinking about going home again. They were getting close and this made Stephanie sad and if she thought about it too much she wanted to cry. She took a sip from the drink and looked around the hotel room. Stephanie wanted badly to kill herself somehow before she got there. Denying something was always easier than facing something. Stephanie wanted to kill herself really badly. She took another sip. There was no way she could face Jeremiah now. There was no way she could face her mother now. She tucked her hand without a drink under her thigh to keep it from shaking. There was a time a few months ago when she had convinced herself that there was a life without ever having to go home again but that didn't last long.

Now she was on her way home again and it looked like there was no avoiding it. She took another drink and watched Maggie as she sat on the edge of the other bed in the room staring disdainfully at the cell phone plugged into the wall. It was only half-assed plugged in and not charging really. They never had convenient outlets in these cheap hotels.

Stephanie smiled after Maggie said this. This might well be the nicest hotel she had ever stayed in, outside of the one she stayed at in Chicago. Maggie got up and unplugged a standing lamp and plugged her phone into that outlet.

They both jumped when someone knocked on the door. It was their pizza.

It was a scary looking pizza from some local place. It looked like they had tried to sell it earlier in the day and then just put it in a box for them. They set it on the same bed and ate it though. It was terrible. But they ate it. It just seemed like women who enjoy sex were training ground for other women, you know? Maggie said out of the blue.

"What?"

"I believe that," Maggie said. She picked the scary looking mushrooms off the pizza. "That guy I talked to earlier? I shouldn't have called him but I did. More professional than personal. Seriously. He's just a glorified copy editor, but we did it all the time and like, this wimpy secretary, homely, conservative, I catch them at his place."

"I swear. The more I sleep with a man the better and crazier the sex gets and the more he wants to fuck someone else." Maggie shook her head. The pizza was okay. The sauce was too sweet. Stephanie stopped chewing her pizza. She never looked at it that way. She thought about it. She looked quickly back into her past at all her lovers.

"Could be," she said.

Stephanie could take or leave sex really. If she wasn't getting it, that was okay, but after she got it she usually wanted it again soon. They exchanged ornery smiles.

"Maybe it's us women that get our rocks off easily," Maggie said. "Men want a challenge." They both half-laughed. Then Stephanie started telling Maggie about Seymour, her first and only real affair, and the 935 thing and that was probably stupid but whenever it was 935 she thought of him.

Maggie thought about something also.

"You going to look him up when you get back?"

"Oh God no," she said. "I'm probably going to jail."

Right then Maggie's phone started vibrating and shaking there on the floor.

Her pizza slice flew out of her hand.

Pot

Outside around the edge of Renoir's pool at the Hampton Inn on the dark side of Lookout Mountain Doc checkmated Charley Younger for the fourth time. Then he rolled out a small stash of marijuana, not a lot, you understand, just enough actually for a bowl or two or three, and it was strictly for medicinal purposes and legal under Florida law.

Doc laughed and it was a happy laugh. He looked around. There was no one around. He started stuffing the ashy green and gray substance into a four-inch white-bone, dragon-shaped pipe. No, Florida didn't allow marijuana for medicinal purposes, but it should.

Instead Doc would buy it occasionally from an old Mexican lady's nephew who lived three trailers down, wore a red headband, and drove a '63 Chevy just like the one he once owned, minus the chrome wheels, rear lifters, and speakers in the back as big around as manholes.

"For medicinal purposes," Doc said, lighting the pipe. He took in a deep drag. He coughed slightly. Old men like him had many aches and pains, he said. He offered it up to Charley Younger.

Charley Younger adjusted the piece of wood in his right hand, looked around. Okay. He smoked pot twice with Jeremiah. One time afterwards they ate a whole six pound pot roast between them and the other time when Jeremiah was upset his girlfriend was going to break up with him. She didn't. They laughed about it though and sat through the only movie they had in the trailer twice. What movie?

"*The Alamo*," Charley Younger said. "It's the only movie I can sit all the way through."

Then they both froze. They heard something. Music. What was that music, in the distance, they were hearing?

All of a sudden, back around the back of the Hampton Inn, as the sun went down and darkness settled over that huge ass mountain, over a short fence and down a fairly steep ravine, there was an open place overlooking the beautiful city of Chattanooga. A fire was lit in a cut out trash barrel. Cars pulled up quietly and people got out and trunk lids opened as the courtship music of slaves from the bowels of 18th century Columbia began to fill the thick humid Tennessee air. That music was called . . .

Cumbia!

A gray haired Mexican with a thick matching gray mustache emerged from the darkness and an old beat up Dodge van, emerged from twelve hours of cleaning plates at a downtown Chattanooga hotel, and began his manic 4/4 spits from his equally aged and beat up minor-key accordion. He was joined by two other minor-key accordion players and two guitar players and several low budget percussionists.

The old man began to sing along with his manic accordion beats. He sang a song about an immortal lover who never left home and always made great tortillas. Laughter and dancers came out of nowhere.

For a brief moment the ghosts of Cumbian music floated down from the heavens and beautiful Columbia and Mexican and Chilean slave girls adorned in plain yet colorful red and yellow and blue billowing dresses, holding candles in one hand, and the end of these long ankle length skirts in the other, shook their hips rapidly, shuffled their feet perfectly, steadily to the pounding staccato rhythms of . . .

Cumbia!

These beautiful ghosts of Cumbia past soon melted into half-shirted young women in insanely tight, insanely short cut-off jeans or ankle tight blue jeans stitched in faux gold who held no candles but shook their delicate wrists as their hips pounded rapidly and their feet shuffled wonderfully to the beautiful staccato rhythms of Cumbia!

The men followed, bandannas waving wildly in the air as they tried to match their women with their hips and shuffling feet. They weren't as good, but they danced around the slave girl of their choice and it was all so vulgar and lower class and here it was now, in the groin of America, and as the fog of Cumbia music past lifted, the candles were replaced with cans of beer in one hand and cigarettes in the other as they danced.

They bumped and grinded their way through the 4/4 beats and forlorn singing, as their multi-colored Converses, the Mexican tennis shoe of choice, covered all their feet, and tapped gently upon the American soil here overlooking Chattanooga as delicately as if they were dancing on hot coals.

As their hips kept moving, and their breasts kept shaking.

Cumbia!

This sexy beautiful form of song and dance came from slaves in Columbia centuries ago and now had swept through Mexico and now was alive in the mountains of America.

Amen.

Seymour looked at the clock he put on the kitchen wall. It was now well past eleven. The clock was white with plain black numbers and green plastic trim. He paid six dollars for it at Wal-Mart. He had wanted a bigger, fancier one with Roman numerals but Rhonda had shot that down. It would look out of place here. She was right. As he stared at the wall he noticed for the first time that the kitchen walls were white painted plywood. No drywall or even plaster in this tin-roofed little house. And the two doors into the house, the one in front and the one in back out to the outhouse, were also doubled up pieces of cut plywood. There was a small window in the front door but not in the back door. The back door sagged a bit and you had to lift it some to lock it. It had gotten the most use in the years from 1946 until now. The locks were large square metal locks with skeleton keys to lock them with. The doorknobs where shiny round and pearl handled.

This was a very simple, very utilitarian southern Illinois farmhouse that didn't even have phone lines in it until now. He remembered his father calling Aunt Edith and Uncle Bud's neighbor to ask her to tell them they were coming to visit. That wasn't a problem, the neighbor said. That must have been in the late 70s.

And Rhonda had to tell him what clock to buy. Seymour needed a woman for such things like sex and clocks and other practical matters and he had come to the conclusion that Rhonda was a very smart woman even if she did drop out of John A. Logan College when she got pregnant with her son. She had wanted to take some business classes and maybe someday move up at the bank.

But about Rhonda and him being together Rhonda was probably right. Seymour wasn't sure how long he could stay here and now, with such a strange lump in his stomach for never being able to see Rhonda again, he probably would do what she said. He would look for a teaching job of some kind in some small ass town around here where he didn't have to explain the iPod and four cheerleader thing and then he would start fucking a thirty year old 4th grade teacher who listened to Regina Spektor and had one bad love affair after another in college and was now getting a little fat but knew when to drink red or white wine.

Seymour smiled as he stared at the clock.

This place, without Rhonda, would drive him fucking crazy.

Even though it was late and he had shut his laptop off he pressed the button and turned it back on. Even with all the twists and turns in his life the last year or two at least he was back on the Internet. He kind of had to piss but the thought of turning on the porch light and walking to the outhouse this late at night didn't appeal to him. He moved his bare foot on the rough vinyl floor and a spot he sat his foot down on crackled.

But he liked this place. If Rhonda would have stayed with him he would have followed through with putting a bathroom in. He had the money to do it. He didn't have a lot of money but he still had earning years left and he had enough to put a bathroom in.

But Rhonda was gone now and this thought left Seymour more than a bit hollow inside. And his ex-wife wouldn't even return his email to tell him how she was doing with her new lover and all. He shrugged. As usual, it was Stephanie he missed when he was alone and thinking about it. Timing is everything in relationships and their timing had been off.

He tried to remember her email address. StephForPrez or something like that. Oh, well.

He typed her name in Google.

Nothing came back. Seymour smiled. That was a stupid fucking thing to do. He looked around the empty kitchen, irrationally making sure no one had seen him do this.

He jumped as if shot when someone knocked on the door.

Pablo Discovers American Freedom

Pablo was curious. He was curious by nature so when the Cumbia band began to play and the mean *patrón* joined the other boys dancing around his aunt he decided he could explore for awhile. He was quick and his tiny chicken legs were strong and his magical tennis shoes, even if the shoestrings were wearing out, carried him quickly towards the hill and up he ran, low and fast, as he dug his fingernails into the dirt to keep him balanced.

He stopped only once up the hill and hid as best his could as two *Estadounidenses* came falling, stumbling by him. One was an old man and the other a special man, with broken hands and a broken face. Pablo, even in the darkness, watched the special man all the way down the hill. The special man almost lost his broken footing but he didn't because God had helped him. Pablo continued up the hill.

Shortly, Pablo was where he could see where all the bright light he saw at the bottom was coming from. His eyes widened. This was America. There was no tall barbed-wire fence around the beautiful blue and white swimming pool in front of him. There was no uniformed guard reading a *revista nena* with an American made assault rifle beside him. Pablo was so excited he could hardly breathe. There was no one around at all. Not a soul.

He could walk right up to the pool. There was still no one around. He approached the pool slowly anyway. He stopped and looked at the yellow light in the square windows of the hotel. There was nobody looking out these windows. The pool was his.

The pool wasn't muddy or even cloudy. It was so clear he could see the bottom. Pablo took off his tennis shoes and stuck his toe in. It was barely cool. More warm than cool so off his shorts and t-shirt came so they would be dry and there would be no trail for the *patrón* to follow back to here.

Back to here in America where Pablo could swim in a pool for the first time and for free and there was no one around who would beat him or kill him for doing so.

In Pablo dove, headfirst. He didn't surface gasping until he was halfway towards the shallow end.

As Pablo emerged from the cool warm clear water, mouth open wide, he took in the most beautiful breath he had ever taken in.

The breath of American Freedom.

Razorblades

In 1895, King Camp Gillette, a Utopian socialist by political inclination and a traveling salesman for a Cork and Seal company by trade, came up with an idea that would revolutionize the shaving business. After opening a bottle of beer and tossing the cap away for about the five thousandth time, King Camp thought—Jesus Christ, if lids on beer bottles can be cheap enough to be disposable, why not make a razor with disposable blades? The light bulb went off and history would eventually be made.

But it wasn't exactly instant because by the late 19th century men were so tired of cutting themselves on the expensive supposed safety razors of the time, they just said fuck it and grew beards (Dostoevsky, Émile Zola, Walt Whitman, for proof of this).

So it wasn't until 1903, with the help of an engineer from MIT, that King Camp Gillette's dream of creating the cheap disposable razor blade came to fruition. The rest would be history. While King Camp would become known as the inventor of the safety razor, he didn't really. A more accurate description would be to call King Camp Gillette the inventor of *freebie marketing*. What would follow would be cheap tiny puzzles and plastic toys in Cracker Jacks, plastic Cinderellas and action figures in Happy Meals, etc. King Camp only wanted the disposable razor blade so he could sell gazillions of the five-dollar razors you had to buy to put those disposable razor blades in. Back then, five dollars was two weeks of wages. And it worked!

Yes, a safety razor with cheap disposable blades was invented back then, and thanks to a turn of the century America suddenly enamored with the possibilities of a clean shaven face, clean shaven underarms, and with the Victorian sanctity of the ankle length hemline receding faster than the German trenches in World War I, well, King Camp made a killing.

But it would not be until 1921, however, that the first suicide by one of these cheap disposable razors would be documented. Her name was Ethel Livingston and, after failing to get a part in a Shakespearean play in a tiny theatre in Yonkers, after shaving her underarms in a bathtub as the Casting Director had ordered all the women who were auditioning for a part to do, Ethel then used the brown little blade to slit her wrists.

They didn't find her body for over two weeks.

When Ethyl Livingston's method of death hit the papers a different kind of history was in the making.

The slashing of the wrists with a disposable razor blade.

Upwards of three percent of the population, worldwide, either try or succeed in slashing their wrists every year using Mr. Gillette's little disposable invention. The number and percentage has remained as steady and proportional, in the last century, as the number of women who decide to terminate a pregnancy.

Yes. Steady as she goes.

Stephanie had already tried to do it once. If her perv peeping tom neighbor hadn't been in the closet that day jacking off while he watched her take a bath, Stephanie wouldn't be standing where she was standing at the moment. She had already tried once to slit her wrists with a razor. Now . . .

Stephanie was looking at herself in the mirror on the bathroom wall of a room in a Hampton Inn. She was naked and about to put on a bathing suit.

Maggie's phone was charged up enough for her to get on the goddamn phone again. Stephanie was nauseous.

She couldn't go home again. She didn't really want to see her son again really. She didn't want to face any of it now and inaction is the easiest of all human activities and she just wished Maggie would shut the fucking hell up and get off that goddamn cell phone.

But there on the counter in a corner was a small blue rectangular pack of 7 o'clock brand razor blades. Thank you, King Camp Gillette.

Back in high school, back when Stephanie was a sophomore and swallowed two hundred aspirins for no good reason anyone could figure out, she remembered sitting up in her hospital bed as a younger doctor told her that sometimes the desire to kill yourself had more to do with metabolism than the mental state or life environment.

The doctor was smiling a bit when he added, "My guess is you will try to do this again sometime."

From how the doctor stared at her back then and after he said this to Stephanie she fully expected him to follow by saying cheerfully, "Good luck!"

Stephanie's next attempt, her senior year, after she knew it wasn't a good idea to fall in love with her volleyball coach and history teacher, after she drove her Pontiac Gran Am into a cement wall at 110 miles an hour, which left her with only a broken leg and a pretty good concussion, an older psychologist, his damp old hand on her bare thigh in the hospital, explained that there was little doubt in his mind that she had somehow been abused as a child. He gave her thigh an odd squeeze (it was her leg that had a cast on it from the knee down and was propped up). He asked her to tell him, in great detail, anything and perhaps everything she could think of that might constitute abuse.

Stephanie stared at the brown ceiling of the hospital room there in Granite City back then.

The only trauma of any kind, she told him, she could think of was having her bare thigh caressed right now by an elderly pervert doctor who was stroking his crotch with his other hand. If he didn't stop she would scream.

The old man looked angry and nervous all of a sudden. His hand eased off her thigh. Then in a stern voice he said something about lying being the perfect antidote for denial.

"What?" Stephanie said.

The elderly psychologist left.

Stephanie rubbed her finger over the top of the little packet of razorblades there in the bathroom of the Hampton Inn. It was pretty much full. She removed one.

Stephanie put on her bathing suit as she heard Maggie talking madly once again about the novel *Black Comanche*. Maggie was still pacing back and forth in the hotel room.

She stopped pacing and stared at nothing in front of her. "No, no, listen! Yes! It's a muscular novel, uh, sort of Gore Vidal meets, oh, Jim Thompson, but no, that isn't right. What?" Her face pained. "What? Fucking Cormac McCarthy? God, Sonny, you know what I think of his stilted pretentious fragments. Fuck! I have to always go back and reread his shit without the quotation marks and all those quote *organic* realists who follow him like fucking southern lemmings . . . Who did you just say? Russo? Who's Russo? Wh—? Oh shit no. Gaa! Yeah, Sonny, nothing like setting the scene of Pulitzer Prize novel with house values in Maine and don't follow with Irving, aren't they both from the same school of bored academic writers without style? Please Sonny. It's the 21st century! This novel has it all. It's, just let me think for a moment . . . " Maggie paced and as she paced she looked down and pounded her forehead with her palm.

Maggie leaped in the air and then pointed at nothing. "Marquez! This guy writes strong sturdy declarative sentences sure, but there are long passages of magic realism. True magic realism! It's brilliant!"

Stephanie nicked her thumb on the razor-blade. It bled a bit. She put it in her mouth.

Maggie was practically jumping up and down as she talked on the phone now. To some guy named Sonny. She was so animated as she talked it looked like she needed to take a potty break. She stopped moving.

"There's this one part. It's about, well, the obvious absurdity of the Vietnam War and all that but there's this *Village Voice* reporter who has snuck onto the base and he interviews Black Comanche about all the Agent Orange him and his unit are dumping every day on villages and was it really as toxic as they were saying it was and shit like that, well, Black Comanche tells him to come back tomorrow. Black Comanche would take the journalist up in one of the five World War II vintage propeller planes they flew and he could watch Black Comanche take out an entire village. He could then write his history making essay 'The Ballad of Black Comanche.'"

Maggie jumped high and surprised Stephanie with the splits and then continued.

"No, just hear me out! So Black Comanche, who come to find out, is totally anti-war really, and not a real serious killer or anything, you know. Did I tell you he's not even a real Indian or anything? His mother was an Aztec Indian, a goddamn Mexican, but anyway, his girlfriend is a Filipino chick who lives with her family in a small Vietnam village so—"

Maggie paused and then her shoulders slumped. "I don't know why she's Filipino, Sonny! It's fucking fiction! I know! I know! Your cute little aging wife beckons. I know that shit. But listen! One more minute.

"So the day before the *Village Voice* writer came, Black Comanche and his crew went around and talked to all the villagers they were friends with and told them to do them a favor and all the villagers loved Black Comanche and his crew so they shook their heads and laughed. They would do it. The whole village got in on the joke, Sonny.

"Then that night Black Comanche and his crew filled up these barrels or containers or whatever with orange juice! Orange juice! They had a huge stockpile of it! Rancid orange juice not even worth giving away.

"Then the next day the *Village Voic*e reporter came back and Black Comanche flew him over the village real low and released—" Maggie laughed loudly— "Orange juice over the village!" (Stephanie, razor blade in her palm, was even smiling)

"And, and the *Village Voice* guy looked sick, begged Black Comanche not to do this evil, horrible, inhumane thing. Kill all those villagers with Agent Orange. Black Comanche told him to shut the fuck up. This was the real face of war, goddamn it! Ha! Ha!

"Then Black Comanche drew his gun, he forced the horrified reporter to stare down at the villagers and, oh Christ! They were all staggering around and pretending to fall over dead, clutching their throats! Several hundred Vietnamese villagers did this! Hundreds. Spread eagle on the ground, tongues hanging out. Staggering, gasping, coughing. Their little big tent hats on and all. The reporter threw up over the side of the open cockpit plane! Maggie paused then screamed, 'The Ballad of Black Comanche!'

"Brilliant! He titled this chapter 'Agent Orange Juice.' What? Oh hell, Sonny, there are twenty, thirty, forty scenes like that. And all written in short chapters. Very refreshing approach. People will love the short chapters on a Kindle, Sonny. They will. Collage fiction rules! Or it will soon!"

Maggie looked now at Stephanie as Stephanie got in her bathing suit. Then told her,

"I'll come too. Shortly!"

Uncle Bud and Aunt Edith

Something startled the chickens. Seymour rose up from the kitchen chair when he heard that muffled startled chicken noise.

He sat back down. He would not be able to see anything in the inky Bible Belt blackness. Rhonda told him just to chill when this happened. Chickens were nervous. You're nervous, she had told him that evening as their bare thighs touched in the feather bed.

It was simple. He missed Rhonda. He wasn't sure how long he could last alone.

Seymour always considered himself a loner but only in the context of a woman being somewhere close in his life.

He stared at the spreadsheet on his screen. He had plenty of money to live here. Even if he kept paying Roger two-hundred-fifty dollars a month he had no bills except a cell phone and a few other utilities. He only had to pay about a hundred dollars to keep his school health insurance. If he sold this place he could move somewhere and get another teaching job. Maybe out of state. Maybe Seattle or somewhere like that.

Seymour stared at the large old cast iron cooking stove. He saw a large black cast iron skillet with three inches of bacon grease in it frying to a crisp several eggs. Over easy.

Then he saw his Uncle Bud, in one morning after feeding all the farm animals, in overalls, his round white safari hat hanging on the wall behind him, wiping his white plate absolutely clean of all egg yolk with a piece of folded white bread.

Seymour heard his Aunt Edith complaining about how every joint in her body was filled with arthritis and how it was getting so bad she one day, may not be able to help Bud in the fields because each year it was getting more difficult for her to climb onto one of their three John Deere tractors, not to mention how it pained her fingers to steer those machines.

Bud never responded to his wife's complaints. He would just finish his cup of black percolated coffee and get up from his chair. He had to get started on the rest of his farm work that would carry him to lunch.

Uncle Bud would die of a heart attack at the age of sixty-nine. He had a heart attack a few years before and the doctor would tell him if he stopped farming and perhaps change his diet he would extend his life considerably.

Bud thought about this. What would he do if he stopped farming? He didn't stop farming and he didn't stop eating two pieces of thick cut jowl bacon with three fried eggs every morning and one afternoon in September when his nitroglycerin tablets weren't helping at all, the day after he mowed clean the area on his farm where he would be buried next to his mother and father, Bud Lanier dropped dead putting one foot in front of the other toward the barn.

Seymour's Aunt Edith would live to be eighty-one and die in a nursing home in Carmi, Illinois.

And now Seymour was here. He didn't want to leave really. The best years of his childhood were here and there were very few opportunities for people to return to their childhood. He would put a bathroom in though. He could at least do that.

Then came the knock at the door.

Nietzsche

The moon was as full as it could be tonight. It hung leeringly right there at the top of Lookout Mountain like it came here all the time just to watch people swim in the pool. Perv!

Stephanie, still twirling the razor blade in her thumb and forefinger with an uncanny precision, stared at the large bruise on her thigh. Her legs were sunk in the pool up to her bikini bottom. She teetered on the edge of the deep end. The water was the only thing at the moment that felt good. She'd been through hell lately. It seemed to Stephanie that hell rose up in her life right when it looked like it would never return again. Her dead lover rose tanned and ugly beautiful out of the far end of the pool and it hit her suddenly that he was dead and that all seemed surreal and well, funny. She had no idea Charley Younger had that in him. She stared at the bottom of the pool.

Stephanie could do it in a heartbeat. Just like she shot Tony and nearly killed that dumb fucking Mexican trying to rape Maggie back at Crabby Joe's that night. Stephanie had an innate ability to do harm to someone. It all went back to the trashcan, she believed. Born in a trashcan and angry about it but sad at the same time. If she had been smarter and Seymour had a clue they would be together and maybe that would have been all right. She doubted it though. Trashcan babies rarely turned out okay. This made her smile. Seymour would have liked her thinking this. She couldn't go home again. She didn't want to face any of it. More than that, she couldn't face any of it.

Stephanie may have heard water swishing somewhere but she was fairly immobile now. This was the state she got in when there was a quiet darkness surrounding her slipping or crashing towards death. Towards taking her own life. She spoke with Seymour about this one time after he had brought her to one huge orgasm with his mouth and then rested his head on her brown stomach he enjoyed so much. They were in moonlight similar to now and blackness was everywhere. Her legs were jelly. She told Seymour why she would slip every now and then and try to kill herself for no real reason and how it had more to do with this state she put herself in than anything else. She couldn't explain it. She recalled suddenly, there with Seymour kissing her stomach how, as a three year old, she had once started marching straight off a cliff overlooking Kinkaid Lake. Her sister tackled her and saved her life.

Seymour stopped kissing her stomach that warm evening in

September way back when. "Nietzsche," he said. Maybe Stephanie did kill herself that time when she was three years old and she was now part of some eternal return and so she kept returning and returning and dying and returning and dying.

He swiveled around and got into a position over Stephanie like he was about to deliver her child. She told him this and he laughed. She loved to make Seymour laugh. Then he leaned over in the gray black moonlight and gave her a very gentle kiss right below her belly button.

"Nietzsche wrote a book called *Gay Science*. If we all knew that whatever we do we will have to live over and over again for all eternity, eternal returns, as they say, then we would just cash it in and end it right then and there." He kicked off first his jeans and then his underwear. He was the only guy she knew besides her grandfather who wore boxers. He was about to give her a long gentle fuck.

"You know something the rest of us do not know," Seymour said as he slowly, very gently started penetrating her. "So the way I interpret that," he said, more than a little out of breath. "If we were to die right now," He eased all the way in. "This would be our eternal return." He kissed her side, right below her breast.

Stephanie eased her hand with the 7 o'clock razor blade in it over to her wrist. With a pause she pushed the tip into the top of her wrist just deep enough to draw a dollop of blood. It oozed up black on her wrist.

She started the incision.

Then suddenly a firm hand stabbed at her hand with the razor blade in it. It was a tiny but strong hand.

It was the hand of a little Mexican boy named Pablo.

Stephanie's heavy lazy eyes finally looked up at the little Mexican boy standing next to her in baggy soiled soaking wet underwear. The knob of his little pee-pee poked through the saggy wet underwear like a little acorn.

With his other hand Pablo pointed his finger straight up into the black sky.

"No!" Pablo scolded.

He kept pointing.

"*¡Dios te está observando!*" He shook and shook until the razor blade came out of her limp fingers." It floated into the clear water.

He shook her wrist again.

"*¡Dios te está observando!*"

He kept pointing up towards the dark sky.

God is watching, is what Pablo was warning Stephanie about.

I Do

Rhonda came back. It startled Seymour so much he banged his knee on the corner of the kitchen table and it was one of those old sharp metal-rimmed kitchen tables with the thin chrome legs. It poked a hole in his jeans. It stung. He winced.

Rhonda barged right in after knocking and frankly she was surprised the door was unlocked because this city boy locked everything down tight usually. She dropped her gym bag and tossed a sweater on top of that and then she looked even more shocked than Seymour, it seemed like. She held out palms.

"Okay, you know, I . . . listen—" She pointed at Seymour, took a deep breath, then ran her fingers through her thin blonde hair, swayed her body some in some sort of body language like she was prepared to explain everything.

She had on his favorite pants. They were very thin, very tight beige painter pants, paper thin actually, she'd had them for years, and yeah that sex thing was always good between them, he had to admit that, but this wasn't fucking New York or even St. Louis for that matter or Chicago, this was cowfuck southern Illinois farm country, Ridgway, everybody was almost gone from this area, empty small houses and old barns were scattered everywhere, small rusty jack hammer oil wells every so often, yeah, but Jesus, I mean, our choices aren't that great and I can really help around here, if this is where you want to be for a while, you know? I mean this is a farm, Seymour. Yes, you're the smartest man I ever slept with, but—

Rhonda sniffed. Her face was a mess now. Seymour's was getting that way.

I don't love him. I don't love my husband. I mean, I'm not certain I love you really, I guess, well, fuck, goddamn it.

Her face was more of a mess now. She stared off somewhere. Then back at Seymour.

You probably like me more than you realize, I mean, the sex that comes first with guys and all before it turns into more than that. But that more than that usually comes, you know?

Her chest heaved and her whole body shook.

Her son was asleep in the car. Rhonda went silent for a minute and then her face got so bloated and red and wrinkly it didn't look like her. Maybe she had totally made a big fucking mistake coming here now.

You know?

Seymour's face was an equal mess.

"No," Seymour said. His voice was weak. He nodded though. He said he agreed with everything she said.

She wiped her cheeks with the back of her hand.

"You do?" She said.

Seymour looked once at the clock on the wall. It was edging just past midnight.

He nodded.

"I do," he said.

Black Comanche Epiphany

The middle-age balding man stopped reading the *USA Today* as he stood behind the counter in the lobby of the Hampton Inn to stare at the busty yet skinny little thing with the bandage on her nice looking leg. She wore a cute one piece bathing suit that looked expensive. She stopped pretty much right in front of him. He started to ask her if he could help her with anything but he didn't. She was completely absorbed in talking on her cell phone. His eyes went slowly up then down then back and she just kept talking so he went back to his *USA Today*.

"No, no. You just don't get it, Sonny. I know when something is bad. Everyone in the business knows when something is bad. Every little English major in the universe knows when something is bad. You know that. But if it's going to sell in the fabled hundred thousand copy category, fuck, who does anymore? Quality fiction is just plain in the shitter . . . What? The shitter, Sonny. It's just a term. Midwestern again, I guess."

Gateway to the Midwest

I got a home now that's more important than you know really I don't just go off with my debit card Nancy found us this place Section 8 apartment with our own bathroom damn I don't really care but she thought it was a big deal she's a doer like my mom really she's working at an old folk's home during the night in the daytime Nancy's at a diner with the best hash I ever had the only time I had it really but goddamn it's good but what I'm sayin' is Nancy got me washing dishes at both places quite a few hours a week really so my debit card is in a drawer Nancy thinks my mom is sandbagging with what she puts on it every month but I don't care Nancy don't either really she just told me what she thought there ain't no sex between us Nancy calls us each other's pets I don't care if sex is gone from me but Nancy says I'd be dead if there was sex in me but I don't think so people can live without it really I think anyway you know but what I like is my bed. I mean it's got this pillow like top and I come home from my jobs about one really Nancy told the old folks home I'd get more done late than that Mexican they say was stealing stuff Nancy said she wasn't stealing stuff she was just quiet but people ain't right Nancy said and I laughed and said like me and she said yeah like you and then she rubbed my head goddamn we are each other's pets is what she always says but what I'm sayin' is Nancy works at the other food place because there's a girl gonna come back there someday and tell her where her son is so we'd have this kid to take care of eventually Nancy says.

It ain't happened yet I have a home and two jobs really not bad for a guy like me with this debit card after Iraq and all.

Granite City ain't that bad. We go down by the river on Sundays and drink beer and look at the Arch. Fuck, that thing is big. Gateway to the Midwest, Nancy says.

Okay.

Hubcaps

The moon was almost gone for the night. The fading gray glow of impending morning turned the trickle of a creek an inky pale blue black neon with utter hopeless black saturating all else upon the canvas of a small clearing where, legs and arms crossed, Stephanie, cigarette dangling from between two of her long thin fingers, sat in a folding chair from Doc's van right along the edge of the creek. The belly of the mountain towered monstrously black behind everything. It was warm and cool all at the same time.

They all survived the evening. The evening of crazy Mexican music and crazy Mexican dancing and enough free tequila to kill a city. Doc took care of everyone though. He kept the Mexican men away from them and them away from the Mexican men. Charley Younger had early on crashed inside the van.

After his morning walk along this strange curling creek winding up towards the mountains Doc sat smoking his pipe on a big dead log not far from Stephanie. He loved the peacefulness of a morning like this. He could live around here. He could. Maybe when he closed this chapter of his life and finally shut off the phone he kept calling and sold his old house. He just might move here. Right here.

Stephanie spoke softly again about her doubts about whether she was doing the right thing or not. Doc scoffed at this. He'd not done the right thing a single time in his life. And he was proud of this. She coughed out a laugh.

They sat smoking quietly there in the morning dark and Stephanie might have done some crying but he would have none of that. He flipped on his cell phone and called his house one more time.

It rang and rang. He stared at it at arm's length. Then he shut it off. He lit another bowl of tobacco. That's all he had left. They smoked all his pot last night.

Maggie and Charley Younger were sleeping hard inside the van there just up a gravel road from the creek.

Everything was fine. Everything was great really. They were alive this morning and moving forward. Or soon moving forward.

They had to wait for the Greater Chattanooga Truck Service Company. They were on their way out as soon as they opened.

There along the gravel road, the van where Maggie and Charley Younger slept so soundly in, was up on cement blocks and the hubcaps, wheels, and its tires were completely gone.

Earlier, when Doc awoke and discovered this, he grinned broadly and said:

"Fucking Mexicans."

Milton

The four Mexican sheep looked up, their weapons of mass trimming, as their whirling nylon blades that cut down the superfluous ugly green and yellow weeds sprouting all over yet another dying industrial American town, went silent suddenly when the house across the street shook as if a bomb had gone off inside.

But it was no bomb. It was a fight. Two American beauties were going at it. Those Mexican landscapers didn't know their names were Stephanie and Nancy. They just knew they were two truly tall thin American *bellezas like in a movie,* one would tell the other as they watched. *A Quentin Tarentino movie. No,* the other one would say. He was an exiled world literature major from the National Pedagogic University of Mexico. *It was like the laundry room scene in* L'Germinal *by Zola,* he said. *What?* the other said.

They didn't know the names of these two *bellezas* but they knew there was a real fight going on in that house.

Behind the house, on the other side of another decrepit street where the pavement was as fractured and broken as any third world war zone, an ominous rusty red rectangular three-story tall factory as long as three American city blocks towered over the house and threatened soon to block out the sun.

The slumbering factory had only a few tilt out windows all along those three blocks, and three stained yellow smoke stacks on top of it billowed out thin trails of gray white smoke.

One of the *belleza's* heads shattered a picture window of the house. The Mexicans, who had dropped their gas-powered trimmers to their sides, jumped as the glass exploded and the head popped momentarily through it. They froze as the dark haired head was jerked back inside.

Those two bellezas were going at it pretty good, you know? One said.

Those two young attractive women had met from opposite directions at exactly the same time at exactly the same spot in front of the house. They were after exactly the same thing. The same possession. The wrong possession, as it would turn out, but the fight was not to be avoided.

The Mexicans should have gone on. Gone on with their Southern Illinois government subsidized destruction of weeds in the City of Granite's small parcel of land at the corner of Fifth and Lincoln. They should have minded their own business, attended to their chores, but there those two tall American women were, face to face, nose to nose, one in tight slightly faded designer jeans and tiny black tank top and the other in short cutoff blue jeans and snug yellow t-shirt, and as they could all see, there were sparks of fire at the ends of their long billowy hair.

The strong Midwestern wind not only blew their long billowy hair around, but also blew up the waves of angry pheromones that burned in the nostrils of those young Mexican men.

The Mexicans had all smelled it before. It was the smell before a cat fight.

Yes.

The only thing missing was a soundtrack.

A lonesome spaghetti western guitar mixed with the snakelike echo of dying cymbals rumbling.

Like, what did you just say, amigo? The other one said to the exiled world literature major. He shrugged.

What those two prototypes of American female volatility were fighting over was right there in the arms of the crazy woman in the backyard, they both wrongly believed. The crazy woman who often talked loudly to herself as the team of Mexicans mowed. Who hung clothes on the clothesline during a rainstorm. Who once got the mail and danced with the mailbox. For an hour or so.

Now that crazy woman sat at an old gray faded picnic table in the back with a little boy.

To one of the cat fighters the little boy was an odd deranged sort of obsession. He represented some bizarre belief in her that now her life was not a total disaster, but somehow that little boy represented some kind of freedom. Freedom, she believed, from the horrors that gnawed all around the periphery of her existence. This little boy would somehow bring a lifetime of abuse, mayhem and random killings to an utter stop. The demons in her pretty little serial killing head would end and she could bring this little boy to daycare every day for 150 dollars a week at the Granite City Kinder Care on 2nd and Jefferson. It was right on her way to work.

Nancy had already looked into it. In fact, Nancy had already put down a fifty dollar deposit and listed the boy's name as Jerry. Her son.

Stephanie, on the other hand, had more grounded reasons anyway. The biggest one being that Jeremiah was her son and she hadn't seen him for probably a year now. And she felt, at least at this moment in time, her head was on straight. Now that she had found out she hadn't killed Tony. Now that Lucy, down at the Main Street Diner, where Stephanie used to work, told her the whole story, more or less, as they sat at a table just across where Nancy sat, on her break from working at the very same diner.

And what about Stephanie getting her old job back? Well, okay, yeah, Lucy said. We just hired Maria though, who couldn't speak American too much but the locals loved her. (Big boob gesture.) People came and went all the time, you know? Stephanie looked around the diner. She looked right through Nancy, who sat very close by listening to it all.

Anyway, Stephanie planned to take Jeremiah back to Florida with her. Back to live with her right there next to Doc and Charley Younger. Yes. Stephanie, as she bristled and puffed up there in front of her mother's house, saw her future with a dusty sort of clarity really.

Unfortunately for all involved that boy Stephanie's mother held was not Jeremiah.

Another window in the house broke. What a fight.

Stephanie dug her nails into Nancy's shoulder blades through a mass of black hair.

Nancy screamed so loud and wretchedly the Mexicans jumped again and so did Stephanie's crazy mother in the backyard. (And did Lucy back at the diner, know anything about Stephanie's little Jeremiah? Well, yeah, Lucy thought her mother had Jeremiah. It'd been awhile, she had to admit. Maybe a year now since Lucy had heard anything. I mean come on, Lucy had moved to Belleville going on six months now.)

The crazy woman, Stephanie's mother, in the back jumped so severely at the scream it startled the little boy she held and he let out a yell of his own. And then he commenced to crying.

Stephanie's mother told little Tony it was okay. It was just the neighbors.

Even though there were no neighbors anymore. Outside of the Mexies who did yard work for the city, she was the last one on this dead block.

Yes, the little boy's name was Tony and yes, he was named after the blind and now dead Tony. Because he was Tony, Jr., conceived as his mother, Stephanie's sister, bent over a Saturn in the back of a titty bar in Sauget just weeks before Stephanie shot Tony blind and crippled and left town on a Greyhound bus.

But these two little boys, Tony Jr. and Jeremiah, weren't even the same age. If those two women in the catfight inside would have just noticed.

They didn't.

No, Nancy and Stephanie were bloodying each other over little Jeremiah, who wasn't even in the backyard.

And little Tony Jr's mother? Stephanie's sister?

She was drinking mid-afternoon shots of tequila as she shot pool two miles away in the Granite City Bar and Grill called Happy's.

She didn't leave her son with her mother much. Her mother had gotten, well, crazy, and even more so, forgetful.

But goddamn it all to hell, sometimes you just gotta get out of the house, you know?

Tin Roof Music

There was a flash of lightning behind the tool shed but the clouds moved elsewhere so they all decided to go fishing.

They sat on the wooden porch swing that faced the catalpa tree Seymour used to climb when he was little. They were looking north across where a field of asparagus that the Mexicans would come to pick shortly was. Rhonda's son couldn't touch the porch floor yet so he just swung his legs as he sat between them.

Up north, Rhonda said, it had rained a long time. It was the rainiest in years and that's why the floods came just a few weeks before Seymour came to town. This startled Seymour at first. He had forgotten all about how his uncle, and now his, farm was located in the Bottoms of southern Illinois. The Bottoms was the flood zone created by the little Wabash and the big Wabash and the Ohio rivers. The Bottoms stretched on thirty miles inland and back in 1937 before the WPA built a bunch of levees that flood left millions of people homeless. Did Rhonda know about this? Seymour was a historian and he even wrote a paper on it once, the '37 flood.

Of course Rhonda knew about it. She was born and raised in New Shawneetown and her grandfather, who was dead now, was one of the people who refused to move out of Old Shawneetown when the government offered to move his house three miles away to New Shawneetown back in the forties. Her grandfather stayed put. Even though he had a free lot waiting for him up in New Shawneetown and thanks to Roosevelt's New Deal, the government would move him, his family, and his small brick house there for free.

But Rhonda's grandfather didn't move. He didn't want to move. He died in that house in 1992 and smoked rolled cigarettes in the attic and cussed during each of the four or five times his property was flooded in those fifty years. He stayed put though. And they built an even bigger levee in Old Shawneetown there where it always crested along the Ohio River.

Now Old Shawneetown only had about two hundred residents and a couple biker bars. Two thousand or so people lived in New Shawneetown three miles away.

"It was a pretty good flood, this last one," Rhonda said. "It hadn't flooded this bad in forever."

As Rhonda talked about it all Seymour recalled a black and white photo of his Uncle Bud, in overalls, in a Jon boat just off the porch of this farmhouse. The land around the farmhouse was covered in water. His uncle was smiling though. His uncle was always smiling. He made the best of everything.

Fishing sounded like a good idea.

Rhonda drove. Seymour pointed out a cat running and stopping nervously in an empty field. The little boy's mouth opened wide as he looked at the cat. He was a good kid. Quiet, but a good kid.

It still amazed Seymour that all of these sporadic farms that dotted the flat, minimal landscape here in southern Illinois were all emptying out. People don't know how to make a living on those farms anymore, Rhonda said, as she drove. She laughed.

"It's too much work," she said. "People don't want to work hard today."

And that was true.

A novel idea hit Seymour suddenly.

"Why don't they just let the Mexicans move here?" It was rich, fertile farmland and if you put your house up off the ground like his uncle did in the 20's, then you could make a decent living. Maybe.

Rhonda laughed. Then she went, "Hmm." Then she said the Bottoms were dying. Or already dead. Seymour stared off at an old farmhouse and half fallen in barn. It might be true.

Rhonda took them off the blacktop and down a dusty gravel road. There were trees for a while on both sides of the road and then the trees opened up to empty bottom flatlands again.

She pulled the car up to a small concrete bridge that seemed to cross just a ditch really.

It *was* a ditch, she said. But a deep drainage ditch.

This is where they would fish. The ditch, for maybe a mile, was filled with fish. River fish. Catfish and sturgeons, blue gill, crappie, and big ugly carp. She pointed. A big brown fin moved in the middle of the ditch water. Their eyes widened.

This was a backwater ditch. The Wabash was just up the road. See that line of trees? That was the Wabash on the other side of those trees and whenever it flooded the backwater trapped fish from the river when the water receded.

The fish would have to work hard to get back to where the ditch finally drained into the river but river fish weren't that smart so in a few weeks they would just die belly up in the oxygen depleted water and then there would be an awful stench along this ditch.

"We can catch all we want before that happens," Rhonda said.

And they did. They found an open place down a ways from the bridge. They sat in wooden folding chairs and used cane poles from the tool shed. Earlier, Rhonda and her son dug up worms from a moist area behind the farm pond.

Rhonda was a little worried that the string was rotten since these cane poles hadn't been used for twenty years or so but evidently nylon didn't rot. Only once did a line break.

They caught more than they could eat in less than an hour. They barely had to put but a whiff of a worm on the hook and jerk! They had a fish.

The boy laughed so much his stomach hurt.

It had rained earlier in the day and fish always bit well after a rain, but these fish were starving anyway, Rhonda said.

She had to take nearly all the fish off the hooks. The little boy's hands were too small and Seymour didn't have a clue. Especially when they swallowed the hook completely, as many of these starving fish did.

They caught five crappie, seven blue catfish, a half a dozen fiddler catfish, too many blue gill to count (they only kept the hand sized ones), and they threw back all the carp.

Seymour and the boy had the times of their lives.

Rhonda was a genius. She knew the Bottoms and what backwater was. And she knew the best place to catch these backwater fish.

When they were done Seymour sat on his porch swing and watched Rhonda methodically clean the fish. Her son fell hard asleep against Seymour so he took him inside.

Rhonda used a large flat piece of wood from the barn and after turning over two round tin tubs she used two very sharp knives and cleaned all the fish.

She tossed the fins and the guts and such in a bucket.

She told Seymour to bring out that big blue speckled pot under the sink.

He did so.

Each fish she cleaned went into the pot. She would shortly fill it with salt water to take the fishy taste out of the fish.

Then she would fry them up tonight too because they just didn't have enough room in the tiny freezer in that old refrigerator anyway.

They ate them all. The crappie were particularly tasty, Seymour thought, but Rhonda wouldn't let her son eat any of the crappie or blue gill because there were too many little bones in them. But he loved the catfish anyway. Rhonda meticulously picked the piping hot white catfish off the bone and piled it on his plate.

They had fried potatoes and a can of corn and a six-pack of Coronas with lime.

No, it probably wasn't Seymour's favorite fancy beer, Rhonda decided when she bought it, but they didn't have much else to choose from at Big John's grocery in Eldorado when she was there yesterday. Seymour smiled. They were just fine.

Lightning flashed again, and thunder rumbled as a soft rain began to blanket the tin roof as Seymour eased himself over and onto and into Rhonda later that evening.

But Rhonda had fallen asleep. She was beat.

Seymour eased out and off of this beautiful earthy naked woman and stared briefly at the gray damp window and then looked straight up into the blackness of the bedroom.

The rain on the tin roof sounded good to him finally. It had taken awhile for this. It had scared him when he first moved in and then for a while it annoyed him but now it sounded so good to him he compared it to music as he lay there. Tin roof music.

Still he was close to hyperventilating again. He needed to get started on his book about, let's see, what was he planning to write a book on shortly? Robinson Jeffers. Yes, he had found a book about an environmental poet named Robinson Jeffers who protested World War II.

So that would be his next book, Seymour decided, as he lay there, his penis going limp. He would write a historical account of the environmental movement from the perspective of radical artists. Since the 1940s, starting with Robinson Jeffers.

Yes. His previous two books tanked but then history books from obscure historians always do.

He needed to get a teaching job also. Seymour closed his eyes and let the tin music slow his heart rate.

Then when he was relaxed he stared at the blackness again and he did this for a long time and then finally Seymour Belmo, badly out of his element, went to sleep.

Back to Venice

Just south of Granite City, just three miles actually from the mother of all cat fights taking place in a house across from the closed down Granite City Tool and Glass Company, there was a little town called Venice. Venice, Illinois. Another dying little town in southern Illinois that once used to thrive alive with middle class prosperity, but now it was a drug infested, weedy old stretch of town that in a matter of thirty years, went from twenty percent African Americans to now well over 90 per cent African Americans. And most of them were unemployed. And most of them didn't care if Obama was in office or not. Hope, along with the jobs, left a long time ago and now Venice couldn't even pay the Mexies to cut the weeds. A Chinese restaurant, a barbecue joint that wasn't open but two days a week and two bars with thick black bars on the doors and windows were all that made up downtown Venice now.

But there on the north edge of Venice, where a stretch of brick homes still remained intact and, for the most part, still had mowed lawns and flowers along the front, an old white man and a crippled dude poured gasoline around the perimeter of one of the houses. Reluctantly the old man broke out each window and poured some gasoline in those too. Gasoline just around the periphery of a brick house may not burn much of anything. It took these two awhile to do this.

Then the crippled dude went out in front of a van and sat in a lawn chair and waited. He was told to wait exactly twenty minutes. Then he would ignite the gas and run back to the van.

In the middle of the street a pretty girl in tight shorts and an even tighter tank top chattered on a cell phone as rapid and inconsequential as anyone like her might do so while standing just outside the food court of some big mall.

She was speaking to someone named Sonny. That girl was Maggie. She told the man on the phone he was full of shit if she planned to go to work for some *Addy Valdez* in the newly created Latino division of some big-ass publishing company. Totally full of shit! She yelled into the phone. It didn't matter if Black Comanche was really a Mexican Indian! THAT WASN'T THE POINT OF THE FUCKING NOVEL, SONNY, YOU DUMBASS!

Then, after sniffling and few times and working very hard, it seemed like, to gather herself, Maggie asked the cell phone very quietly but firmly if somehow Sonny didn't still love her just a little.

Silence.

She eased into a rabid moan into the phone.

Back in the Arms of the Lord

Marty Robbins, greatest of all country music singers in the last century (if you exclude a couple hundred others), hero entertainer to the likes of Merle Haggard, Pete Townshend, and Johnny Cash, was not only a great country troubadour but also the first person to get banned from the Grand Ole Opry for bringing a trumpet player into the house (evidently, as many of those kind often said, the trumpet was not a country instrument, but a nigger instrument). In addition to all that, the great Marty Robbins was also a successful racecar driver and the first person to undergo triple bypass heart surgery in 1969 (about 25 years before Lipitor).

But of what interest is Marty Robbins to the ending to *As God Looked On?*

Asleep in the arms of the Lord . . .

Gleaned straight from the "Ballad of the Alamo," the greatest religious ballad in all cinematic cowboy history, the late great Marty Robbins sang the most ambiguously humanistic religious refrain of any lyric of its kind. Everyone who died at the Alamo was, as the credits rolled by:

Asleep in the arms of the Lord . . .

There's a Lord all right but the concept of eternal sleep is a humanist one. Thank you, Marty Robbins.

(Can't you see all those Christians sleeping like little babies for all eternity and the Creator pointing to his kind with his finger up to his ecclesiastical lips with a SHHH . . . don't wake them up, Man. It's their reward . . . They asked for it . . . The party's going on in the next room.)

But Charley Younger wasn't thinking about any of that as he lay curled fetal at the end of the long gravel with the grass in the middle driveway that led up to Seymour's old southern Illinois farm house.

Asleep in the arms of the Lord . . .

It was this bizarre re-enactment of the ending to the movie the Alamo that had sent Charley Younger catatonic there in front of Doc's van.

Asleep in the arms of the Lord . . .

It's all Charley Younger could hear. He had watched that movie a hundred times and counting (a hundred and three times to be more exact) and here it was. This was a modern reenactment of the ending he was always dreaming of. The greatest ending to the greatest movie of all time and now he was near comatose on the ground.

Asleep in the arms of the Lord . . . .

The Catfight continued . . .

Well into the afternoon and to hell if their *patróns* got on them. The workers were the first to congregate around the house and then they came in threes and then tens, and shortly hundreds, from all over the town, all over the area, from miles around, they were all around the periphery of the house pushing themselves up to look inside and shaking their heads and whispering and more head shaking.

They climbed on the roof. They helped each other look inside. They held each other to keep from falling for just a glimpse inside.

It was one hell of a fight going on inside that house. One of the *bellezas* had pulled so much hair out of the head of the other, it was wrapped around her wrist and her fist. Blood bloomed everywhere on both of them. The dark haired one had broken the nose of the light haired one. It didn't slow her down one bit. She leaped up and pulled the dark haired one down literally out of the air and with just her foot broke the other's ribs. The crack of those lithe, strong ribs could be heard for miles. It hardly fazed the raven haired *belleza*.

It was something. They should call 911, someone whispered. They all just looked at each other. They couldn't call 911. They were all illegals. That's right. Illegals knew only to use 911 to say one thing (it was a long standing inside joke):

Hello 911 operator.

Can I help you?

mi viaje aquí (my ride's here).

A Cause Defined

And it was, *hombre*. Those two *bellezas* in there, those two Zola French women in the laundry house in Northern France smack dab in the pre-industrialized age of fear, it was all about the human condition, or more truly the class struggles of humanity as they fight for their rights in a system of misery and oppression, dude. Yes, it was titillating all right, like that naturalistic 19th century breast exposed, a touch of blood for nice lovely color, look at the raven haired *belleza*, the craziest *belleza*, look in through that dirty old window at her tight jeans slashed open so bad her pink little undies glowed radioactive, but they were fighting for something, a cause, our cause, *hombre*. Those two are true blue Mexican *soldaderas*, *Adelitas,* each one. Go run now, spread it to each and every one what these two *soldaderas* are fighting for, dude, our cause *hombre*, and it's all about territory, this was down to the basics, the basics of a revolution, this country here right now is dead, man, this country is ours, this is our America now, stinking of decay and dead ends and the picture needs some color added, you know, like our restaurants, man, splash the gray. We are nowhere, nowhere near the sea of Cortez, that bloody Spaniard bastard, nowhere near the never-ending fields of corn (They were just up the road actually), nowhere near the salad fucking days I read about it in the American magazines when I rode my bike to the library in Oaxaca, this here is two *soldadera* cats spirally conquering hate and death, this is four Spanish tanned sinewy lean legs entangling, four sexy exclamation points of a cause defined.

But *amigo*, we haven't arrived with them yet. This is nowhere. We need better weapons than small gas engines turning spools of nylon. We need our numbers to swell as big and overpowering as they did when they passed through the white man gates at Ellis Island. We don't have to scrape together pesos to pay our way onto those Cortez ships and eat each other's shit for three months just to get our freedom. We just got to know how to swim or wade or run in the dark.

Fuck that nigger bitch white lady governor of Arizona. You think she's ate a clean meal since she passed her fucking law in her fancy Arizona country clubs or restaurants? Our brothers and sisters, the only people on this continent who can cook a decent meal, are taking care of that, dude, that wrinkled up mouthy old lady has ingested the piss and semen and sweat and spit of a cause defined.

Fuck, man.

Is that one belleza dead? Did that slam kill her?

Flames

It was burning now. Doc had instructed Charley Younger to dump the two red containers of gasoline from the van all around the foundation of the house then light a match and get back. Charley Younger lit the gas with a wooden match. It took him several tries. You know the story of his thumb-less hands. Nothing was easy. But he got it lit.

Doc stood outside on the porch for a while. He tapped his home phone number into his cell phone. It was set to 'speed dial A' on his old cell phone.

Doc listened carefully. Through the living room wall he heard the ringing.

It was the real phone ringing. There was still the same beige with gray buttons phones he bought new in 1981. One was in the living room and the other in the bedroom.

His wife didn't answer. Of course she didn't answer. Weeds grew all around the house and in the yard now. The old man who used to mow the lawn, who lived next door, was too old to trim anymore.

Doc smiled. When he lived here he didn't trim very well either. His wife trailed behind him and finished the job.

Doc noticed how old everything was now. Dirt and dust and dead bugs were thick in the corners of the old aluminum overhangs on all the windows.

Doc wasn't smiling anymore. He loved this house. He loved those old overhanging awnings that were noisy when it rained. A lot of people in the 70s loved those old aluminum awnings. All they did really was block out the shade trees now.

He fought an impulse to dial one last time.

Instead he went inside and let flames engulf him as he sat in a folding chair in the living room. He lit his last Cuban cigar and crossed his legs. It was how he had planned to end it all someday all along.

Ellis Island

Columbus may have sailed the ocean blue in 1492 but it was in 1892 the most important plank was dropped on American soil. And who was the very first person to cross that plank?

Annie Moore!

Annie Moore, a fourteen-year-old lass from the county of Cork in Ireland, accompanied by her stuttering dyslexic brother Anthony, and her rather dimwitted other brother, Phillip, became the first people to be processed at the most famous immigration station in the history of America. Ellis Island.

For all you history buffs out there, the very last person to be processed at Ellis Island, after the Republicans had passed obscenely strict immigration laws that reduced the flow of 12 million immigrants into America to a trickle, was a drunken Norwegian sailor named Arnie Peterson. Arnie, after drinking himself silly in a pub in New Jersey on the evening of November 18th, 1954, passed out and missed his tramp steamer back to Norway. By Arnie's account, the Captain, an angry ex-member of *Arbeidernes Kommunistparti,* the Norwegian Communist party, did not wait very long . . .

Arnie Peterson, the very last recorded immigrant to be processed, also uttered the last recorded words of an immigrant passing into America through Ellis Island. He uttered:

"Are there any other Norwegians in America?"

Mildred Feinstein, the last worker to record and document the last immigrant to ever cross into America via Ellis island, after reflecting on her ten-year tenure there, replied, "Not that many really."

Ah, but way back before then, back in 1892, five hundred years after Columbus sailed the ocean blue, Annie Moore would be the first of over twelve million souls who would pass through this island spigot and into a new life.

When Annie, in her peasant's scarf and long button up dress and high black laced boots demurely walked down that plank the Governor of New York, along with many others, were waiting for her. There was a band with a tuba playing.

They were waiting for her with something special. Something that would mark this historic event appropriately.

The Governor handed Annie a shiny brand new ten-dollar gold coin. Incandescent light bulbs popped off like fireworks. It made her brothers cower. She just stared at the coin in her palm like it was magic.

Annie, if myth had it correctly, would place this beautiful shiny gold piece under her pillow every night, and thank the Lord God Above each and every night of her remaining existence, for bringing her to this incredible new world.

Every single night until she would pass away.

Well, that's not how it happened. The truth always trumps fiction any day. So let's do the math . . . Annie was homeless and she had no money whatsoever when she crossed over into America. She also had two younger brothers, who weren't exactly skilled labor potential, to take care of. Yes. By today's standards, that gold coin would be worth about 5 thousand dollars in 1892.

Annie cashed that gold coin in faster than a New York minute.

As anyone would have done. Bless her heart.

While it was a momentous time there on that island back in 1892, America would lose track of Annie about as quickly as she had traded gold for paper.

There were reports, decades later, that Annie had married some German fish market owner just two blocks away and had eleven kids by him before she hit thirty. (Right. Travel three months on a freighter to the new land and marry a German fishmonger two blocks away . . . Please.) There was also another report of an Annie Moore who died in Fort Worth, Texas in 1924. (Right. Everyone knows there are no Irish in Texas . . . These were, no doubt, the same people reporting her putting five thousand dollars under her pillow every night and thanking the Lord.)

No, the real Annie Moore took her money and did what many of the Irish, still reeling from the effects of the potato famine a hundred years previous did when they hit American soil: She ran.

She ran from an Ireland that had, in the span of two hundred years, become almost ninety-seven percent Catholic and thus, predominantly dirt poor and continually told God wanted big families so fuck away and keep the kids, *hombre*. It was the sanctity and blessed nature of life.

Annie Moore left and when the teller handed her all that paper money she lit out of New York by horse and buggy so fast, she didn't even remember crossing the Brooklyn Bridge. (No, I didn't, she later told to her husband. You had to. It was the only way across that way. I swear, I didn't. I would have remembered . . .)

Annie Moore drove that horse and buggy so fast through the eastern states and part of the southern states she swore she never slept a wink for five long weeks. Not one wink.

But she knew where she was going. The Catholics may have taken over her country and the potatoes may have killed most of them off when they came up rotten, but it was her Gaelic background that spoke to her heart. It was a Gaelic song of contentment that was the siren that would lead her to where she was going. Frankly, at first Annie wasn't exactly sure where it was she was going, but as the Chinese say . . . if you don't know where you're going, any road will take you there.

And she was going. And she was following the song of her Gaelic heart.

Where the two rivers meet in the heart of the land
Where the two rivers meet in the heart of the land
I'll carry my Gnáthóg Aingeal (two angels)
And pitch a sacred tent under Ancamma's hand . . .

Ancamma was the Gaelic God of water. As abruptly as Annie had plowed off into the heart of America, she stopped finally. Right in the heart of America. Right on a bluff overlooking where two great rivers met. The Wabash and the Ohio.

Annie Moore had arrived.

A Haiku Family

No, Doc and Charley Younger didn't burn up Doc's house. That was all metaphor, dear reader. That all happened in Charley Younger's head. On the road trip up to find Stephanie's son and extend their haiku family even further Charley Younger listened to Doc talk and talk about his wife and his house and how Doc threatened to burn it all to the ground and there was these red plastic gas containers in the van so Charley Younger imagined a big fire that would finally get Doc off the subject of his dead wife. And then they could all move on.

But nothing was burning. It was worse than that. Charley Younger was curled tightly in the big passenger's seat of the van with his fists tight and his fingers buried deep in his palms. His head rested against the window as he stared at Doc's old house in Venice, Illinois. The house was a fairly small rectangular house and it did have those old aluminum shutters on the windows. A rusting, gray metal fence surrounded the house.

It clouded up suddenly and began to rain a bit. Charley Younger tapped a button and the window eased down a couple inches and sure enough. The rain hit the shutters with a noisy thud like distant gunfire. Charley Younger could never actually recall hearing distant gunfire but that is how Doc described the sound of rain on aluminum shutters and that seemed right.

The rain didn't stop the pretty Maggie from standing outside the van in the deserted street and talking on the phone. She was again talking to someone named Sonny. And when she wasn't talking to Sonny she was on the phone talking to her sister or mother about Sonny. She liked to talk on the phone.

What was worse though than burning down the house was Doc.

When he got to the house he was having trouble breathing. Charley Younger thought maybe he was having a heart attack or something and he asked Doc if he was all right.

Doc smiled at this as he stared down a street he had lived on for almost forty-two years. No one, Doc said, who had been in this van lately was all right. This made Charley Younger smile also.

Doc was just upset. He was home again for the first time since leaving for Florida and his wife would not greet him at the door. He stared a moment down the street and could not bring himself to look towards the house. His eyes stayed on the street.

Then Doc began to cry. It was a low cry at first and then slowly it became a very horrible sounding cry that made Charley Younger dig his fingernails deeper into his palm and the blood came even heavier and he closed his squinty eyes even more and pressed even harder against the rain splattered window.

There was nothing worse, Charley Younger decided, than hearing such an old man cry. Charley Younger closed his eyes. Doc kept crying and when Charley Younger thought he was about to stop crying Doc would roll out another round of low growling cries.

Maybe this was good. Maybe Doc was getting it out of his system and then shortly they would all head back to Daytona Beach Shores to the only island trailer park in the world and Charley Younger could clean the trailer and Doc would come over and they would play chess and twice a week Stephanie would come in and sleep in her room and they would all watch old movies together sometimes and she would fall asleep and he would stare at her pretty face just a moment and this is what Jeremiah had called a haiku family.

Jeremiah, after taking a college class one time studied haikus and he said he had an assignment to write a haiku. He only wrote one. It was about how Charley Younger and Jeremiah had the smallest family there ever was:

> *Our house has Charley Younger and me*
> *There ain't no one else*
> *It's just a haiku family*

Jeremiah had thought this was a funny haiku poem but Charley Younger didn't. It would stick with him. Jeremiah called Charley Younger family. When Jeremiah died Charley Younger kept hearing this poem in his head. It was all the family Charley Younger had. And everyone needs family. The Chinese family considered Charley Younger part of some weird extended family and they would take him back to work since no one did his work better. And that was good.

But Jeremiah was Charley Younger's family. And he was gone now.

Charley Younger thought about telling Doc about the haiku family poem but he didn't. He wouldn't understand probably.

Doc stopped crying finally. They just sat there silently in the van for a while.

All they could hear was the rain thudding on the aluminum shutters and occasionally Maggie's excited voice cursing at someone or something again.

As God Looked On   251

Finally, Doc said, "I think we can go home now."

In his dull, deadpan, retarded voice Charley Younger said, "I'm all over that."

Doc started the van.

Chopper 5

The Mexicans came from all around to the house. They piled into busses and old pickups all along Cherokee Street in St. Louis and from the plains as far away as Indiana. They crawled off roofs and ladders and put down their rags and stopped doing dishes. There was something more important to attend to at this very moment. Two *soldaderas* fighting it out in the house in Granite City.

That something was history.

Oblivious to the Mexicans was the *thud-thud-thud-thud-thud* of Chopper 5 high above them.

Chopper 5 was reporting it all. A thousand, no five thousand, Chopper 5 reported. (Or were there just over a hundred?)

But it was a sight to be beheld, they said. Something was going on in that house and what did they hear being shouted out?

Soldaderas!

Soldaderas!

Google it for God's sake, Larry, the news chopper driver said. You got the damn smart phone. I don't know how to spell it. I just heard it. I heard it again! Look down there!

Freedom fighters from the Mexican Revolution. Female freedom fighters. Women who were excluded from the Mexican history books by a chauvinistic, patriarchal church-led government but kept alive through the oral history of every generation of Mexicans since.

Soldaderas fought as hard as their male counterparts and some believed even harder.

Google it yourself. *Soldaderas*!

Like piles of worker ants, the Mexicans poured into the yard there in Granite City from all directions and formed orderly lines to get their six-second view inside the windows of history.

The two *soldaderas* were going at it like mad women. Slamming each other into walls, ripping out hair, gouging eyes, breaking ribs and limbs, running maniacally at each other and colliding with such force the house shook Mexicans off the roof. End tables and two coffee tables were smashed like matchsticks. One had to pull both feet from another window, glass flying everywhere.

Thud-thud-thud-thud-thud . . .

It can't be but they were doing it. There were white robed priests (?) hanging from every window into that living room giving each Mexican, as they came to peer in, a wafer.

The Bread of Christ.

History was being made. Even though one was Cuban-Chinese and the other Irish.

Those two *soldaderas*, bloodied and worn down were fighting for, as would be told around the campfires as far down as Argentina in the years to come, the freedom for their people.

The freedom of people to live.

The freedom of people to live wherever they wanted to live.

Amen.

Myths

Someone even called in a Mariachi band but when they got to that house in Granite City the mass of Mexicans were starting to leave. (And besides, the stupid gringo guitar player from the Central West End, who was filling in, couldn't get a cab to take him across the river anyway.)

So they just stood there with their *sombreros* on, instruments ready as the crowd began to leave. One started to play and the others frowned him down. But they all knew something was up. Something serious was in the air. They didn't have to be told anything. They may only be a parttime Mariachi band but they weren't born yesterday.

The fabric pulled over the mattress of history was right in front of them.

Inside that house had raged the Mexican battle of the new millennium. Two *Soldaderas* had stood up to and fought savagely against what else? American Oppression and Imperialism.

The people of the new American millennium now had a new battle cry, a unifying rage against a brutal machine! Soldaderas!

It was how myths were made.

And the Winner Is . . .

What actually happened was Stephanie, on top and straddling a savagely beaten and bleeding Nancy, herself equally beaten and bleeding, had finally won.

There was absolutely no strength left in Nancy to continue. And very little in Stephanie for that matter. Cushion stuffing from old cheap 70s furniture floated thick and light in the air. Sunlight streaming through one of the broken windows made the stuffing glisten. All three lamps had been shattered and one was throwing off sparks. Every window had been destroyed.

None of the two paintings, one of dogs playing poker, and the other of a sad but beautiful Jesus, were still on the wall. Smashed and shattered.

A hardback copy of a Bible was teetering half inside the smashed in glass of a 20 inch Zenith console television. (Several Mexicans, with their cell phone cameras, made a point to take a picture of the bible sticking out of the television. It seemed important and was immediately put on YouTube.)

For a moment Stephanie eased herself down to lay atop Nancy breast to breast. Their mouths almost touched. Nancy had a fillet knife in her hand. Stephanie had Nancy's arm pinned down though. When Stephanie caught her breath and her strength returned enough she planned to take the knife out of Nancy's hand and bury it in Nancy's chest.

Nancy figured as much. She had lost. Fair and square. Slowly, ever so slowly, since her index finger was so badly broken bone stuck out, Nancy moved the blade of the knife the reverse of how she had been holding it. She offered it to Stephanie.

"Jerry's your baby, ain't he?" Nancy said.

Stephanie started to say something, but couldn't at first. She managed a swallow.

"Jeremiah," she said.

"You win," Nancy said.

Slowly, Stephanie eased herself off of Nancy. They ended up side by side, on their backs, wincing in pain and seemingly barely breathing.

There was a strange silence for a moment in the house. All the Mexicans, at least, had gone.

Then someone spoke. It was male voice. It was Nancy's pet friend.

"Nancy," the voice said. "You think maybe we outta go home now?"

The Old Man and the Donkey

Seymour had his two lists made for the day. One was for the things he had to do around the farm and the other was for ideas he had for writing a history book about the immigration experience.

He had decided to write about the immigration experience out of a certain naivety about it all, but after seeing the rows of Mexicans bending over for hours at a time on both sides of the road leading up to his farm he had come to his epiphany about his new book.

And then when he went for a long walk and ran into that elderly lady who lived on a ghost of a farm about a mile down the road who claimed to be Annie Moore and who also claimed to be over a hundred and thirty years old and how she was really just a ghost when you stopped and thought about it because there was someone coming soon that she could pass the torch to.

The torch?

Yes, the torch, the old lady who claimed to be Annie Moore said.

Seymour offhandedly Googled Annie Moore later that evening.

The coincidences Seymour was seeing after spending several hours reading about Annie Moore and the Mexicans out front were just too many.

He was a historian after all. Or so he believed.

So Seymour had his two lists ready for the day.

Out the window the blue and white bus at the end of the road startled him again. It had been there before, but regardless, each morning, it seemed out of place on this his farm.

But it was just the bus that brought the immigrant workers to pick asparagus.

There was also an old donkey tied to a fencepost halfway down his long driveway but that never startled him anymore.

The donkey was named Legion. It belonged to an old man who came every third Wednesday of every month to fish in Seymour's pond and, the old man said, to seine for crawfish.

The old man was named Henry. The crawfish, he said, he would use to fish for catfish in the Little Wabash River. Henry was pushing ninety and had been a very good friend of Seymour's Uncle Bud. They used to go fishing together all the time and once in a while they would stop in a bar in Shawneetown for a shot or two of whiskey.

Occasionally Henry, on his way to the pond, would forget that

Seymour's Uncle Bud was dead.

"I'll catch him next time," Henry would say.

"You bet," Seymour would say.

At first Seymour didn't know why Henry brought the donkey, but after a while he figured it was to steady Henry on his walk to Seymour's farm. It was about a half a mile walk.

Henry told him one time he used to ride the donkey to the post in the middle of Seymour's driveway and that he used to come every single week for many years but now he wasn't able to get on the donkey so he only came once a month.

Henry had a very large head, enormous ears, large bulbous hands and fingers and his body had shrunk up to about a four and a half foot frail frame. His skin was so pale and white as to be near translucent. His eyes appeared to be peering out of tiny black holes. It was as if gravity and his swelling appendages were slowly pulling Henry to his death.

Seymour took a deep breath as he looked out his window at his front yard and the bent over Mexicans picking asparagus and the donkey tied to a post halfway up his driveway. Sometimes he would almost have a panic attack over this new life of his.

He took another deep breath.

Rhonda would be home from work at the bank soon. She would first pick up her son who stayed with her mother most days when Rhonda worked. Then she would stop at the grocery store probably. She had sent him a text earlier that she wanted him to grill hamburgers this evening. That sounded good.

Seymour enjoyed Rhonda's company. Her little boy was a very sweet kid. He was well-behaved and a little too quiet but Seymour had been a quiet kid also so he didn't think it was worth worrying about like Rhonda did sometimes.

Seymour would find it very hard to leave Rhonda now. He thought about it once in a while and occasionally he would find some distant teaching job on the Internet but he was growing attached to this minimal fucking farm even. This farm from his childhood. This farm that, at the moment, still didn't have an indoor toilet.

He was working on that. Seymour had on his list to call someone in Eldorado about an estimate for a septic tank installation. That had to come first, Rhonda said.

He was working on this. Rhonda had said they probably only had room for a shower and a toilet but that would be wonderful.

Yes, it would be.

An Ice Cold Sombrero

The rusted old van rattled and moaned as it wound slowly down that broken street in Granite City like it was on its last gas-combusted breath. It wasn't. It creaked and coughed to a stop in front of the house it had dropped Stephanie off at earlier in the day. She told them to leave for a few hours.

A crippled man stepped out first and looked around. Then he held one of his bloody palms in the other, leaned against the fender and stared down and became a crippled person still-life.

An old man in bright yellow Bermuda shorts and a black Brian Jonestown Massacre t-shirt hopped out next. He nodded as he looked around. Something odd had gone on in that house since he dropped Stephanie off and they spent the last few hours at the Fairview Heights Mall. (He bought himself a new Tablet. He always wanted one. They had an Android on sale at Sears. He had no idea if it was a good one or not. It looked cool though. It was blue. When he got back to Daytona he would have to get his wireless hooked up right). The old man wound his way around the front of the van and hiked his pants up and nodded as he stared at the house. Every goddamn window was broken in that house now. They weren't when he left. Jesus Christ.

There was also a huge bright white sombrero on the front step of that house. It was about as big around as a hula-hoop and as tall as two stacked big coolers. This was odd. A couple of moments would pass and before the old man would step inside and carry Stephanie back to the van. He would kick the sombrero out of the way and son of bitch. That sombrero was cold. Colder than death. Seriously. He didn't know what to make of this. He soon forgot the ice-cold sombrero completely.

Broken Things

Stephanie's mother eased into the house after everything had settled down and she couldn't hear things breaking. She held the little boy half over one shoulder. He played with a small blue rubber bus. He drove the bus over her bony shoulder blade. She walked gingerly over broken things. Her face slowly eased into pain as she stopped and squinted as she stared down at her daughter. She asked her if she was okay.

Stephanie coughed weakly. So weakly it came out as a small breath. "Not exactly," she said. She stared at the boy. It wasn't Jeremiah. During the ass-kicking they had both given each other Stephanie caught glimpses of the boy through the open kitchen door. It came to her finally.

Jeremiah wasn't in this house. Her mother slowly looked at the boy, then back at Stephanie. She kind of figured out Stephanie at first thought this was her son and not her sister's. Her mother could do nothing but stare through Stephanie at this realization. Stephanie knew her mother and this look wasn't a good thing. And of course her mother couldn't tell her the truth. Couldn't tell her that little Jeremiah, not a day after Stephanie left Granite City on a Greyhound Bus, was taken away by Tony's mother. No. She didn't have the heart to tell her daughter that her biggest battle was yet to come. Her mother said something else. She was just wondering if Stephanie would help her clean up her house.

Yes, she would.

Then Stephanie's one eye that wasn't blurry locked on the one thing that hadn't completely been knocked off the wall of this room. It was on the wall just over her mother. It actually had been jarred loose and flew so high it hit the ceiling and then managed by some miracle to find a hook hanging on the wall that caught the little cord behind it and kept it on the wall. Upside down.

It was a clock. The time had been turned upside down also.

It wasn't the real time.

But the clock read 9:35 in upside down time.

Stephanie's non-blurry eye went wide. She knew where her son was now. No one had to tell her.

Frida Kahlo

Is the greatest Mexican artist of all time. She was all Gabby Valdez, captive legal Mexican immigrant, could think of as she stood in the Mexican line on the west side of the soon to be historical driveway. Resilience over affliction. That was this new *soldadera* and what was happening was epic. The new Frida Kahlo. Who cared if this magical woman could draw? Her tiny long legs and broken yet beautiful face was now sailing with the wind down past Argentina and beyond. On the wings of Frida Kahlo. Who miscarried in Detroit and killed herself in the name of art and who smiled as her body eased through the crematorium. Frida Kahlo drew the breath-taking heart-aching "Henry Ford Hospital" (1932) and "My Nurse and I" (1937).

This beautiful strong woman, who needed help to put the little boy on the donkey, who marched proudly back down the gringo driveway with her boy on a donkey, as both lines of Mexicans, having risen from their bent-over asparagus picking postures and saluted just like at the Alamo, she was the new Frida Kahlo.

It would become the truth.

The Last Cigar

Oh, it came down rather quickly actually. There were a few clouds in the dull dry blue sky and they were getting darker by the minute. The chickens were stirring. They knew something was up.

And something was up.

The van pulled ever so slowly down the long L-shaped driveway with the thick green grass growing in between the big ruts that always bottomed out Seymour's Jetta.

The van stopped just behind the blue and white bus. Something was thick in the dry, Midwestern air. Something was about to happen.

Why else would a one hundred and thirty year old woman be sitting in a lawn chair in front of that blue and white bus facing the driveway with the donkey in it? This is where Stephanie had somehow told Doc how to get to. At least he thought it was the right place. Stephanie hadn't gotten out yet. If she even could get herself out.

Doc and Charley Younger got out and looked around. Even they could tell something was about to happen. Doc pulled two lawn chairs out of the back of the van. He and Charley Younger sat in them right next to the very very old woman. Doc asked her how she was doing.

She didn't take her eyes off the driveway. If she still had eyes. They were lost in a mass of snaky thick sunken wrinkles in a small round face. She looked downright dusty in the lawn chair. Except for the donkey there was nothing else going on really. And the donkey wasn't doing anything really either. There were Mexicans bent over and picking away on both sides of the driveway. A small boy lost in some play world on the porch of the old farmhouse was waving his arms and making motor noises.

"I'm about to die," the old woman said. Her voice was soft but strong.

Charley Younger and Doc looked at each other. Doc shrugged existentially. He took out the final cigar he had brought along just for this adventure. He knew he had saved it for something.

He flipped his silver dolphin lighter open. Lit his cigar.

Spotting

Rhonda put everything she got at the store away and then left out two *Dos Cervezas*, big ones, that they had on sale in the liquor department, and while she didn't really care for Mexican beer probably Seymour would like them. He seemed partial to expensive beer so she brought home usually anything she found on sale. She leaned hard against the kitchen table. Oh my she was tired. She was spotting today and her head hurt and there had to be a better way of dealing with people she worked with. There just had to be. Especially one in particular. And right now she wanted badly to have that indoor bathroom. They just had to get that in. She wanted a nice hot bath. She missed nice hot baths. She might even think of leaving Seymour to get a nice warm bath once in awhile. She laughed at this thought.

Rhonda straightened up suddenly. Someone was yelling.

The Donkey

Wind whistled loudly through the sparse trees behind Seymour's pond. Everything else was quiet. Yes. Once again the old man had walked home and left his donkey in the driveway. He would either have to walk it home as he had twice before or Seymour could leave it standing there as he had accidentally done in the past. The old man didn't give a shit one way or the other.

Something moved somewhere. Seymour looked around. He could not see the old man who used to know his uncle and was now so old he forgot his uncle was dead and occasionally left his donkey tied to a fence post along Seymour's driveway and walked home alone.

Jesus Christ.

The first time Seymour started to take the donkey home he stepped in a huge pile of donkey shit that was hidden in the grass.

Seymour jumped. He heard someone yelling.

(Remember the Alamo?)

The Mexicans all stooped over and lining both sides of the long driveway picking asparagus, straightened up. All together. They hadn't really noticed the old van pull up behind the blue and white bus and they noticed even less two people, and old man and a crippled man climbing out of the van first. But the *patrón* and his bus driver bodyguard did notice the two las niñas get out of the van. Especially the one who wasn't so beaten up, the one with a handful of paper in her arms. They were very interested, in fact.

The girl with the stack of paper in her arms was naked. Stark naked. The *patrón* stopped leaning against the bus alone with his iPhone, put the phone in his shirt pocket and smiled. The bus driver, who had stepped out of the bus, was also smiling. They muttered something between themselves.

It was the beat up *nina* who staggered some. The old man almost got out of his lawn chair. He asked her if she was all right. She was.

Until she let out a yell. Jimmy was at the opposite end of the driveway. In the front yard playing with an Iron Man doll and a water pistol.

That's when the Mexicans all rose up.

That's when they froze and all of them had already heard about the *soldadera*.

It was her.

Jimmy

Okay so as I saw it I don't remember a lot of it but it sure sounded like she was yelling my name. I didn't know her. But it sounded like my name anyway. It sounded real clear that it was my name. Seriously. I didn't know until I was grown that she was trying to yell Jeremiah! Jeremiah! Not, Jimmy! Jimmy! Because that was the name of her kid and all and my mom was just standing there, mouth open and I guess a little shocked by it all. The donkey, the Mexicans, and that naked girl had climbed on top of that old van and it was windy that day and the naked girl liked the wind because she was letting a few sheets of paper at a time fly out of her hands and those sheets of paper were almost like in the jet stream or something flying high into the air like those pieces of paper had wings and that made this naked girl real happy and I don't remember much what she was yelling but I do for some reason remember something she kept repeating. It was this:

"Not a fucking dime out of this one, Sonny! You cocksucker! Not a fucking dime!!"

It was weird, I tell you. And what was weirder about it, well, all kinds of things were weird about it. I thought the other girl was yelling Jimmy but her jaw was broke and her teeth were loose and her mouth was full of blood and that pretty girl limped down the driveway after me and I was clutching my mom's leg and also See Mee's leg. That lady was crazy yelling Jimmy! Jimmy! Jeremiah! Jeremiah! Wow.

But not a Mexican moved when they stood up. They became Mexican statues. That was pretty weird too. And I didn't notice it but my mom tells this story about that crippled guy and how he shot fifteen feet in the air and then landed on the ground totally completely catatonic when those Mexicans all rose up in unison because he had watched *The Alamo* so much and here was another ending he would later say it was exactly the real ending and come on now that's very weird but the weirdest thing was See Mee and how sad he looked. I've never seen him look so sad. His face had sunk down to around his chest he was so sad. You know when someone is really sad and shit man, he was the most sad I would ever see him.

And Mom noticed this too. She held his hand but that wasn't doing any good for nothing. They should be laughing about all this but Seymour wasn't. He was so sad he looked about to collapse. He looked so sad both my mom and me got worried. We should be laughing. This was all so damn funny. It was a quiet farm usually and now a naked girl sending paper flying high into the jet stream and a girl yelling my name and stumbling along like some drunk down the driveway towards the house. Did I tell you about the old man who just blew cigar smoke up into the jet stream? He didn't say anything but he would shake his head occasionally and blow smoke. And I had no idea if that was a scarecrow sitting next to him or some old woman. Yikes. And the Mexicans. Fuck.

But Seymour, man, he wasn't laughing. Not laughing at all. Mom and me really got worried when we saw his body shake when he tried to sigh. There were tears in his eyes. More than tears. His eyes looked like they were sitting in shot glasses of water. Man, was he sad. Goddamn.

And then he spoke finally.

"It's okay," he choked out. Then Seymour took my hand and this surprised my mom and me.

"It's okay," he said. He pulled me along. "It's okay, Jimmy," he said. We headed down the driveway. Seymour was taking me down the damn driveway!

We would meet the girl halfway.

We met the girl at the donkey.

Martians

This land is your land and this land is our land now. Yes, it was and while all that went down in the Land of Lincoln southern Illinois between the two great rivers of fertile empty soil I out ran my aunt. I could feel the balls of my feet hit my ass I was running so fast. I stopped only once because I was so surprised to see it.

It was an outhouse. A wooden outhouse. Behind the farmhouse where all the action was taking place. I had come all this way right when my great family had finally gotten an indoor toilet and now in the land of endless opportunity there was a house with an outhouse.

My aunt slapped me hard up against my face and nearly knocked me off my feet.

"Pablo! ¡*tonto el culo*! Run, dumbass!"

And I ran. We didn't stand at attention and watch the *soldadera* and the donkey and stuff. It was our chance to escape the *patrón* and so we cut and ran.

The *patrón* and his lackey had their eyes glued to the naked girl on the van. The rest of them watched the *soldadera*.

We didn't stop running until we got to an old rundown barn two three four miles away I don't know but we ran on the adrenaline of freedom.

We were free. This was our land. Now my aunt would get a job in a restaurant and I would pick this old barn clean of all that got in our way and the dust of our land was American dust. I breathed it in deeply.

I would grow up and own the place.

But that day we ran through a half open barn door and the sun shone through and we were too tired from running but each step I got closer, I got more scared and scared because we were going to get caught and the *patrón* would beat us and I was so scared my tired legs shook.

And just when my aunt was about to pick me up and comfort me between her ample yet firm breasts she let out a scream and swept me off my feet and we both were screaming so loud and stumbling and staggering against the barn wall. We were caught.

There across the room stood two Americans. They stared at us and we were too frightened and startled to stare back and we cringed and yelled. My little head was buried deep into my aunt's chest. I kept screaming.

Then finally my aunt stopped screaming. I kept screaming. These

Americans knew the *patrón* and we would be dead and tortured first and then dead. It was over.

God would just look on.

Then my aunt spoke.

"Pablo, Pablo, stop it now. Pablo, little one. Please. You think we were looking at Martians or something. Please, please Pablo. Enough."

She tried to pry me out of her bosom.

"Pablo! Stop it!" She pried me finally away. She told me to look.

I looked. I looked finally and there the two Americans were.

There across the room, nailed into the far barn wall was a full length oval golden trimmed beautiful though cracked mirror.

It was dusty and shiny all at the same time.

The two Americans who had caught us looked at us and smiled.

They kept smiling and looking at us until the smiles turned to laughter.

We were looking at ourselves.

The End

Their eyes met and it had been a long time and all Stephanie could think to say was to ask Seymour if he was still listening to "My Bloody Valentine" and this crushed Seymour as Stephanie stood here now leaning against the donkey as such a broken down bloody mess. He didn't even want to know what happened.

"Yes," he tried to say. "I kind of like the Dandy Warhols a little better now, but—"

They both tried to smile. Stephanie's eyes were on the little boy. Of course it wasn't Jeremiah. Her eyes went to the woman at the end of the driveway. Then Seymour.

Seymour went off somewhere. His eyes were open but he didn't want to look anywhere.

He didn't want to see anything at the moment.

He could hear the wind and he could catch an occasional sound of a piece of paper rustling as it flew high into the air.

Finally he felt the tugging on his shirt by little Jimmy. He liked to ride the donkey when Seymour brought him this far.

They both reached down and helped him on the donkey. Stephanie untied the donkey.

The two lines of immigrant workers stiffened. They knew what happened next. Some even saluted. They were not only remembering the Alamo, but the dawn of a new age. The *soldadera* had won.

Someone's iPhone played a drum cadence as Stephanie and Seymour marched the little boy on the donkey down the driveway.

Jim Harris is the author of two previous novels, *Nowhere Near the Sea of Cortez* (2001), and *A Bottle of Rain* (2007). He taught college for 26 years and stopped in 2006 to focus on writing novels. *As God Looked On* is his third published novel and his next novel, *Broken Arrows*, is in progress and is about the lost atomic bomb off Tybee Island, Georgia in 1958.